# DEZI GOLDEN
## *The Kris*

I0675288

The Kris
Dezi Golden

ISBN-13: 978-1-7376566-5-4
Also available in Ebook

# Also by Dezi Golden

**BreathHealer**
BreathHealer Book I
BreathHealer Book II

**Standalone**
The Kris
Guide to Living with CPTSD
Soul of a Tantric
In a Weekend
My Hero My Love

Watch for more at https://www.dezigolden.com.

## To Lou...

Because you saw the black belt in me before I could. Thank you beloved teacher. May we always walk gently.

# 1. Kilt Built

Marney blinks slowly opening her eyes. She waits until her focus comes in and recognizes the subtle curve of his tush. Sean lays breathing softly on his stomach, his face buried in the pillow. *Wow, he is fucking righteously sexy!* She grabs the sheets tighter to her and moves closer to press her lips to his shoulder. The ceiling fan moves her hair so that it tickles her cheek...but she likes the feeling. She likes how her whole body feels! Sean is amazing. The man can make love. He can fuck too, but he's too authentic to just fuck. Marney likes that about him. In today's day and age, it's not easy finding a genuine man.

She frees one hand from the sheets and runs her fingernails down his gorgeously sculpted back. Sean responds by inhaling then turns toward her with a sleepy smile.

"Can't sleep Marns?" He whispers. Sean looks at her with his deep blue-eyed gaze...compassion in his eyes. The way he always looks at her. Like she is the only one he sees. Marney loves this look.

"Sorry." She attempts a smile. He leans and meets her lips with his own. He holds the kiss for a moment, then kisses her again, deeper. Marney can feel her body begin to stir again. No man has ever affected her like Sean. Just his kiss is all it takes.

He pulls away slowly and moves to turn on his side to face her, "Want to talk about it?"

"Naw. It was just a bitch of a day." She snuggles closer to his chest. Sean knows not to ask more. He wraps her in his arms and waits.

"Deucen was being a douche again."

He chuckles, "Deucen the Douchebag."

Marney smiles. Sean repeats the title she had given her pudgy, chauvinist boss years back. Terry Deucen, Chief of Police for the Olman Police Department. Class A dick. He doesn't care for Marney or the fact that her father was his predecessor...and he shows her by riding her ass. He sucks as Chief, and he knows Marney knows that. She *doesn't* suck as a detective, and she knows he knows that too. Everyone knows that. That's why she gets ninety percent of the cases...and has solved all but two in her nine years as a detective. Deucen went from patrol right to the chief position. He has no respect for his six detectives because he has never been one. That's politics though. Marney always thought he just sucked the right dicks for his high level position. He loves to allude to her being a cop only because of her daddy. She put her time in though. No ass kissing...or anything extra curricular. Hard work and a supportive father is what it took. She knows Deucen hates that.

"Yup, Deucen the Douchebag..."

Sean caresses her hair, running his hand through her dark brown strands. He loves the way her eyes and her hair accentuate each other. Marney is the most beautiful woman he has ever seen.

"It's hard enough doing this job, putting up with the guys razzing me day in and day out, but then, sitting in his fart-smelling office, listening to his whining about how I "offended" some fucking piece-of-shit criminal..."

Sean laughs softly. He loves how Marney's brain works.

She smiles, "Are you laughing at me?"

"No...not at you babe."

"I'm sorry, I'm just having a bitch-fit. I'd much rather hear about your day." She reaches up to touch his cheek. Her eyes meet his gaze in the low light coming through the window of her bedroom. Marney loves Sean's face. Her real-life version of a Chris Hemsworth....but Scottish, not Australian. Good breeding in Marney's book. With a name like Sean Faherty and muscles upon muscles...he is her pot-o-gold leprechaun. He is "Kilt-Built" as she calls it. He doesn't see it though. All he sees is Marney. And to Sean, no one tops Marney.

"Nothing to tell. Same shift, same drunks. Another night of Olman's boring boozers." His voice softly echos in the room.

"Well, that sounds much more interesting to me than druggies, gangsters, thieves, and criminals." Marney loves how simple Sean is. How simple he has designed his life after returning from Iraq. Affordable house, easy bartending job, loving Scottish-American family. He's seen the worst parts of the world...completing top secret military missions, healing his wounds and his brilliant mind...leaving it all behind, never looking back. She has the worst parts of her world in her face every day and the only leaving it, is in his arms.

"You know what sounds interesting?" He whispers.

"What?"

"Me taking you away from this awful day of yours...again."

"Oh?"

"Yeah." Sean reaches in and kisses her. Marney moves her hands up his back and pulls him close. She never passes up an opportunity to feel Sean make love to her. He takes away all the big bad stuff...with his own big stuff. Marney smiles beneath his lips, moving under him so she can feel his perfect weight and his hard thick manhood as it burrows into her. The awful day finally disappears for good...

Her cell phone vibrates against the nightstand. A feeling of deflation hits her for a split second and Sean mumbles "no no" while pushing her arms up and over her head, holding her wrists with one hand and using his other to hike her knee up around his waist trapping her. Slowly, sensually, he thrusts deeper and Marney forgets about the phone. She is losing control again...*how can he keep this up?* She knows it's been long enough since her last release, she is ready for another. She volleys in her mind that this will have to be the last one tonight. After all, she needs to walk and function at work in the morning. By the sounds of it though, work may come earlier than morning.

The cell buzzes again and before Marney can look over at it, Sean distracts her by changing his rhythm and kissing her deeper. She smiles under his lips as he picks up the pace and starts his pelvic magic. She knows what he's doing and she joins to meet his movements so they can climax in unison. They communicate flawlessly in bed...and out of it too.

Sean moves just a little faster, thrusting perfectly with a little staccato flick using his pubic bone to entice Marney's clitoris even more. She kisses him deeper and delights in the thought of their music...knowing the beloved crescendo is arriving. She can no longer take it, she lets go...Sean's breath stops and his body tenses along with her, both crashing over the edge in consummate timing with hers. His tongue plunging into her warm, waiting mouth. Ahh........ecstasy...

\*\*\*

Marney steps out of the shower and grabs a towel to dry off. Looking across the room at Sean, entangled in her sheets, makes her want to blow off the call...but she can't. John O'Malen will call back fifty times if she doesn't get her ass in gear. He is such a persistent little prick dispatcher...yet, good at his job. Marney likes when cops are good at their jobs.

She throws her hair up in a ponytail, delighted in her decision to not wash it so she can enjoy the lingering scent of Sean's cologne for awhile longer. Quickly, she dresses in jeans and a t-shirt, pulling on a blazer and boots to hide her guns and knife. It's a nightmare trying to conceal weapons under clothing in New Mexico. It's a hot state. Even at two in the morning.

Marney bends down to kiss Sean's head, running her eyes down the Adonis she must leave sleeping in her bed sheets. *Jeezus...I'm so lucky*...She smiles and turns to go.

# 2. Andres Diaz

Marney quietly shuts the door and locks it. After scanning her entry way, property and driveway she hops up into her truck taking a quick look in the back as well. It gets real dark in New Mexico at night. The desert is just that way. Bright all day, pitch black at night. Stars blazing bright from the contrast. Marney is always on the lookout for criminals and critters...twenty-four seven. It's just a cop thing, especially at her personal residence.

"Okay O'Malen, what's the scoop?" Marney calls in to the front desk dispatcher.

John O'Malen sighs, "Marney Jade...nice of you to join the party."

"I texted you John, has it been ten minutes yet?" Marney doesn't really want to play, but she knows the midget dispatcher at Olman P.D. needs his attention. The job is also incredibly boring at night...unless, of course, there is a DOA call.

"Jade, you need to call me...NOT text me miss..."

"Bite me John. I'm not in the mood for your Napoleon complex bullshit. What've we got?" Marney half-smiles knowing she can get him to throw a tantrum if she keeps it up. John is harmless. Truth is, she cares about the little shit, feels bad about his height challenges. He gives her crap all the time but behind her back, he is one of the more respectful critics. She has heard the things he says about her. In a nutshell, he thinks she is a genius detective, but wishes her fresh mouth shut.

"Now see, why ya always hafta go there Jade? Always with the short jokes-"

"-is Deucen there?" Marney cuts him off with a threat to go chain-of-command over his head. She chuckles at his sensitivity toward height when she was actually referring to his temper.

"He's been notified! That's who told me to call you first Marney! He wants you in charge of this one...again!" John raises his voice.

Marney knows it's serious if Deucen put her on the case. It'll cause problems with the other detectives on shift, but she is Olman's top closer. Ha...and to think she might have some down time after closing the Sandevan's case last week.

"Okay John, again, what have we got?" She pulls out of her driveway and drives off slowly trying not to wake her entire neighborhood. Gerda, Marney's 1973 Dodge pickup, is not the quietest of vehicles. She's old, sputters at times, and is vociferous.

John exhales trying to compose himself. "Earlier today we had a female report her husband missing. It took patrol a bit to get a hold of his employer and get the location of his job, he installs cabinets...anyway, he is over in one of the new development houses in Drona Ranch...he was installing kitchen cabinets in one of the two-story units...the big ones ya know?"

"What else?"

"Well Marns....it's...gross."

"Gross John? So, not an accidental death?" Marney suddenly feels it's going to be a long week.

"Well, you're the detective, detective..."

Marney wants to stop losing brain cells on John. Enough attention has been given. "Fine. My ETA is seven minutes fart-face. Make sure you sign me on."

"You have to sign on tac Marn-" She hangs up on him and smiles to herself. John hates when she makes him work.

She shifts Gerda and reaches to turn on the radio. Picking up the receiver she speaks into it, "District seven, seven thirteen on tac and en route. ETA six minutes." She signs on to make John happy.

"Received seven thirteen." His voice is low. He's angry and relieved all at the same time.

Shifting Gerda again, she looks over at the computer screen and sees her position posted. Now all the patrols and whoever else is watching sees she is available on shift. *Here we go, something gross...*

An interesting thing about the desert is that it's so dark at night, that when spotlights are brought in and used, the sky lights up like a carnival. Marney can see the glow of the crime scene five minutes out. Which makes her wonder if the rest of town is curious and on their way there as well. With this being a new development, she hopes not.

She downshifts Gerda and turns into the main street of Drona Ranch. It's pretty. Suburban living. There are only three houses under construction with the rest of the streets still empty lots. Marney knows this is a nightmare for a crime scene. She pulls up, parks and begins her assessment from her seat. Entry and exit ways into the houses are the newly paved streets, obvious doors and windows, but after that only flat, dark desert. No cover, no trees, no nearby structures and no other houses for about a mile. Marney looks up, there are no cameras because there are no street lights yet. So far this is a perfect set up to commit a crime and leave quietly without being seen.

"District seven. Seven thirteen onsite." Marney puts the receiver back and cuts the engine. She jumps down out of her truck and begins to scan the vehicles parked along the street in front of her. The house is taped off with bright yellow crime scene tape. The perimeter is wide which tells her the first responding officer is Theo Blair. Marney likes working with Blair. He's a good cop who can follow orders and get things done.

Marney pulls her badge out of her pocket and hangs it around her neck. Next, she pulls on plastic gloves and readies to do what she does best.

*Sidewalks-clean. Footprints-none. Up to down, left to right....nothing. One, two, three, four patrol cars. My brother's work van. Ambulance. Two public works vans with spotlights. Jeezus, do we have enough people here?*

"Well, if it isn't Jadelock." Patrolman Richard Dawson turns as Marney approaches the corner of the crime tape.

"Dick." She nods in greeting.

He fakes a smile, "Its Richard...Dawson to you."

"Like I said...*Dick*." She smirks.

Marney points to the tape and waits for him to lift it. She ducks under it and pauses to scan the dirt up to the house, "Well, Richard...its detective to you. *Not Jadelock*. Blair first responder?"

"Yeah...wait....how'd you-"

"Thanks Dick. Good job securing the tape bud. We wouldn't want it to be stolen." Marney takes her sarcasm and continues up the sidewalk, careful not to disturb any evidence. She knows with all the personnel already on scene that it's near impossible it isn't already in some way contaminated. Olman is not used to a crime scene, so everyone on duty finds their way to the address out of plain curiosity. She decides she will put most of them to work and kick the excess out.

Marney gets to the door and sees Patrolman Theo Blair standing with a clipboard just as he should be. "Hey Blair."

"Detective Jade. Good to see you. The scene is all urine pee pee." Blair cracks a joke and starts flipping through to his notes so he can answer her questions he knows she will soon fire off. Marney likes that Blair is a happy guy and thorough...he seems to enjoy his job. Ex-military cops are always better at the job than the college grads. School rookies come with so much ego and not enough street or world smarts. Veterans come with real-world experience and less attitude generally. She hated patrol when she was in it...even though she was great at it. Too much politics, paperwork, and making the public miserable. It's a good job for some, but for her it sucked. She did it, but only because she had to, to get to the detective unit. The worst part was putting on a uniform everyday that most the public did not respect. It was like a bullseye or target for her. Now, in plain clothes, only the criminal public hates her...as they should.

"Okay, what've we got?"

Blair takes a breath, "Looks like our missing person Andres Diaz. Wife reported him missing when he didn't return home from work at four. Your brother is running the fingerprints on his mobile out in the van. Appears to be a twenty-nine year old, Latino male. Eyes stabbed, tongue removed, hands removed, and genitals completely gone. From what I know, only your brother has touched the body."

Marney looks Blair in the eyes and sees what she knows she will see from every male working on this case...terror. She looks over at the body across the room. No one is near it, but a pathway and evidence is already marked. She can tell that it's been a quick glance body. Too gruesome for most to really look over for long. Now she understands why John kept saying it's gross. For men, it certainly is.

"Genitals gone huh, well now isn't that special." Marney takes a long breath. "Okay, I'm going to need you to get with dispatch and express how confidential this is...basically, tell O'Malen to stop telling officers its "gross" so that they breeze by to sneak a peek. We don't need more curiosity coming over here and contaminating this all-ready fucked up scene." Marney waits while Blair starts writing her list.

He scribbles then looks at her, careful not to look over at the "other" side of the room. "Okay."

"Next, get Dick out there to stop playing with his...and do more than guard the freagin' crime scene tape. He is going to have to secure the scene from KZW so this doesn't end up on the morning news before we are ready. I know that little shit, Stacy is already on her way over here with her damn cameraman."

"Okay."

"Has my brother said anything to you yet?" Marney's little brother Liam is a genius crime scene investigator and her greatest ally with solving Olman's cases. There aren't many people she trusts, but Liam is one.

"He hasn't moved the body yet, if that's what you mean. Just said he would be right back."

"Okay, good. You're gonna have to get patrol out of here. Whoever doesn't belong needs to go. And Blair...I don't need to explain to you how important it is that this doesn't get out. You've got to talk with your officers about keeping their faces shut on this. This could be big news for Olman...and we don't need it. Small towns can become big news real fast."

"I agree." Blair is still writing.

Marney can see the new construction home is far enough along and the electricity has been wired and installed. "Were the lights working when you guys responded or-"

"No, we called and had them turned on."

"Okay, then get Gibens on the vertical and horizontal scanning. All surfaces need to be fingerprinted." Marney knows it's a long shot to expect fingerprints other than the contractors and workers that have been in and out of the house. Just her sense of the killing already told her whoever did this...is too good to leave a fingerprint behind.

"Okay."

"And, what time did the wife report him missing?" Marney knows cabinet installers usually work during the day when there is enough light in the houses. Electricity is not often turned on too soon because the developers don't want to incur the costs and don't need it until appliances and lighting fixtures are completely in. This would explain the compressor, plugged in, over to the right.

"Her first call was at six o'clock. Said he is never late for dinner. Then again at ten. We found him at eleven twenty-two after his boss called the P.D. back with this location. There is nothing out here."

"I see." Marney knows the wife said he did not return at home as expected which means he was a six to three employee. Typical since New Mexico is too hot to work in after four o'clock.

Blair looked over at Diaz and then back to Marney, "When will he start to smell?"

Marney could tell Blair had already been standing at the crime scene way too long. It was going to be a long night for all, "Not for days bud. You've been around enough bodies to know that." She smiles at him. Theo did not like smells. He can do any part of the job...smells pissed him off though.

"Love my job."

"That's the spirit bud. Hey, Jennings already photograph clockwise?" She tried to change the subject to get Blair back on track.

"Yes, he's outside now. Entries, exits, surroundings, street signs, empty lots and area desert. It's a nightmare."

Marney agrees, "Not the best scene, that's for damn sure. Make sure he photographs any spectators who may have shown up to gawk."

"District seven, seven zero one onsite." Deucen's gruff voice comes in low over Blair's shoulder radio.

"Shit." Marney isn't in the mood to deal with her boss just yet. "Okay Blair, you know the deal. I'm going to go visit with Mr. Diaz for some time. Try to keep Deucen away from me."

Blair chuckles, "I'll try."

"Thanks."

*Body supine, sawdust covering most of anterior...marks on floor to right, obviously hit from behind then turned over. Right eye vertically stabbed, double-sided lacerations means double-bladed knife, next left eye slashed horizontally...hmmm odd...next tongue was pulled and sliced off...some still left, mouth open, left hand picked up by finger and removed with one swift slice, diagonal laceration from left side of wrist to lower right side wrist...next right hand removed...same, upper to lower...probably backward slash. Stomach in tact...down, down....wow, penis and scrotum removed with pants still on. Left to right jagged slash pattern...most likely a left-handed assailant-perhaps a sawing type motion? Legs untouched, knees extra sawdust...fell to knees then to face. Possible strike to posterior skull...didn't see it coming. Shit....gotta roll body to see if tongue, hands, and genitals are under body...naw, just ask Liam. Definitely gonna find a blow to the head or neck, assailant wiped footprints...smudges in sawdust pattern toward sliding glass doors-*

"Jade."

*Balls!* "Sir?" Marney stands and pivots, careful not to touch the body. She looks over at her boss...trying to stifle a laugh. *This guy! Is he really in his fucking pajamas?*

"What've we got?" Deucen puts on rubber gloves, like that will help.

Marney steps back away from the body and follows the marked path across the room to her boss hoping that going toward him will keep him from going toward the body and getting his funky mothball smell further into the scene. "Not quite ready to surmise sir but it's safe to say homicide at this point. No way this could be an accident." She hates having to sound simple, but that's what Deucen can handle.

"How do you mean?" Deucen looks down at her like he always does...even though she is very near his same height. If men could be fired for staring at tits...Deucen would be the first to go. Marney calls his left eye is "sexual" and his right eye is "harassment".

"Eyes stabbed, tongue removed, hands removed...and genitals gone." Marney speaks matter-of-factly because it pisses him off.

Deucen's eyebrows raise, "What?"

Dispatch obviously did not share the "gross" parts of the scene when calling Deucen to notify him...or he wasn't paying much attention. By the looks of his attire, he wasn't thinking too clearly. Marney notices the smell of cigar on Deucen, which is only a little better than the smell of his old-lady-mothball-trench-coat.

Marney waits for the information to sink in. It's just a given, men are going to have a hard time with the details of this case. "Yeah, pretty sure there is a posterior skull wound...by the size of this guy. When I'm done my anterior assessment I will roll him."

"Well, what are you waiting for?" Deucen sounds crass.

"Liam is outside running the prints to make a positive I.D." Marney always waits for Liam before touching the body...since he knows what to look for. She continues scribbling her notes so she doesn't have to make eye-contact with her boss. He has a face she just wants to punch.

Deucen lowers his voice, "Oh, how is the little flamer?"

*Definitely a face needing punching.* Marney sighs. She hates dealing with Deucen's homophobic comments about her little brother. It's these little things he does and never gets fired for that pisses her off the most...but she also knows he is in the closet and expresses himself in this way to hide it. Most cops talk a lot of shit, it's part of coping with the job, but Deucen could land on the stand some day with the rules he breaks.

Marney lowers her voice too, "I'm not going to answer such questions Chief. What people do when the lights are off or in the privacy of their own homes doesn't bother me."

He smirks, "Well, it should."

Marney's stomach turns. There is a dead body lying in the middle of the floor and this nipple-head wants to talk about her gay brother. "I'm only concerned if there is a crime or a dead body."

"Yeah...okay." He huffs his stupid laugh.

"So, back to our DOA here. You may want to hold off on a news conference or alerting the media at all." Marney waves her pencil from Deucen's head to feet reminding him of his ridiculous outfit.

Deucen grimaces, "Well, obviously Jade. We need a positive I.D., notification to the family and the body to be in the coroner's office first!"

"Yes, sir...of course." Marney smirks to herself. Playing dumb will surely make him feel superior and perhaps light a fire under his ass to leave...and get some work done.

"Well, get your brother's ass in here and get me some answers. I'm gonna need something by morning!"

Marney nods, "Yup."

Deucen abruptly walks back out of the house feeling all special about giving her orders...and Marney feels relief at the stupidity leaving the room.

# 3. Body Roll

Liam wanders back into the house...paperwork and more of his tools in hand. He has our photographer with him.

"Hey Marns. How goes it?"

"Hey bud. What'd ya find?" Marney's missed him. She wants to tousle her little brother's hair like she used to when he was younger...but that would surely not go over well.

Liam places his equipment down on the kitchen cabinets that are not completely installed. Standing in one spot, so as not to disturb evidence, he reaches to hand her the printout verification from his fingerprint results. "Yup, that is one twenty-nine year old, Andres Juan Diaz."

"Okay good." Marney looks over the paper.

"Well, not for the wife and kids." Liam opens another suitcase of fun tools. Marney loves all his gadgets and work toys.

"No, not for the family. We'll give it another hour before notification...then we'll bring the wife in for an interview."

Liam smiles at his sister, "Yeah, nuts gone is pretty personal...crime of passion maybe?"

"Never know little brother...never know. You almost ready to roll the body?" Marney puts her pencil and pad in her back pocket.

"Yeah. You like that knee to face plant impression in the sawdust?" Liam's eyes light up. He loves his job.

"Uh-huh. I'm betting blow to the head to incapacitate. This guy has no defensive wounds. Didn't see or even hear it coming."

Liam nods, "He must have really pissed off the wrong guy."

"Or girl." Marney is going with instinct. It's never failed her in the past.

"Woman? Really Marns?" Liam stops to stare at her. He knows how Marney gets with solving crimes...he would never say it but, he understands why everyone calls her Jadelock. She hates the nickname, but she can't deny that she has a gift of figuring things out.

"Liam, it's not just the balls missing. The penis, scrotum, hair....everything! Cut clean off with one slicing-type motion. You can't tell me you wouldn't consider a woman." Marney squints her eyes.

Liam plays devil's advocate, "He's a tall dude Marns. Remember, in my world...men can get angry enough to dismember...ya know?"

"You've got a point brother, you do but, other men, gay or straight, don't usually castrate. We women...we love cock-"

"Hmmm..." Liam purrs.

Marney tries not to laugh, "until it hurts us, either violently...or in a cheating manner."

"Still though, don't you think this is excessive?" Liam cringes and pulls at his pants.

Marney smiles again, "Liam, we work in homicide, everything is excessive. My point is, even though it's exuberant...a woman might have less care for this type of castration...since she doesn't really know what having a dick feels like."

Liam nudges his sister's shoulder, "Its heaven sista."

Marney laughs out loud, "Yeah, okay. I'm not having this argument with you again little man. I told you, when you can spin out multiple orgasms like a woman...then we will talk."

"Oh, but I can Marns...Rodg is a-m-a-z-i-n-g in-"

"Liam! I will not listen to your ramblings about Rodger. At least wait until Christmas dinner so you can make proper memories embarrassing Dad and Asner." Marney laughs again, harder than she should and Liam joins in. Marney loves working with her brother. He's a hoot and makes such heavy crime scenes a little easier to handle.

"Okay, okay..." Liam snaps his gloves.

Marney scans the room again, everyone is hard at work as she needs and without her having to delegate. She's worked hard at getting a system down for her crime scenes. It's so nice to see things running smoothly. "Alright, let's do this."

Hours later the sun is up and blazing. Liam and Marney have done all they can at the scene and have the body on the way to the coroner's office. Liver temperature indicates time of death between two and three the previous afternoon. Andres Diaz appeared to be cleaning up and ending his work day when attacked so Marney is betting it was closer to three. There is a decent sized gash in the back of his skull that has a slight vertical shape. The mark appears to be coming from a lower position to upwards, which tells Marney that the suspect is shorter in height than Mr. Diaz. She will wait for the coroner's report before saying so...but it doesn't mean she won't be looking for a suspect that's shorter...and possibly female. Smaller, less physically strong suspects, generally try to bring down their victims quickly and without a fight.

On the way to the station to interview the victim's wife, Marney braces herself for the next few hours. She never enjoys seeing people in pain, especially surviving spouses.

She calls Sean. The thought of him cooking himself breakfast in her kitchen, drinking coffee, and reading the news on her laptop made her want to drive straight home. Sean is her favorite person. Has been for seven years. No matter how much time goes by, he makes it feel like the first year. She doesn't know what it is...he is just *that* kind of guy.

Marney dials his number. Sean picks up after the first ring, "Hey." His voice is morning-sexy.

"Hey. Did I wake you? It's eleven."

"I'm at the counter Marns...just a rough night baby."

Marney has a twinge of guilt mixed with flurried passion wave through her lower region, "Oh yeah. Rough life...you trying to make your girlfriend forget about her stressful job and all."

Sean smiles, "Any way I can help."

"Oh, well thank you sir."

"My pleasure. So you okay today?" Sean sounds genuine.

Marney smiles at his shift, "On my way to the station to interview the suspect-slash-wife of a DOA, formerly a missing person, now a homicide victim."

"Hmm, sounds fun."

"Well, it could very well be. Guy was sliced and diced Sean." Marney knows she can tell Sean her most classified of information, and it never goes further. He is all about loyalty and integrity. The best kind of man in her book.

"No shit."

"Yeah, in places no man would ever want a boo boo. If you know what I mean." Marney uses her best sweet southern accent.

Sean quiets for a second. "Seriously Marns?"

She smiles to herself knowing this is the reaction she is going to get from every guy who hears about the case. "Yeah, not an accident. Olman's got one real pissed off murderer on its hands."

Sean's voice softens, "Oh...I guess you could say that."

Marney knows he gets sad when she has a real doozy of a case. He misses her even though he never complains. "Yeah, I hope douchebag handles this well in the media...or else Olman could be smack-dab in the middle of a shit storm. It's not every day there is a case like this in New Mexico and it's been a long time for Olman. For a murder anyway."

"Yeah, since what...2009 with the Lee shooting?"

"Well, that was self-defense. No we haven't had a murder in Olman since...about 2007. Lots of deaths, but murder...no." Marney realizes this can be quite time consuming.

Sean takes a sip of coffee, "Well, how ya holding up. You want me to cook you some lunch?"

"No thank you. I'll call you when I can okay?"

"Okay babe. Be safe."

Marney pulls up in front of the station, "Will do. Hope you have a great day at the bar."

"Ha! If I can walk." Sean laughs and makes Marney laugh too.

# 4. Juanita Diaz

Marney bypasses all the patrol, dispatchers, court personnel and public by going through the back entrance to the detectives unit. Slouching in her chair she lays her head back for a moment. She just needs to breathe for a minute and then she'll call dispatch and tell them she's onsite.

She looks across her desk and sees a cup of coffee on Chris's desk. *Oh shit, Chris is back from vacation today! Oh man, what a day to return to work. Missed my partner. Wonder where he is...* Her phone rings.

"Detective Jade." Marney replies softly.

"Goooooood morning Marney! Ya have to fucking let us know when you're onsite girl." Freda Jackson practically sings the entire sentence to Marney on the other end. Freda has been the daytime dispatcher for over thirty years and has the mouth of a trucker.

"Hey Freda. Just trying to get a minute alone."

Freda cackles, "Girl, we all tryin ta get a minute alone. You ain't special."

Marney sighs, "Yeah, thanks. Hey, any idea where Shean is?"

"Oh Chris? I'll find that shitbag for ya no problem." Click. Freda hangs up.

*Oh lordy.* Marney looks at the phone then hangs it up. *Here we go.*

A few minutes later, all five missing detectives come strolling into the office. Chris Shean is in the lead, Rick Davenport is next, then Jimmy Hoss, Leeana Kazib and Joe Radden. All with cake and coffee in hand except for Chris who has two pieces of cake, one of which he places in front of Marney. Chris bends and kisses the top of her head.

"Wow, thank youpah-tna." Marney says in her gruffest western voice. She is relieved to see him. He's been her partner for over four years, and they work together like coffee and cream.

Chris sits down in the chair next to her desk instead of the chair at his desk two feet away. "Welcome doll. So I hear you are the big bad detective in town...again."

"You mean WE are the big bad detectives in town...nice to see you back. Gotta a lot of work to do today." Marney takes a huge bite of icing then scrunches her nose. *Yuck! Way too flippin' sweet.*

"I see. Freda just said there is a hysterical woman crying in interview room three. Please tell me that isn't for us." Christopher Shean is Marney's partner and best friend from childhood. They grew up on the same street, went to the academy together, ended up detectives the same year, and have saved each other's lives more than once. Chris is huge. In a sexy way. He is about six-foot-four and three-hundred twenty pounds of badass cop. He carries only one forty-four magnum to Marney's two guns and one boot-knife. He much prefers to use his hands than his gun. He drives a green mini-cooper which makes Marney crazy because he doesn't fit in it. His home is a houseboat on Olman's only lake and he lives with his bulldog named Lucy. Marney loves Chris to death and if he wasn't so much like a brother to her she would probably be married to him. Except of course for Sean, who makes her heart flutter. Among other things.

"Yup. She's ours."

Chris takes another bite of cake, "Aw shit, seriously? Is this the DOA on Cameno Drive?"

Marney decides the cake is better than the icing and picks it out with her spoon, "Yup."

"Homicide?"

"Yup."

"Wify-poo is the first to be questioned huh?"

"Yup."

"You want me to start with the questioning? Play the big softy cop so you can come in strong mid-way?"

"Yup."

Chris smiles, "Glad we could have this conversation Marns."

"Yup."

"Okay, okay...you can fill me in now." Chris pings her with his spoon wiping icing on her nose.

Marney cracks up laughing, "Yuuuuuup."

"You missed me huh?"

"Yup." Marney smiles again, realizing she is short-word answering like a dude.

"Oh, if it isn't Mr. Watson and Jadelock in flirtywood." Leeana Kazib breezes by Marney's desk on the way to her own.

Chris scowls at her, "Lee Lee, don't you have some old ladies to arrest?"

"Bite my ass Shean!" Leeana actually stops to speak through clenched teeth.

Marney huffs a laugh at Chris's reference. He's only been back from vacation an hour and he is already teasing her in his special "Chris" way. Leeana Kazib has been a thorn in Marney's side for years. She takes every opportunity to badger Marney, almost like a bully on the playground. Marney could care less...but Chris takes it very personal, and turns on his protective skill. About a month ago Leeana made a bad call by working with a narc that tipped off his supplier...so basically she busted into a house with only two old ladies having tea. It was the big joke for awhile and Leeana hasn't lived it down yet.

"Uh...no, I think I'll pass on that Kazib." Chris winks at Marney, he is usually less cruel. "Yo ass needs to stay in those muffin-top jeans thanks."

"What up guys." Jimmy Hoss walks by with a mouthful of cake.

Marney nods, "Hey Jim."

He heads to the other side of the room and Marney sees Joe and Rick whispering in the corner like two little school girls. The gang is all in one room. This doesn't happen often.

Marney takes a last bite of cake leaving the icing in a blob on her plate, "Okay partner, we have to get our shit in gear. By the way, who's cake did I just eat?"

"Hell, if I know...someone named Jean?"

Leeana walks by again, "Its Jean Carter's birthday dip-shit...the court clerk down the hall?"

Chris smiles at Marney again. Pleased with himself for pissing her off. Marney decides it's time to head into the conference room to brief Chris about the case. Otherwise, this could take all day to complete a conversation. Way too much activity in the detective's unit today. She waves him in and closes the door behind them.

Twenty minutes later, Chris and Marney stare at the video surveillance camera for interview room three. Juanita Diaz has had an hour to cry and use what looks like a whole box of tissues. A large pile of sogginess has formed in the middle of the table. She has her head down in her arms and painfully lifts it to wipe her eyes every few minutes.

*Ugh. I hate this part.* Marney pulls Chris's shirt. "Come on big daddy, let's do this."

"Yup. Time to squeeze the Charmin." Chris jokes and Marney laughs. Now its all about playing good cop, bad cop.


Three hours later Marney and Chris emerge from the little interview room. It was clear to Marney in the first five minutes that, Juanita "Jenny" Diaz, did not kill her husband...although she did have motive.

"Alright Marns, I'm gonna hit the head and get a cup of coffee...you want anything?" Chris is exhausted already and feeling the effects of coming back from vacation into a shit-storm.

Marney nods, "Yeah, that'd be great. We need to sort out our notes. I'll meet ya in the conference room in ten okay?"

"In ten."

Marney heads to her desk, happy that the interview with Mrs. Diaz is over. The woman is a mess, but far from being a vicious killer. For one, she isn't smart enough to orchestrate such an act, her alibi is solid, and sadly, she just learned of Mr. Diaz' three other conquests.

After making a few calls Marney realizes the affects of getting up too early are setting in. She feels it deep, behind her eyes and decides after meeting with Chris, she is going to head home. This is going to be quite a little mystery to solve...so she's going to need her rest.

Chris stomps into the conference room, two cups of coffee in one huge hand, and his notes in the other. He gives Marney the eye roll.

"Deucen corner you?" Marney huffs a laugh.

"Yeah. In the freagin' john too. I'm suddenly wanting to be on vacation again in my little water paradise. It's like the hyper-vigilant piece-of-shit wants the whole case solved after just one interview."

"I know but, he's gonna have to wait. This one is tricky."

"Your damn right it is. The guy didn't make good friendships from what the wife says...and although I'm not getting the kill vibe from her, she sure had enough motive to do him in." Chris slurps his coffee.

Marney nods, "I agree, but she is in a worse situation now...with no husband and another kid on the way. She needs the fucker alive more than dead."

"Yeah, I was thinking that too. Man, you are kick-ass with the standoffish bitch cop part Marns. I was impressed." Chris play-punches Marney in the shoulder. She laughs.

"Okay, what've we got?"

Chris clears his throat then flips to the first page of his notes, "Well my take is that this guy was a first class dick. I mean he had to be a level one sociopath Marns. Marries too young, moves her far away from her family, his family here hates her, he's a big-time momma's boy, he cheats on her left and right, puts his hands on her so she miscarries...twice, brings women home while she's working, tells her to get out when she walks in on him screwing them, throws her out, takes her back, knocks her up again. Now, she's four months along...and he's dead...and missing his penis."

Marney smiles at how Chris's mind works. "Well, I am pretty concerned with the enemies he made at work...not to mention, the women he slept with behind his wife's back. Anyone of those women could have wanted him dead...or their husbands could have paid him a visit.

"True. Shit! How are we suppose to track down all his hoes, if the wife didn't even know where he was meeting them...and the whole penis thing-" Chris cringes.

"I know C, the dick and balls is a huge issue. Let's not forget the eyes, tongue and hands are at play here too."

"I know Marns, but his whole package?"

"Christopher! We have seen our fair share of sick shit over the years. This is just another psychopath for us to catch right?" Marney tries not to laugh. They are both very overtired.

"And it's gone. The dick, balls and tongue are gone. I mean why leave the hands cut off and lying nearby but take the other cut off shit?"

Marney chews on her pen. The missing parts has bothered her some, "Yeah, that is odd. My guess is the hands were left behind so we could identify his prints quickly...but taking the other stuff?"

"What are you thinking? I know your brain has been going and going..." Chris waits.

"I don't want to say just yet. I'm hoping this is just an odd homicide by a really pissed off killer. It strikes me curious that some body parts were taken from the scene. That's more of a serial killer behavior...you know, souvenir-type psycho shit." She scribbles another note.

Chris sits back against the chair, "Oh Marns, you're not telling me...?"

"I'm just saying this could go downhill real fast. I had a call from my federal buddy and he says there is nothing in the database about missing genitals since 1974, and that sicko was executed. And as for New Mexico, that toy box killer was sentenced to 224 years but died of a heart attack in 2002, 2009 was the 11 bodies up north, and that

1980's dude only had minimal ties with our state...what was his name Little or something?" Marney is rambling and Chris is wide-eyed.

"Shit. I hate when you get a "sense" about things. Do you really think we will have to call the feds in on this?"

Marney chuckles, "Let's just hope it's a one-and-done okay. Now give me what else ya got." Poor Chris. What a way to come back from vacation.

# 5. Salad and Whiskey

Marney steps into the dimly lit bar and her eyes immediately find the tall, sexy man she is in search of. Sean has his back to the door...and she doesn't mind. The owner, Cherie Daytone is behind the bar as well, serving up a tall one to Old Man Benny, a regular. Marney smiles at the view of Cherie's wrinkled cleavage peeking out of a bright pink baby doll t-shirt. Sean is right about his boss's taste in teenage clothing. *It's too much.*

Marney scans the room to make sure there are no new faces she needs to worry about. It's only six o'clock so the bar isn't real busy yet. Sean looks up and sees her. His face lights up and a sweet smile appears. Her day has suddenly gotten better. He nods for her to sit at the end bar stool and starts walking in that direction. She makes her way to meet him, happy none of Olman's P.D. personnel are here. It's always a risk coming into Daytone's because Deucen could show up at random. Marney, unfortunately, caught Deucen and Cherie in the throws of their truck-in-the-woods passion years back on patrol one night. It's never been mentioned again, but Deucen knows she knows, and Cherie knows she knows. Marney wishes she didn't know...or see it, for that matter. Cherie giggles and flirts when Deucen pops in from time to time, so Marney has a feeling the affair has continued through the years. Sad for Deucen's wife, but common for a cop like him. There are good cops and then there are cops...like Deucen.

Marney takes her blazer off and hangs it on the bar stool. She steps up and Sean's lips meet hers as she finds her seat. *Damn he smells good.*

"Ultra?" He offers and Marney's heart warms to the sound of his deep voice.

"No. Nothing unleaded tonight. Seagram's, rocks and a huge greek salad, please." She smiles at him and then nods to Henry and Rod a couple seats down.

Sean smiles, "Rough day get rougher babe?"

"It's better suddenly." Marney winks at him and he turns with a smile, to get her order.

*At this time, all we know is that...*

Marney cringes and looks up at the news on the television. She recognizes Deucen's voice and sees his fat face on the screen. She heard he had done a short news snippet about the body being found in the construction house at the Cameno development. She's happy to see he chose a suit instead of his god-awful baby blue pajamas. Cherie gawks at the screen smiling like a doofus and Marney shakes her head and laughs. At least Deucen kept quiet and didn't say "murder" or "homicide". It buys Marney a few more days without the press up her ass...or the FBI for that matter.

Sean serves Rod another draft, wipes his hands and then walks back over towards Marney with her drink. "How's your body holding up after all the hours? Chris make it back from vacation alive?"

"I'm feeling like a truck hit me but nothing the treadmill won't erase. Chris never even left the houseboat. Said he and Lucy just chilled. Fishing and sleeping...that sort of shit."

"Wow, that sounds more like a weekend off, not a week's vacation." Sean laughs.

"I know right? He really needs to get out of Olman sometime. He just might after this case. You should have seen his face today. What a way to end a vacation."

"Anything you want to tell me?" Sean lowers his voice. Marney loves how he is so in sync with her.

She starts to talk but sees Cherie walking toward them so she stops. Cherie hip bumps Sean and puts down Marney's salad. "Hey girl. Here ya go."

"Thanks Cherie. I'm famished."

"Well, eat up hon and don't you worry about giving him back. I can handle these old farts tonight, myself." Cherie aims a thumb towards the customers at the bar and smiles while walking away.

"Ooh, got you all to myself then, huh?" Marney smiles at Sean.

Sean crouches in, "Hurry up and eat your rabbit food and I will show you the new paper towel dispenser in the men's bathroom. It's automatic." He waves his eyebrows comically.

Marney laughs out loud at Sean's cheesy line but considers the thought. It would be really nice to be with him right now. "Open your mouth Sean."

He obeys and Marney fills it with a forkful of salad. He muffles, "Is that a no?"

She smiles, "It's never a no big boy. I just prefer to go home and wash the nasty crime scene off of me. Besides...you smell divine, I don't want to ruin that."

"Hmmm, then I'm going to have to wrap up early here...before someone falls asleep on me."

She chews and swallows a mouthful. *Yum, food.* "I'll wait for you. My place okay?"

"Sounds good. Now let me get back to the guys here. I think they all come in just to see what Cherie is wearing each day." Sean caresses Marney's cheek as they share a laugh. Marney enjoys his sense of humor.

A half hour later, she pulls into her driveway and turns off Gerda. Her cell phone rings and she knows it's Deucen. *Ugh.* There is no way he would just let the day end well. She's happy he didn't show up and badger her at Daytones. It made her little dinner with Sean so pleasant.

Marney fills Deucen in on what she knows. Without results from the coroner's office or more completed interviews yet, there isn't much to discuss. Deucen wants to see her first thing in the morning in his office for a briefing. Marney rolls her eyes because the information will be the same in the morning as it is right now. *Such an idiot.*

She strolls in the house and throws the mail on the counter. She heads into the bedroom and changes into yoga pants, a tank and sneakers for a run on the treadmill. Marney loves to run, it clears her head...and keeps her svelte figure. It also helps her keep up with her very fit lover!

Forty-five minutes later, Marney is showered, shaved and happily sitting up in bed researching what kinds of knives make the wounds she saw in Andres Diaz's eyes. She knows the coroner will probably have the answer by tomorrow, but something really resonates with her and the wounds on the body. Marney knows she has seen slices like this before but can't quite remember where. *This is gonna be interesting...*

Two hours later, Marney wakes to a figure standing over her removing her laptop from her chest. Instinctively, she reaches for her holster attached to the side of her nightstand.

"Marney!" Sean whispers quickly and she retreats when she feels his warm hand on her face, his voice familiar.

Her eyes focus and she sees his beautiful face, "Oh hey." She hates that she does that. It's instinctual after years of working with Olman's worst.

"Baby, it's just me."

"Oh, I am so glaaaadddd..." She reaches for him and Sean bends to kiss her. Running her hands along his neck she wraps her arms around him and pulls him down onto her. She is so happy he came home early like he promised. She loves that Sean keeps his promises.

Marney kisses him long, parting his lips to explore his mouth with her tongue. His cologne lightly fills her nostrils and she inhales the scent of him, waking her so nicely. He responds by wrapping his hands around her then pressing his pelvis down, parting her legs. Marney purrs then, wrapping her legs around his waist. She can feel him grow excited and knows he wants to be out of his clothes...as much as she wants him out of his clothes. Moving her hands down his back she tugs at his shirt pulling it out of his jeans. Sean deepens the kiss and moans softly. Marney's body pulses in response to his voice, she wants him. Sean starts to pull at her nightie. Marney pushes him, turning him over onto his back and straddling him. She moves his arms up and hikes his shirt over his head. Next she unbuttons his jeans and tries to move off of him to the floor to remove his boots. Sean softly grabs her and shakes his head in protest, not wanting her to move from his lap. Pulling her in to kiss him again, he reaches to unfasten the clasps between her legs. Sean loves her black lace nightie. Gently, he lingers there, slowly moving his fingers inside her in swirls, treating her like she is the fragile queen he believes she is. Sean is firm but so kind with Marney, he has so much respect for her and he lets her know it. With his free hand he removes her lingerie up and over her head, throwing it to the floor so his hand is free to caress her breast. Marney throws her head back in an attempt to catch her breath. His hands are so warm and adoring. There is nowhere she would rather be at this moment. Marney finds his waist and pulls his jeans down, then his boxer briefs...freeing his glorious manhood. *Jeezus, he is perfect.* She lifts up on her knees to try to get off his lap again to remove his shoes, and again he protests, this time pulling her back down slowly onto his aroused shaft, sensually sinking into her velvet silkiness. Marney lets out a soft moan and Sean pulls her head to him pressing his lips to hers. Suddenly, the day simply disappears into unrelenting rhythmic passion...

# 6. Perfect Dysfunction

Marney slouches in her chair and exhales. Her desk is a complete mess. She picks up the pile of pink phone messages and rifles through them until she finds the one from her brother. *One week into this bitch of a case...he has to have something for me.* She picks up the phone and dials Liam.

"Jade." Liam's voice cracks.

"Hey Jade...it's Jade. You okay?" Marney laughs.

Liam's clears his throat, "Oh hey Marns, yeah just tired. How goes it?"

"Ugh, the whole week has been nothing but Diaz dysfunction. One family member after another and still no big breaks. The in-laws hate the wife, the wife can't stand the husband's family, the siblings hate each other, the coworkers can't stand him, the girlfriend could be more than one, everybody wants to point the finger at the other, and they are all in pain...it's a bloody nightmare."

"Sounds like it."

"And the guy was not very likable. The more I learn about him the more I see how anyone could have had a reason to do him in. Chris and I have to bring in his boss and coworkers again. I'm tired of talking to everyone twice." Marney sighs, "So far though, I'm not getting a real strong murder vibe from anyone."

Liam says, "I didn't think you would. Family members and acquaintances murder, but they don't usually dismember and take body parts as souvenirs."

"True. But then again it is murder...I mean what's normal?"

"Right." Liam chuckles. "Hey, how about lunch? I'm headed over to Gina's for a cheesesteak. You game?"

"Yeah, sounds good. I'll see ya in a few."

Twenty minutes later, Marney slides into the booth across from Liam.

"Hey I ordered for you, that okay?" Liam's eyebrows raise.

"Oh yeah, that's great thanks."

"Okay, so Doc Fine told me on the way out that we all need to meet up at four o'clock today...go over his report of Andres Diaz."

Marney sighs, "Oh good, so he's finished?...now maybe I can go somewhere with this case."

"Marns, it's only been a couple days." Liam smiles, defending his boss.

"Liam, I wanted this shit solved in the first forty-eight hours." Marney slides her blazer off.

Liam huffs, "You can't solve everything in the first two days. Spoiled Jadelock."

Marney flicks a straw at her brother. He catches it and laughs in surprise.

"So how's your man?" Liam flutters his eye lashes. He has always adored Sean...too much.

Marney frowns, "Things are great."

"I bet."

"They are. Can't complain about Sean. He is the most uncomplicated thing in my life." Marney accepts the water the waitress places on the table and reaches for another straw.

"Thing huh?"

"You know what I mean Liam."

"So, any future plans? I mean it's only been like ten years right? It's been at least six months since I last asked." Liam sips his coke.

Marney wants to kick him under the table, "Seven. And we aren't like that. What's wrong with just enjoying a life together? Why do we have to have future plans?"

"Don't you want something to look forward to Marns? A bigger house, maybe some kiddies?"

"No Liam. And I do have things to look forward to...every night." She smiles curtly.

"Yummm, like Sean abs...or Sean glutes...or Sean di-"

"Liam!" Marney cuts her brother off, "I'm going to call Rodger in two seconds if you keep talking about my boyfriend like that." She picks her cell phone up from the table.

"Oh, please do. Rodg loves to discuss Sean."

"You suck Liam..." Marney stops talking when the waitress puts her plate down in front of her and silently wishes there was more about the case to talk about.

"Yup, you know it sister." Liam steals her french fry and let's out a hearty laugh.

# 7. Cause of Death

Marney pops a piece of mint gum into her mouth to try to mask her nasty fried onion breath from lunch. Chris stomps in and takes the chair next to her while Liam sits across the conference table from her. It's best he is far away from her because he is testing her patience today. She squints her eyes at him daydreaming about sliding across the table and putting her brother in a headlock. It's been way too long. She looks down at the end of the table and sees Douchebag Deucen on his cell...a headlock would be appropriate for him as well, but then again his roadkill hair piece would fall off grossing her out. She erases the thought from her mind.

Olman's Medical Examiner, Doc John Fine, steps into the room looking disheveled. His pathologist, Jeremy Lockly, follows him in holding a stack of paperwork. Liam works with them but is not a paperwork guy, he is more hands on. Jeremy takes the seat next to Liam and smiles, Doc Fine sits at the head of the table opposite Deucen, way down the other end of the room.

Doc Fine's scratchy voice cuts into the room, "Okay folks, lets go over this Diaz case quickly, it's backed me up substantially. I need to get back to the other deadies. Jeremy, could you please pass out the report?"

Marney watches Jeremy respond quickly to his mentor. He's proved to be good at his job...but he gives her the "I-have-someone-locked-in-my-basement" vibe. Deucen frowns as he skims over the first few pages of Andres Diaz' autopsy.

"Okay, cause of death is blunt force trauma to the posterior skull at the external occipital protuberance. Eyes perforated with double-edged type sword sagitally through pupil, iris, sclera, and superior and inferior eyelids. Mid-to-anterior of tongue removed with same weapon. Hands, missing from body, removed with same weapon separating the scaphoid carpal area from the radius, most likely from a swift chop of the weapon since the lacerations were contused and from a lateral-to-medial movement. Probably from the first quarter of the sword near the handle...not so much the tip..."

Deucen clears his throat and opens his mouth to speak. Doc Fine ignores him and continues. "Okay, okay...oh yes, the penis. Alright, the external male genitalia were removed at the base of the scrotum in a more sawing type movement...through the clothing...and slowly if you will."

Marney looks and scans the room. Not one male looks up from their paperwork. Jeremy swallows and Marney smirks just a little. *Too funny.*

"Uh, oh yes, from a left to right slicing movement. And the way the skin is severed, I would deduce that the bottom, thicker part of the weapon was again used." Doc Fine turns a few pages. "Jeremy?"

"Um, yes sir....and latex residue was indeed found on the groin skin, the clothing, as well as the lips, cheeks, forehead and right side clothing. Which leads us to believe the suspect was wearing gloves and turned the body from prone to supine." His voice quivers, he does not speak as confidently as Doc Fine.

Marney asks, "So where abouts on the clothing were the latex deposits?"

Jeremy is ready, "Ms. Jade, it seems the right hand was about the ribs and the left hand at the ilium...err hip area if you will. So on the victim's t-shirt and also his jeans...by the waist."

Marney could see the movement in her head. The killer hits Mr. Diaz from behind, he falls on his face and then is swiftly turned over and....mutilated. *Interesting...* She flips through the next few pages of the autopsy report and lingers on each photograph. *This was murder plain and simple...but why would the killer do all the horrible parts after the victim was knocked out? Not so concerned with seeing the victim in pain as in seeing him humiliated maybe?*

"Jeremy, were there any other bodily fluids...or fibers?" Marney asks.

"Only the victim's blood, his hair, his own sweat, his own clothing fibers...and then the latex powder. Nothing else from the suspect...it's almost as if...well, it's as if the killer was in some sort of decontamination suit." Jeremy huffed a small laugh and looked around as if he had just told a joke.

Marney got him, even though no one else at the table was even listening. They were all looking through the photographs. Even Doc Fine was onto the last portion of the report and writing notes on his big yellow pad. These are the small details that help Marney solve cases so quickly. So, she is definitely listening.

Liam chimed in, "So far, every fingerprint at the scene has been accounted for. It's been a nightmare since over twenty-eight contractors have been in and out of the house...but not one fingerprint, or piece of dirt or sawdust found shouldn't be there. Even Diaz' fingernail scrapings were all from the scene...and his own DNA. All footprints around the body were cleverly smeared so we could not get a footprint for anything other than those workers that were suppose to be there."

"Hmmm, okay." Marney's wheels begin to turn faster. She is starting to get a real sense about things...and knows she is dealing with one intelligent killer.

# 8. Freyja

Limping from the pain in her hip, she slowly makes it to the edge of the fire pit. In her right hand she has the lighter fluid and with the left hand she reaches into her satchel and removes the blood-soaked body parts in the clear plastic bag. She holds them high and turns them left then right. She marvels at what's left of Andy Diaz. A slight smile appears as she thinks about how such a small penis assisted him in his own ill fate. His dumb brain, wandering eyes, nasty language, and un-pure hands, which she left behind, helped too, but it was his cheating that sealed the deal. *If only he had kept it in his pants...Mr. Grower not a Show-er...* She chuckles to herself and squirts the bag with the lighter fluid. The little canister makes a funny squeaky sound when all the fluid is expelled. She throws it in the pit to free her hand then reaches for the matchbook that reads Olman's Shelter Services on it. With a flick she lights the whole matchbook and watches the flame settle. One movement ignites the bag and she watches it fall into the pit. Next, she disposes of her latex gloves, sure to turn them inside out and send them down the pit with the lit matchbook.

Stumbling a few steps back, Freyja takes a seat in her old ripped up lawn chair. She sinks down and lays her head back, lifting one foot and then the other to rest on the side of her homemade fire pit. She looks up to watch the smokey remains of Mr. Diaz genitals and tongue just wisp through the air thinking how she had saved a few more hearts by her heinous act. That even though Juanita will mourn for some time, after it is all over and passed, she will be able to move on to the life she deserves...and never have to endure the pain of her sociopathic-narcissist-cheating husband again.

# 9. The Puffies

Chris holds the door for Marney. She scuffs her feet all the way to her desk and slams down into her chair. Exhaling a breath of air, Marney's bangs flutter. Case exhaustion is setting in.

Chris smiles at her, "Well, that was a fuckin' crap-shoot."

"Not one of those puffies did Diaz, Chris! I mean I could tell in the first five questions...and then interrogating them for hours after just...ugh...fuck..." Marney is annoyed.

"I know kid, but we gotta do what we gotta do." Chris sits forward to remove his blazer and Marney smiles. "What?"

"You know, lucky thing I was in the room, puffy number two there was practically licking your neck." Marney puts her feet up on her desk and readies to begin a relentless teasing assault on her partner.

Chris secures his gun in his desk drawer and leans back, "I thought she was going to start humping my leg after all that lip stuff she was doing. Do girls really think that shit is sexy?"

Marney laughs, "Couldn't tell ya. I'm not into the stripper-lip stuff. That's why I chimed in though...I could see she was messing with your concentration." Marney raises her eyebrows at Chris.

"She wasn't messing with my concentration Marns, she was freagin' turning my stomach!"

"You sure you weren't getting a little knob movement down in your nether regions C?" She motions towards his waist area across the desk then ducks when he throws a paperclip at her head.

Chris makes a face, "Ew, no. What I can't understand Marns, is how this guy had these three girls on the side...and they are all overweight!"

"Well, think about it Chris. He meets them all in bars, flatters them with his stories of how he loves "thick" girls, admires their "voice", gets them to take him to their places...and eventually has them paying for his shit...while keeping them hanging on with the promise of love and marriage...and his wife never knows." Marney stands and stretches.

"Yeah, they did all have that in common huh? They got duped big time. I'm going to check out all their alibi's, but I gotta tell ya, any of them had motive to do him in."

"I agree, but I'm not feeling it. None of them knew about the other, nor did they know he was married. And, the tears...all the tears were real. They weren't even mad at him! Especially puffy number two. She's had the longest relationship with him, so you can tell she is the most affected. Now, the wife...how could she not know about the others? Poor chic should run out and get tested asap!" Marney starts to pull her legs up and stretch. She feels its time for a run. The stress of the day is getting to her.

"Hmmm..."

"I think I'm going to pay her another visit. I want to get a better idea of who she believed her husband was."

"Okay, well I'll meet you back here tomorrow with what I find on the alibis. What, say...noonish?" Chris secures his gun back into his holster and puts on his jacket. It's already four o'clock, time to call it a day.

Marney straightens her desk and locks it up, "Sounds good. I'm gonna head home and get me "some run-n-sean-time"." She smiles wide.

Chris salutes, "Yeah, you do that. Tell my bro I say hey and to call me about fishing this weekend."

"Oh, I will." Marney flips her hair back in a sexy motion and Chris rolls his eyes.

# 10. Female

Marney arrives home and smells something delicious. It's her night to spend at Sean's place but he texted her that he was making dinner for her at her house. From the smell of it he had made Italian food...her favorite.

He's not in the kitchen or the living room so she does the next logical thing and searches for him in her bedroom. The room is warm and smells of vanilla oils and water. *Oh he's in the hot tub....yeah!* She secures her gun at the nightstand and calls to him.

"Sssseaaannnn?"

His deep voice is music to her ears, "In here babe."

Marney pushes the door open and delights in the sight of him naked, reading, in her jacuzzi tub, "Hey there, can I join the party?"

Sean looks up from his book, "Well, I would hope so. I've been waiting all day to see you."

Marney thinks, *oh screw the run...this is much more appealing.* She walks into her closet to disrobe, "It looks...and smells like it. I love when you have the night off from the bar."

"Chicken Parmesan okay?"

"Okay? It's more than okay...it's knob-sucking-worthy!"

Sean lets out a huge laugh.

Marney loves his laugh...and that he gets her humor. "Yes?"

"Rough day huh?" He says after composing his joy.

"Why, because I love when you cook for me? And, I love to give you man-praise for it?"

"No sweetie, because of your edge." He locks eyes with her and then glances down her perfect figure and up to her eyes again. A smile appears on his lips and he gets the sex look.

Marney laughs, "My edge?"

"Yeah, you're extra edgy on the overload days. Creative words flow from those pretty lips."

"Really?" Marney is intrigued by his observations, but not surprised. Sean is very tuned in. She loves how he just lets her be who she is. Fowl language and all. Its a cop coping thing and she knows he gets it because of his own military coping. He has his more under control...now that he doesn't have a killer to catch anymore.

"So?"

"So what?"

"How much did that poor brain have to absorb today?" He puts his book aside and reaches for her.

Marney steps into the tub on one side of him. He reaches up to hold and guide her waist. She puts the other foot in and straddles him looking into his beautiful face. Sinking down onto him, feeling the hot water...the day washes away and she holds his face to kiss him deep. Sean pulls her closer and groans in a way that ignites all her senses. It's so nice to be desired by such a generous, good-looking man. She kisses him long and reaches over to push the button for the jets. Her edgy day descriptions can wait until later.

"Another?" Sean holds the wine bottle above Marney's empty glass.

She reaches to hold the base, "Please."

He pours then leans back in his chair to finish the bottle into his own glass. Marney smiles lovingly at him admiring his plush black bathrobe. *Hmmm he is man-sexy. His tan neck peeking out at the top of the collar...his arms unfolding into beautiful hands.*

"That was truly wonderful Sean, thank you so much for dinner." Marney is sincere.

He sips his wine, "My pleasure." He wants to say more about pleasure but decides it speaks for itself. He reaches his foot under the table to rest it on the soft skin of her dangling foot. The other is up on the chair covered in her own bathrobe. "So the autopsy and the puffies huh? That's a pretty full day Marns."

"Yeah, back at it again tomorrow. So Chris says hey. Mentioned something about you two fishing at the lake this weekend. Wants you to call him." Marney takes a long sip of her wine. It is continuing to warm her joints and finish what the hot tub and Sean started.

Sean looks at his cell but decides he will call Chris later. He wants to spend as much time with Marney as he can...while she is still awake. He knows she works so damn hard on these cases, the hours are crazy, so when he can have her smiling and laughing with him at home he savers every minute making her priority. But, he also knows she loves her work, "So tell me...what are your thoughts on this whole Andy Diaz thing?"

"About the case?"

"Yeah, I know it's early, but knowing you, there is an idea of what happened circling around in that brilliant mind of yours." He sips again from his glass.

Marney is flattered, "Thanks. Well, if I go with my gut, I'm thinking that Andy Diaz got himself offed because he has terrible man-behavior...and not so much by the wife or three girlfriends. You can't go around just using people and it not come back to haunt you in some way."

"Okay, so he was an ass...that karma paid a visit? Are you thinking one of the husbands?"

"Only one of the girlfriends is divorced, the other two are college chubbies...not really enough to-"

"Oh, well maybe an upset brother, boyfriend or father?"

"Maybe, Chris is looking into it. I'm feeling something else though..." Marney starts to chew a little on her thumb nail.

"What do you mean?"

"Something darker...I don't know. Vengeful but for different reason."

"Why babe?"

"The body."

"The body?" Sean sits up.

"Yeah, the way the body was treated postmortem. The message. Not a message to us per say, but like...like there was a lesson to be taught." She puts her foot down and smoothes her bathrobe out against her thigh.

"So you think there was a message? Was there a note or any clues you didn't mention?" Sean thought she had told him everything, she usually does. He loves that Marney trusts him.

She shakes her head, "No...it's more in the silence of it. It was swift, quick, no mess...but brutal no less. Not so psycho. I mean it's psycho...but in a different way. Personal. There was no message written in blood, or grand theatrics, it was more like an ending. And it wasn't as if the killer wanted him to be tortured either, I mean all the mutilations were done after the blow to the head. Swift, clean and meticulous almost."

"And?"

Marney was quiet for a good minute and then she spoke, "I'm feeling like this killer is female...and sending a message."

"Female?"

"Yeah. Weird huh?"

# 11. NSG

Marney knocks on the trailer door of Mrs. Juanita Diaz. There is a tin type sound to the door, not your typical deep thudding knock sound. The house is not new by any means but, it looks as if someone cares enough to clean up and plant flowers. Marney steps down and continues to scan the area, and the neighborhood, while she waits for an answer.

Juanita opens the door and peeks out with swollen eyes and and a tissue in her hand, "Hello Detective Jade."

"Hi Mrs. Diaz, would you have some time to speak with me out here." Marney waves a hand toward the lawn furniture. She would prefer to not go into the house. Peoples houses give her the willies. And they almost always smell.

Juanita's eyes enlarge through the blood-shot ostentation, "Am I in trouble?"

"No ma'am. Just more questions...and some potential new information for you."

"Oh, okay. Make yourself comfortable. I am just going to get my cigarettes."

Marney nods. *Great, cancer-sticks and a baby on the way. Nice lady.*

Juanita Diaz is tall and slender, not bouffant like the girlfriends. Marney wonders what Andy Diaz was thinking cheating on her. She is pretty in a tired-mom type of way. Then again, not everything is about looks. Marney thinks about Sean for a moment. Even if he was overweight, bald or missing limbs...she wouldn't cheat on him. Sean is just *that* kind of guy. He keeps you faithful...because he is first. *Best kind of guy.* She takes a seat on the metal chair and smiles to herself. He is the kind of guy that could keep a girl even if she was blind or deaf. It's his energy. His touch. The way he treats people. He brightens the world with his presence. Well, her world anyway...she wonders how she would feel without him.

"Would you like a beer detective?" Juanita sniffles into a tissue as she stops on the second step. "It's just going to go to waste now."

Marney puts a hand up, "Oh, no thank you. Never on duty."

"Oh, yeah."

Juanita sits across the table from Marney and lights a Newport cigarette. "Sorry, my nerves are just shot."

"I can't imagine Mrs. Diaz. Look, I'm not here to rattle your cage again. I need more information from you is all."

Juanita is cautious, "Okay?"

"Alright, now I may have to hurt your feelings here but it's important to the investigation. Do you understand?" Marney is firm but still has compassion. It's helped her a lot in her cases. She usually lets Chris be the softy cop, and she the dick, but sometimes it's necessary to switch roles.

"Well, have at it. May as well get most today's crying done before I have to get the kids from school. I have to be strong for when they cry, ya know?"

Marney watches her closely and nods, "Okay, Juanita you indicated that your marriage was not great and..."

"No it wasn't...and if you're going to tell me he was cheating...well, I wouldn't be shocked." She wipes her nose with a wrinkled tissue.

"Well, then I won't shock you."

Juanita locks eyes with Marney, "Seriously? That mother-fucker was such an ass!" Marney realizes Juanita is in fact shocked and probably survives on her own denial.

"From what we know of...three other somebodies."

"Three!" Juanita takes a long drag on her cigarette then wipes another tear shaking her head.

Marney feels bad, "I'm sorry Mrs. Diaz. I can't reveal who they are or how I found them..."

"It's fine detective, I really don't want to know. I don't have friends here, so I know it's none of my friends or relatives, or anyone I would be running into, unless the show up to his fucking funeral. I wouldn't be surprised. What else can my kids go through right?"

"If it makes you feel any better, they had no idea he was married...or about each other." Marney attempts to soften the blow.

She huffs, "Well, that doesn't make me feel better detective and I am not surprised. Andy was very sneaky...narcs are."

Marney watches her and waits, hoping she elaborates. She doesn't and instead pulls another tissue out of her jean's pocket. Marney takes a small pad out and a pencil.

"Narcs? As in a CI or rat?" Marney waits.

Juanita swallows, "No, none of that cop bullshit. Andy would never go to the cops for anything...and he wasn't a criminal, or a druggie or an alcoholic. Well, he did drink, but he didn't get crazy drunk or hit us or anything."

"Okay?" Marney is confused.

Juanita laughs a small laugh, "He wasn't an alcoholic or a druggie, he was worse...he was narcissistic." Her voice lowers.

Marney searches her face and frowns, "You mean like full of himself...omnipotent...like a conceited thing?"

"Worse. Like the full-blown disorder thing! A fake....a complete fraud. The worst kind of personality disorder. Sociopathic. The kind that gets ya....well, nevermind." Juanita looks completely disgusted and Marney can see the cheating knowledge is sinking in. She is shutting down emotionally.

Marney says, "No, go on...please tell me what you were going to say."

"Lady, I would need a lifetime to explain this fucking disorder and what it's done to me...to my soul...my life! People think it's just some fly-by-day label that psychologists and psychiatrists throw out there. Just another fancy fucking word to put on paper and then prescribe medicine for. The problem is there is no cure, there is no goddamn medicine. The bigger problem is it's an epidemic...in relationships, families, generations and at almost the root of every addiction or problem within dysfunctional families. In my opinion, it is the most devastating of any situation. I mean...look what's happened!" Juanita's hands begin to shake and Marney can tell this woman is super charged on this topic. She wonders if Mrs. Diaz is overly emotional from being told about the other women...or if she could actually...have some tendencies towards...murder due to the abuse from the disorder she describes.

"So, your husband was diagnosed with this disorder?"

Juanita nods, "Yes, years ago."

"Do you know by whom?"

"Dr. Susan Cordova. She runs our group." She takes another drag on her cigarette. Hands trembling.

Marney scribbles notes, "Your group?"

"Yes, remember I told you and your partner that my Mom watches my kids on Wednesday nights so I can go out with the girls?" She makes eye contact with Marney.

Marney admits, "I do remember you saying that, because I remember wondering why Mr. Diaz didn't watch the kids for you. But, I had assumed going out with the girls meant for fun or drinks."

Juanita sighs, "Well, Andy was too busy working overtime, so I thought, to watch my kids so my Mom helps me out. My group is more about survival than fun."

"Survival?"

"Yes detective. This disorder is no small manageable condition. It destroys lives." She looks down at her hands, "I mean look at all that's happened. It's one of the statistical outcomes...murder, I mean."

Marney is intrigued now, "What do you mean?"

"NPDs. Narcissistic Personality Disordered types destroy those around them...the ones that love them the most. In the end they either end up replacing everyone who no longer serves them, replacing old family with new, drive their spouse or loved one to suicide, killing themselves...or well, you know. It's a huge disorder behind crimes of passion." She waves her hands at Marney's notepad.

Marney asks, "It's that bad?" *Is this women confessing..is she making my job suddenly easier?*

"Detective, you wouldn't believe me if I told you. No one does. Our society just thinks its another thing to brush under the rug. And, no one....understands until they live in it!"

Marney looks at Juanita for a moment. She starts to feel bad for her.

Juanita drags long on the end of the cigarette, "Sociopaths set their targets up for failure. There's triangulation, arguments, and lies that consume the relationship. At one point, I tried to rationalize Andy's strange behaviors as insensitive or accidental. But that just didn't work. Especially, when the children came along. So then you have to consider looking at the painful life events from the perspective of someone who is actively working against you, from beginning to end. Narcissists hate anyone who is whole or good. The better you are the fucking worse it makes them feel about themselves...so they have to make you feel like crap. Less then them in some way. It starts to explain everything, from the personality mirroring all the way down to the identity erosion. Sociopaths are cowards who see cheerful, loving people and feel overwhelmed with envy towards them. So they seek to destroy from the inside out, to convince themselves that *they* are superior—that love and compassion are weaknesses."

Marney interjects, "Wow, it seems you have done your homework Mrs. Diaz."

"Oh, I had no choice. It was either learn or die. Thank goodness for my group. I've learned over time, to be a survivor."

Marney hears it again, "Group?"

Juanita ignores her and continues, "With education about the disorder, we realize that the sociopath can unintentionally end up setting us free, on a journey to discover all that we have to offer to this world. And this is the irony in their arrogance: by attempting to destroy us, sociopaths only make us stronger."

Marney frowns thinking Mrs. Diaz is a little strange. She waits, then asks again, "Group ma'am?"

"What? Oh yeah, I had to seek help...so Andy wouldn't destroy me. He had me convinced I was the problem in our marriage. He nagged me to go get help, convinced me I needed a head shrinker...and I actually believed him..at first. I needed to find strength for my kids, but in seeking help I learned it wasn't me after all...the problem I mean. I was contributing of course..." She smiles. Marney can see the woman has some self-esteem...and loves her children. Although she doesn't fit the profile of a killer, she certainly had reason to dispose of her husband. A cheater is one thing, but Marney was starting to understand Mr. Diaz was a much deeper bag of tricks...and Juanita was with the deep bag for over ten years.

Marney scribbles more notes, "So what sort of group are we talking?"

"NSG...it's Narcissistic Survivors Group. It's run by Dr. Cordova. She was first our couples' therapist. She diagnosed Andy with his NPD...but, he told her she was a whack job and stormed out one day. I decided not to. I wanted to learn...I wanted to fix me."

Marney sat back and flipped the page of her little notepad, "What do you mean fix you?"

"Well, I always felt there was something wrong with me...for putting up with Andy's abuse. Friends would say, "Why do you stay Jenny?" I knew deep down our dysfunction couldn't be so successful without my contribution." She huffed and picked a stick out of her flip flop.

Marney realizes Mrs. Diaz is a lot more intelligent than she let on in her initial interview. Marney looks her over from head-to-toe again...then at the little trailer she lives in...the planted flowers and neatly placed lawn furniture. Juanita is actually pretty neat and tidy even though she doesn't have much. Marney feels sorry for her.

"How did you do, Mrs. Diaz, with learning these things about your marriage?"

Juanita half-smiled from the left corner of her mouth, "It's like stubbing an already-broken-toe detective...like a burn on a blister."

"Oh?"

"Yes, when you are in a life like this you just try to survive each day making fucking lemonade out of your lemons ya know? Then, when you do finally get help...start to learn the whys and whats of this horrible disorder...the fucking childhood wounds that start decades back, why you attracted to such a person, how you accept, ignore and move on day after day...well, you go through shock...then grief...then anger. Its a fucking co-dependent roller coaster ride from the co-dependent roller coaster of hell." She drags on her cigarette and Marney feels even sorrier for the baby in her uterus.

"Hmmmm." Marney is writing some notes and thinking how this sounds like a few cops she knows.

Juanita huffs a laugh, "Yeah, when you begin to learn how stupid you are, ya kinda go through a real pissed off angry stage...almost like 'knowing' is worse than not knowing."

Marney frowns, "What do you mean?"

"It's hard to explain, but learning about narcissistic personality disorder is almost just as bad as dealing with it...I guess because even though you know better...you still put up with it."

"Know better?"

"Yeah, because of the addiction."

"Okay?"

"You see detective...narcissists are only successful with co-dependents. Everyone else gets the hell away from them and can't supply them with attention...but me...I'm a fucking co-dep. My brain is made for shit like this. Like that saying, only the strong survive...or

God only gives you what you can handle. Well, I just got tired...ran out of forgiveness I guess. I don't want to be one of the strong ones anymore. And now look, I have to bury my husband...like shouldn't this be easier? Well, it's not easier detective, this fucking sucks. Like I went through it all for what? Some fucked up lesson?"

Marney stares at Juanita Diaz not knowing what to say. She feels like she just got twenty years worth of education in ten minutes and if anyone logically would've put Andy Diaz out of his misery it could've been her.

*Damn.*

# 12. Dr. Cordova

Marney waits in the boring beige waiting room of Dr. Susan Cordova's therapy practice. The office is small, depressing almost, with no receptionist. Marney can hear voices on the other side of the door and since the clock is winding around to the next hour, she's hopeful someone will soon emerge from the door that says "Please do not knock, Dr. Cordova is in session". Since there was no answer when she called, only voicemail from the number Juanita Diaz supplied, Marney figures she will chance it and see if she can interview the good doctor...unannounced.

Suddenly, the door opens and a tall blonde women, forty-something-ish, breezes in quickly. "Oh, uh hello. Can I help you?"

"Are you Dr. Susan Cordova?"

"Yes."

"I am detective Marney Jade of the Olmanson P.D., would you have time to speak with me?" Marney stands holding her badge out.

Dr. Cordova glances at it and then at Marney's face. "Give me one second to finish up in here. I will be right back Detective."

Marney watches her saunter back into the office and shut the door. The doc didn't exactly say yes...but then she didn't say no either so Marney figures it's worth the wait. She sits back against the contemporary red couch and takes a breath. Its a long shot to get a psychiatrist to talk with you about a client. Marney thinks how she should have Chris with her since he is better with the ladies.

Moments later a man emerges from the office door, looks at Marney, then scurries out the front door. He reminded her of the little, old man that lived a few houses over in her development. Short, round and visually hyper. Like he was late in taking his afternoon Xanax.

"Detective? Please come in." Dr. Cordova shouts into the waiting room.

Marney notices diplomas framed on every wall, dark wooden furniture and dim lighting. The room is dismal for an environment of healing. If that's what the goal is here. In all her years, Marney can't recall anyone revealing their talk therapy healed them.

Dr. Cordova motions to the chairs across from her desk where she is typing away, instead of the couches in a separate seating area. "Just give me one second to put this appointment in and I'm all yours."

"I'm sorry to disturb you Dr. Cordova, I-"

"Susan please. My clients all call me Susan." She peers over the top of her tiny glasses that make her look a little like a Mrs. Beasley doll.

Marney smiles politely, "Well ma'am, I am not here inquiring about being a client, I am hear to ask about Juanita Diaz."

Susan stops typing, "Poor Jenny. I feel terrible for her."

"So she is a client of yours then?" Marney thinks this is too easy.

"Yes, she is. Which I can't discuss in detail as you know Detective but, she has allowed me to tell you she is a client as well as a NSG member."

Marney is scribbling away on her little lined pad, "Group member? Is this the NSG group?"

"Yes. We meet once a week. Jenny has been in it for two years now." Dr. Cordova continues typing away leading Marney to believe she isn't just jotting down an appointment on her calendar. She smiles at the thought that Dr. Cordova could possibly be instant messaging or emailing someone for help...or perhaps Deucen to verify her credentials and employment at Olmanson P.D..

"And how is she doing in this group?" Marney tries.

Susan smiles sweetly, "I'm sorry I can't discuss any progress type of questions."

*Fuck.* Marney moves on, "Okay, can you explain the nature of this group then?"

"It's a closed group, so no we can't have visitors or spectators if that is what you are thinking. It's a specialty group for abused women with the purpose of survival and healing from serious narcissistic personality disordered individuals they are living with."

"So only women?" Marney watches Susan's face.

"Yes. While the concept of narcissism dates back thousands of years, narcissistic personality disorder only became a recognized illness within the last fifty years. Of that, 6.2 percent have lifetime NPD, with rates greater for men at seven-point-seven percent than for women which is four-point-eight percent. Significantly, more prevalent among black men and women and Hispanic women, younger adults, and separated, divorced, widowed and never married adults. NPD is associated with mental disability among men but not women. High co-occurrence rates of substance use, mood, and anxiety disorders and other personality disorders are also observed. With additional comorbidity controlled for, associations with Bipolar I disorder, post-traumatic stress disorder, and schizotypal and borderline personality disorders. Similar associations are observed between NPD and specific phobias, generalized anxiety disorder, and bipolar II disorder among women and between NPD and alcohol abuse, alcohol dependence, drug dependence, and histrionic and obsessive-compulsive personality disorders among men. Dysthymic disorder is significantly and negatively associated with NPD as well."

Marney exhales somewhat annoyed at Dr. Cordova's rambling, "So in all that Dr....err Susan, you are saying what?" Marney doesn't have much respect for those who spat off a bunch of crap to try and show their intelligence rather than just answering a damn question.

Susan smirks, "Basically, women are more abused by narcissistic personality disorder then men so...I only have women in the group at this time."

*Jeezus! Why couldn't she just say that fifty fucking seconds ago?* "Okay, understandable. Have men been invited and just not gone or-"

"No, I would create a separate group for men...if it were warranted." She closes her laptop and sits back in her large leather swivel chair.

Marney writes more, "What can you tell me about Mr. Andres Diaz?"

"I have no comment on that Detective. I didn't know the man too well. He didn't continue couple's therapy after the first few visits as Jenny has told you."

"Oh?" Marney watches her face. So they have talked...and obviously in the last two hours since Marney was already with Juanita today. How interesting.

"Well, I wasn't surprised. Narcs hate talk therapy unless they can manipulate the therapist into being their ally...it's the if-you-aren't-with-them-you-are-against-them thinking they have."

"So, you are confirming Mr. Diaz was a narcissist?"

Dr. Cordova smirked, "Yes. I did diagnose him with the disorder detective, which Jenny told you, but to get much more out of me, you will have to come back with a court order, or warrant or something...." It's not uncommon for psychiatrists to become too involved with their patients. Marney takes a good look at Susan, from head-to-toe, to see if she gets a sense of her being a murderer. It would be so interesting if that were the case. *Olman would have it's first super-fucking-hero psychiatrist...ridding the town of dysfunction...*

"In group, many times, we don't use names. Some of the ladies even change the name or sex of their abusers. It makes them feel more protected...especially if children are involved. They will say it's their mother for instance instead of their spouse...or boss." Dr. Cordova randomly changes the topic.

Marney thinks this odd, but the whole disorder and group strikes her as odd. And the perceived seriousness of it. She's heard of narcissism, like back in college when studying greek mythology, and then here and there throughout life, but this is the first time she has heard of a support group designed specifically for it. "Susan, couldn't these ladies go to an Al-anon or AA meeting and get the same thing?"

Dr. Cordova smiles, "Well, that's how it used to be...but, times are changing."

"Why is that? Money? Insurance billing?" Marney has to ask.

"No, in fact the group is free. I don't bill for that time each week. And to answer your why, it's because NPD is usually the foundational issue for such conditions as alcoholism, drug use and abuse...which those other meetings address. My group addresses family of origin issues, co-dependency, survival and change. A "breaking-the-cycle" type of approach." Dr. Cordova stands up.

Marney is scribbling away, then turns when there is a faint knock at the door.

Dr. Cordova excuses herself and walks towards the door as it opens. "Oh, hello Freyja. Come in. I am just finishing up and will be out of your way."

An older women, in her mid-sixties enters pushing a cleaning cart. Marney notices she is short, limps and makes eye contact for only two seconds or so before going about her cleaning duties. The old woman seems very disinterested as she flaps a small trash bag in the air to open it. Something about her swift movements strikes Marney as odd. It's as if from the waist down she is in slow-mode and old and achy, but from the waist up she is quick as shit. *Hmmm...*

"Detective Jade, I must apologize. I have an appointment I can't miss-" Dr. Cordova walks back to her desk and bends down to get her purse from the bottom desk drawer.

Marney stands, "Oh, I do apologize for interrupting your day. Could I call and make an appointment if I have more questions?" Marney realizes how this sounds and looks towards the cleaning lady who is watching her with glances between dusting the furniture on the far right of the room. Although Dr. Cordova spoke to her in English, Marney frowns wondering if "Freyja" understands the language. She can't quite ascertain the women's nationality. She has dark skin and black hair with white peppered throughout. Marney is guessing she is of hispanic decent, or maybe more native indian.

Dr. Cordova smiles, "Sure. I can try to squeeze you in if there is more I can help with. I am fully booked until the first of the year, but I'm sure we can schedule a lunch or something. Leave me your card."

Marney stands, puts her business card on the desk and shakes her hand. She can tell by the handshake that the good doctor is not very interested in anymore questioning. "Okay great. Well, thank you for your time then."

# 13. Another One

"Marns, that's some crazy shit." Chris gnaws on a toothpick with his wide-eyed glare.

Marney nods while typing, "Yup. Gonna be even weirder trying to explain it to the douche who demands these daily reports...doesn't even read them."

"Aw man, he will never go for this psycho babble. What is it again...narcissism group what?"

"Narcissistic Survivors Group. You mean he will argue it with me even after the doc confirmed Diaz' disorder? Why ever would you say that my fine partna man? Cuz douche number one is a NPD type as well?" Marney uses her best swedish accent.

Chris laughs, "Bingo babe...you know how he gets when our case shit hits home..."

Marney chuckles.

"What?"

"No, I agree. Hey Chris? You gotta hit the head?" Marney wheels her chair to the printer.

"Yeah...hey, how'd you know?" Chris twists his face and puts his hand on his stomach.

"Well...you said shit twice and...it smells a little funny."

Chris smiles and sees Leeana Kazib coming towards his desk, "Hey Kazib? You smell popcorn?"

She inhales deep, takes a whiff, then wrinkles her nose, "Aw gross you fucker!"

Chris ducks as Leeana swings at him with a pack of papers in her hand. He maneuvers out of his chair and heads for the bathroom laughing hysterically.

Marney loves how Chris antagonizes Leeana. *Maybe one day she might actually develop a sense of humor.*

*\*\*\**

Sean runs his lips down Marney's back. She let's out a soft moan that sweetly echoes in his dark bedroom. Thrusting slowing forward he exhales warm breath into her ear and Marney grabs the satin sheets in her fists. She wants to beg him in some way, the pleasurable torture is more than she can stand, but no words come to mind. Again, he retracts slowly and she moans anticipating another wave of pleasure. Then....her phone beeps. *Nooo...*

*\*\*\**

Watching Sean's muscular glutes leave the room, Marney reaches for her cell. There are five missed calls, and a text:

# Another gross one. JO

Marney lays back rolling her eyes and resting them on the streak of light on the ceiling. John O'Malen just ruined Marney's entire week...*err year. Another gross one means serial killer for sure. No, this isn't happening.*

Marney springs up and out of Sean's amazing king size waterbed. It smells like Drakkar...and of Sean. Two of her favorite scents. She texts John she is en route when really she is only on the way to the shower.

## 1. 14. Mike Noonan

The body is a few days old. It smells ripe and is swollen like a tick. Marney stares, heart racing. Mr. Michael Noonan presents with a stab wound to the heart, front teeth knocked out, tongue removed, hands removed yet nearby and...penis and scrotum...removed and gone. Marney dreads the process of this and any killings after. Olman will now be under the microscope every day...until this psycho is caught.

"You know what this means Jade?" Chief Deucen clenches his teeth and speaks to Marney as if she is in trouble. *How does he appear at every crime scene? Does pudgy never sleep?*

Marney shows no emotion but makes eye contact with her overly emotional boss. She chooses not to answer him. She isn't remotely interested in Douchebag Deucen's impression of Captain Obvious. She instead, slows her racing heart with a deep breath and again scans the garage to continue her job. Mr. Noonan wasn't reported missing, rather, found by his young wife when she turned on the lights in her garage to get a roast out of the freezer to defrost for an upcoming family dinner over the weekend. Between hurling up her guts out in the driveway and crying, she has explained how she did not one, but two shifts, at the local deli she works at, an alibi that is checking out so far...for the last three days she hasn't seen her spouse. The last time she saw her husband was in bed, 6:00 a.m. in the morning when she left for work on Wednesday. Another wife not surprised when her husband did not return home for days. Marney could only guess that their marriage was on the rocks...and Mrs. Kerry Noonan is most likely in the NSG!

"Jade! I'm talking to you." Deucen is beginning to perspire from his forehead.

"Sir, I have a job to do. I would suggest you make the phone call to the FBI...before any more time passes." Marney keeps her cool and tries to breathe through her mouth to ease the rotten egg stench permeating her nose. A three-day-old body is not the most desirable situation.

"Fuck! Do you believe this? Fucking FBI case now in Olman-fucking-New-Mexico!" Deucen stomps out of the doorway like a spoiled child almost colliding into Chris, who looks disheveled with his hair sticking up on one side and a t-shirt on under his blazer.

Marney looks over, "Hey C...you're gonna love this."

"Whoa! Smells peachy Marns...oh crap, Marney is this guy's nuts gone too?" Chris stops abruptly. His large hands come up and run through his hair as his brain engages. Stress appears from all directions and rests on his forehead.

"Yup."

"Aw Marns....no, no, no, no, nooo...." Chris rarely looks unhappy...but his face goes pale and disbelief washes over it.

"Sorry bud, Olman just hit major mode." Marney bends down squinting at the damage done to Mr. Noonan's teeth. Looks like something the butt of a knife or gun could do. The teeth are snapped off high near the gums and Marney can tell the nose was bleeding as the body expired.

Chris takes a deep breath, wrinkles his nose and then reaches for plastic gloves, "Okay, here we go."

"Yeah...gonna be quite a ride."

*** 

Marney leans back in her chair and cringes as it creaks with twenty-some years of age at its joints. Chris has his feet up on his desk and his head hanging back off the back of his own chair. He is staring up at the ceiling. The station is quiet at five in the morning and Marney can tell Chris is trying to brace himself for the next few months...mentally wrap his mind around it. It's been a long time since New Mexico had a serial killer....and a first for Olman.

The door to the detective's unit opens. Six-foot-four, two-hundred thirty pounds of forty-something-year-old FBI agent steps in. Marney turns and locks eyes with one of the most handsome men she has ever seen. *Fuck.*

"Howdy." His voice is deep but smooth.

Chris plants his feet to the floor and stands, walking over to put his hand out. "Hello, Detective Christopher Shean."

"Good to meet you Detective, Mike Taylon, FBI." Mike Taylon's hand meets Chris's and Marney can't tell whose is larger. It's like two giants readying to fight in the same arena. She feels almost invisible.

Chris motions towards Marney, "Uh, this is Marney Jade...lead detective on the case...err cases..." Chris fades off realizing the seriousness of the now, serial killer situation. The FBI is standing in the detective unit. There is no going back to just "a murderer in Olman" type headlines.

Marney stands as Mike Taylon rushes to shake her hand, "Nice to meet you ma'am." His eyes are soft...and almost gray.

*Ma'am? Wow, manners.* "Hello." Marney thinks she should say more, but words escape her as Mike Taylon's fierce gaze locks on her. Her skin feels warm, his gaze warmer.

Mike looks down at Marney, "So, it looks as if Olman has it's first serial killer?"

Marney almost winces with the words. Detective work is so much more interesting when not so high profile...and done without the help of the FBI, no offense to Mike Taylon. "Well, it would appear that way." She almost sounded condescending...but her voice was smooth.

"Or perhaps a copy cat?" Mike huffed a laugh to try and lighten the mood.

"Not sure if that would be better sir, we have two dead bodies inside of three weeks." Chris interjects breaking Marney's stare at Mike Taylon.

Mike turns to Chris, "Yes, that's what I understand. Looks like we have our work cut out for us." He turns back facing his body toward

Marney again. His eyes dance as he watches her. "Do you like pancakes?"

Marney frowns, "Uh..."

"Pancakes it is! Okay, it's morning, we have two cases to discuss and I can't think without pancakes. Where is the best place for pancakes here?" Mike claps his hands and turns towards the door.

Marney looks at Chris, Chris looks at Marney...then the two of them grab their blazers and head toward the door too.

# 15. Rundown

"Okay puppies, what do we know?"

Marney watches Mike and how he runs his finger down each side of a sugar packet. So far, Mike Taylon is very laid back and light-hearted for an agent. Almost too easy to be around. Almost enjoyable. She expected a more stuffy, disciplined agent. One with a hidden personality. Mike seemed to have his personality out there for the world to see two miles before his body shows.

The waitress brings a pot of coffee and three coffee cups. Chris pulls out his notepad, "Okay-"

Marney interrupts, "So Agent Taylon, no partner?"

"Mike please, call me Mike. She's on maternity leave if you can believe that. Man, is she going to be pissed." He lifts his eyebrows and chuckles while pouring each of them a cup of coffee.

"Why is that?" Marney if curious to know more of why Mike says the things he says. Chris kicks her lightly under the table. She ignores him. "Is this your specialty?"

"Well, everything is my specialty. But for good ole' Tracy...I guess it'd be our third serial case together." Mike is sounding more southern as the morning progresses. Marney isn't letting up.

"More for you then?"

"More what? Oh serial cases? Yeah. I've been at this for a long time darlin'. You're gonna love the ride." Mike sits back stirring sugar into his coffee.

Chris interjects, "Really? Is there a lot of the serial things going on then?"

"Well, there is more than you think. A lot of cases don't even get to the media. That's what I'd prefer here. Those damn reporters are just trying to do their job, I know, but they make ours more difficult. We're gonna try and keep this quiet for as long as we can."

Marney likes the sound of that, "So, how many of these cases did you say you've worked on?"

Chris looks at Marney confused. Mike smiles politely, "I didn't say actually, but enough to help you out detective."

Chris says, "So, I guess we have some pretty psycho killers in this country then huh?"

"Naw, it's worse in Russia. But, in the world of serial killers...yeah, psycho is a good word, sociopaths are almost there...but, psychopaths are actually successful." Mike clears his space and lights up when the waitress places his food in front of him. Marney watches him and the boyish grin he shows as he marvels at his pancakes. By the size of Agent Taylon, Marney can tell the man is an expert at eating. She can't help but notice how he somehow puts it all in the right areas. He is football player big...but in shape.

"Well, this is a first for Marney and I." Chris offers.

Mike looks at Marney, "Oh?"

"Yeah, so we are all ears."

Marney looks at Chris wondering why he is brown-nosing so much. He is usually pretty calm.

"Well, I hear that you both are damn good at solving Olman's cases...the best in the department." Mike eyes Marney again. She sips her coffee and shrugs a bit. She certainly never hears that from her boss, but the numbers indicate they are the best.

Chris continues, "Well, I would have to give that credit to Marns here." He points at his partner.

"Yeah, Jadelock is it?" Mike smiles.

Marney sighs, "It's just Jade...that's some-"

"It's a lil' nickname Marney doesn't really like-" Chris starts to tease.

"Chris and I solve over ninty percent of our cases...so we do well. Good teamwork..." Marney kicks Chris back under the table as a mild warning. Mike changes the subject.

"Okay, so give me the rundown so far. What are your...uh, deductions?" He take a huge mouthful of pancakes and Marney watches maple syrup ooze down one side of his salt-and-pepper colored goatee. She fights the urge to reach out and wipe his mouth with her napkin.

"Are you familiar with narcississisiss....what is it again Marns?" Chris starts to stuff his own face and Marney wonders what it is with giant men and their carbs.

"Narcissistic Personality Disorder." She watches Mike, he wipes his mouth and nods.

"Studied it in the academy like a century ago, why?"

"So far we've been on a trail of a group that meets to discuss...err survive family members with this sociopathic type disorder...and I am willing to bet Mrs. Noonan is probably involved in some way as well. It's like a co-dependent's anonymous group, if you will." Marney takes a bite of her omelet.

Mike uses his fork to cut another huge wedge of pancakes, "Let me guess, wife of victim number one is in this survivor's group because hubby was an ass...and now you are thinking wife number two may have ties." He stuffs his mouth again.

Marney likes how his brain works, "I am headed back to the station to interview Mrs. Noonan. I am betting she will know what I'm talking about when I ask the NSG questions...which doesn't look good for the little wives club."

"Could be the doc no?" Mike watches Marney.

Marney realizes Mike is not lazy and unlike her boss, has read her reports from the last couple weeks. She is impressed. "Could be, I interviewed her but didn't get the murder vibe."

"Hmmmm."

"Could be at the control panel." Chris muffles through his food-filled mouth.

Mike nods, "Right, some docs are on that ego trip and like to put things in motion. They use the minions to do their dirty work. Almost a little narc themselves yes?"

The thought had crossed Marney's mind. Mike Taylon was beginning to grow on her...they think alike. She is almost enjoying her breakfast with the two hungry ogres.

"Okay, so take me through everything you've got and we can see where we're at and how to proceed." Mike leans back and readies himself. Marney notices he doesn't write anything down and wonders if he has one of those minds that just remembers every detail...in every order.

She gets her pad out, "Okay."

# 16. Kerry Noonan

Mrs. Kerry Noonan couldn't be more than nineteen years old and a hundred pounds soaking wet. Her eyes are swollen, almost shut, with grief. She watches Marney, Chris, and Mike enter the room and hugs herself in an oversized New Mexico hoodie. Marney gets a hyperthyroidism vibe as she runs her eyes over Kerry Noonan. She is almost too thin.

Mike makes the necessary introductions as Kerry shakes hands between sniffles. Everyone takes a seat and Marney can suddenly feel the fatigue settling in around the back of her eyes. She really isn't in the mood for a three-hour interview and prefers to go home and sleep...with Sean.

"Okay Kerry, so tell me...your husband ever bite you?" Mike noisily pulls out a chair and flops down all two-hundred-fifty pounds of himself into it, eyeballing Mrs. Noonan into insecurity. She looks appalled and stares at him. Marney can tell that even though Mike seems like a nice southern fella...he plays bad cop real well. It's refreshing that she doesn't have to do it this time.

The room falls silent after Chris and Mike finally stop moving in their chairs. Marney watches Kerry. She moves her eyes from the table, up Mikes frame and to his face, "Yes."

Marney watches Mike, she is impressed with him. More than she likes to admit. He has it...the look, the attitude...the sexy self-esteem that isn't too over-the-top, and the experience. She searches his face, trying to find something she hates...she can't. In fact, she doesn't at all like how she is feeling about him. The guy is charismatic. Strong, tall, muscular. She squeezes her eyes. *Knock it off Marney! Pay attention.*

"Leave scars on ya?" Mike is on a roll.

"Yes, sir." Kerry looks down, embarassed.

Marney chimes in, "You've been married how long Mrs. Noonan?"

Kerry turns her head to Marney and softens her voice, "Two years."

Mike fires off another question, "Start biting you before or after the wedding?"

"We didn't have a wedding...but yeah, after we were married. Not all the time, just here and there."

"But always where the marks could be hidden correct?" Mike seems to be reading from a script he's got in his head. Chris stares at him in awe. Marney knows he is getting to the missing teeth part. She would ask the same questions, just not so early into the interview. Mike convinces her he is a "no-bullshit" kinda guy. She makes a mental note that she needs to be more direct...then maybe interviews would go quicker. She feels like Mike is getting somewhere.

"Yeah."

"Yes?"

"Yes, sir." Kerry wipes her eyes.

Marney knows Mike is leading her in his line of questioning, which the right lawyer would have a field day with, if it were a trial. She decides to take a chance, "Mrs. Noonan, how long have you been in NSG?"

Kerry turns her neck and locks eyes with Marney, "What? Did you guys spend the last few hours investigating me?" Her voice is soft...like a child. No one moves. She blows her nose then says, "Since it started in 2012...you been checking up on me or what?" Kerry Noonan's voice is raising...she is curious. Marney's hunch was right.

"Do you know Juanita Diaz?" Marney watches Kerry's eyes, wondering if the two might be close.

"Yes, I know of her. I don't know, know her...she hasn't been back to group for awhile."

Mike asks, "So you two aren't friends in any sort of capacity?"

"No sir, and what's said in the group stays in the group. I know her as Juanita only. Then a couple week's back someone was talking and mentioned her last name too. We usually only go by first names or nicknames."

Chris stops writing for a minute, "So, discussing her or her recent grief is not discussed in the group?"

Kerry turns to answer him, "I didn't say that. But what is said there...stays there. Are you guys thinking there is something similar with our husbands?"

Marney remembers seeing Kerry at Andres Diaz' funeral with a large group of women...around Juanita. Kerry is starting to show she is going to be tight-lipped about things. She is young, but a little more put together than Juanita Diaz. Marney can't tell if this is due to hiding guilt...or loyalty to the group. Either way, this group is definitely moving into the spotlight. Marney ignores her question, "Uh, how many women in your NSG Kerry?"

"I don't know."

"Roughly?"

"I don't know, I never counted."

Chris interjects, "Mrs. Noonan can I get you anything? Coffee or water maybe?" He smiles his most charming smile.

Mike asks, "Mrs. Noonan, when does your group meet?"

Kerry falls silent for a moment.

Marney feels sleep coming on strong and knows she needs to get some rest soon. She begins to put her pad and pencil in her blazer.

Kerry clears her throat, "Coffee thanks...Wednesdays, and I want a lawyer."

*Fuck.*

***

Marney drives home slow. She doesn't like that she can't stop thinking of Mike Taylon. *What is it about this guy?*

Her eyes blink slow, she shakes her head to refocus on the road...only a few more minutes and she will be in her bed. Ahhh, sleep. She smiles with the thought of sleep. Beautiful, sweet...sleep.

Her cell rings on the seat next to her. The screen reads "Dbag Deucen" and Marney huffs a small laugh. She signed off shift an half hour ago...there is no way she is answering his call now. Besides, Mike Taylon is in the station. She figures the two of them can spend time together while she gets a solid six hours with no interruptions. It's gonna be a long winter by the looks of things...so there is no rush.

# 17. Drinks

Marney finishes concealing her last weapon in her boot and emerges from her closet. It's seven o'clock and Sean is already at at the bar working. She missed the entire day with him, but the sleep felt so good and was very needed. Her phone beeps:

# Meet me at The Palms for drinks? MT

Marney frowns. She's heard FBI agents stay at The Palms hotel when in town. She didn't realized Mike Taylon had her number.

# Chris there?

# No.

# Shld I bring him?

# No.

Marney gets a swirly feeling in her stomach and feels she should tell him no. Then again, he is the agent in charge of Olman's now serial killer situation...and she is kind of curious as to what he wants.

# Be there in 12.

***

Marney walks through the front of The Palms hotel. It's a nice place on the east side of Olman. Not too fancy, moderately expensive. She mouths "bar" to one of the two front desk girls. The more aware one points to the other side of the lobby. Marney walks towards a lit up doorway with a sign over it that says "Retreat Bar & Grill". Inside she scans the room. It's a nice bar with Billie Joel music playing and the pleasant smell of sirloin steak in the air. Mike Taylon is sitting in a booth toward the back exit door and waves her over.

Marney makes note of the twenty-three other patrons in the bar and their general demeanor. Seems like an older crowd...calm. She relaxes a little and approaches his table. Mike stands as she comes near. She slides in across from him, slightly uncomfortable to have her back to the door, but more uncomfortable with his gentlemanly nature. They were cops after all, not on a date.

"Hey Detective Jade, glad you could make it."

Marney notices he has a glass of whiskey on the rocks in front of him, "Marney is fine."

"Okay Marney. What can I get you?"

"I'll have an ice tea. I've got to go to the station and get some paperwork done." She smiles slightly.

Mike smirks, "A whiskey it is then." He waves over the waitress. "You like whiskey right Marney."

Somehow she feels he already knows the answer. She watches him.

Mike sits back against the booth and looks at Marney. He wipes his goatee and then places his hand around his drink. "Marney, I figure we should get to know each other a little bit...looks like this case is going to take some time."

"Oh? And why is that?"

"The getting to know each other part...or the case taking time?" Mike's eyes dance.

Marney sits back, then decides to take off her blazer knowing her gun is well concealed in the back of her jeans. She doesn't answer.

Mike continues, "Well, I would like to know a little more about you if we are going to work closely to catch this wacko and solve the case."

Marney finds this humorous, "Well sir, we both know you have been through my and Chris's file...as well as the case files, so what more do you need to know?"

"Okay Marney, let's not do the sir thing. It's Mike. And you're right, I have read over what I have been provided. Chris is a pretty straight forward guy. Good cop. You both do great work. Seems like your boss is an ass but your other coworkers have respectful things to say...especially about you."

Marney is pleasantly shocked, "Okay."

"Let's see. You weren't on patrol a day passed five years, good run of that but detective work seems to suit you better. Over ninety-three percent of your cases are solved which puts you in demand when anything challenging comes along. Daddy was a good cop, kept his nose clean, retired in enough time to still do some fishing and find himself a new wife. Mom died when you were twelve, she was tough but not enough for the big C. You have an older brother named Asner who works offshore rigging, and a little brother named Liam who works crime scenes, many times alongside of you. None of you are married...odd, but okay." He sips his whiskey as the waitress approaches and orders another for himself and one for Marney. When she leaves Marney waits for him to continue but he doesn't. He just looks at her.

Marney looks into his eyes. He is mesmerizing...and correct so far. He waits.

She takes the bait, "Gay."

His eyebrows lift.

"My little brother. Liam? He's gay. Has a lover named Roger. My older brother...wants a family but he and his lady of eight years are too comfortable...so who knows. My father loves his life of fishing, romancing Glenda and living in his log cabin in Reuna. We get together for weekends and holidays, talk once or twice a week. None of us kids are married...probably because we saw Dad struggle with Mom's illness and death...being a cop an all." The waitress delivers their two drinks. Marney sips hers. It goes down smooth. Mike is still watching her.

"Okay...and you?" Mike can't help it.

"Me what?" She smiles knowing full well what he is asking. Why he asked her out for drinks.

"Why haven't you taken the plunge into the depths of the marriage abyss?"

"Who says I haven't?" She is coy.

Mike smiles at her, their eyes lock.

Marney blinks first wondering why she finds this banter fun, "I have my reasons."

"Okay, that's fair."

"And you?"

"Oh, are you curious?"

Marney sips her drink, "Just want to know who I'm working with I guess."

Mike's smile fades, "Widower, five years. Got a twenty-year old daughter. College. I enjoy my work."

Marney watches him, "I'm sorry."

"She loves engineering...my daughter. She can figure out all that mechanical shit. I stick to figuring out people." He laughs.

Marney is direct, "Was it illness...or accidental?"

Mike's face goes cold, "Sudden." He stops there and sips his whiskey again. "So, have you got someone?"

Marney squints. She knows he knows the answer to that...especially after spending some time with Chris after she left the station to get some sleep. She can even bet Chris mentioned Sean was his best friend...she plays along. "Yeah, I got a guy."

Mike smiles and nods. Marney can't ascertain what he's thinking. "Good guy?"

"Yeah...he is. Not out to hurt anybody, takes care of his parents...fought for his country, treats me like gold." She sips her drink to pause.

"Nice. Gotta respect that."

"Yeah...hard to find in this world." Marney baits him.

Mike takes it, "I agree...especially with what we do."

"Hmmm..."

Mike takes his blazer off, "Speaking of what we do, how are you handling these two cases?"

Marney wonders if he got the answers he needed and if this is turning into a work meeting now...from whatever it was. "Well, it went from a murder to a serial killer in the span of three weeks so..." She smiles.

"No, I mean how are you feeling about it all?"

Marney feels exposed...even more so than the personal questions about her life. Mike looks compassionate, caring almost. She blinks not knowing what to say.

"How do you feel you want to proceed?" Mike looks genuinely interested.

She suddenly feels important. Like he really wants to work with her...not in front of her. "Well, I'm definitely heading toward this little private group first...if it doesn't go anywhere fine but I can't ignore my gut on this one."

"Do you do that often? Ignore your gut I mean?" He smiles.

She smiles back, "No...not too much."

"Good. People who go against their internal signals distrust too much. I have a feeling you solve a lot of your cases with that good gut of yours."

"Meaning?"

"Meaning...well, just keep it up. Whatever your strategy, it's working." Mike tips his drink towards her for emphasis.

She feels somewhat flattered.

"That is why Ms. Jade, you solve most of your cases yes? I'm going to need your gut if we're going to solve this bullshit."

Marney smiles at Mike's teamwork attempt. Again, she agrees with him. He is turning out to be cooler than she thought. *Who says FBI agents are dicks.* She nods.

Mike moves on, "So tell me more about this NSG. I mean I read your reports for Deucen. The facts are nice and all...but, whats your take on these women?"

The waitress comes over to check on the table. "Darlin, I am starting to feel this whiskey too much, would you mind bringing me one of those sirloin steaks, medium rare with a baked potato and a side of broccoli? How bout' it Marney?"

Marney finds his mind, and how it works, amusing. She is actually enjoying herself and she's starving, "Uh, yeah that sounds really good."

Mike holds up his fingers, "Make that two okay ma'am?"

Marney turns to the waitress, "And could I have a water with lime please?"

"Ah, you a lightweight girl?" He laughs.

Marney sees Mike may have had a whiskey before she showed up...he is starting to look very relaxed and his pupils are dilating. "No, I just prefer to digest my food with water. The whiskey is great though."

"Okay, let's make that two waters with our meal okay?" Mike joins the digesting idea.

The waitress nods and disappears. Mike shifts in his seat bringing his foot up to rest on his knee. Marney notices his chest through the unbuttoned opening of his shirt where his tie used to be. There is some hair that is beginning to get a few grays in between. Not too much...just enough. *Very nice.*

"Okay, you were going to tell me your thoughts on Narcissist Survivor Groups...err at least the one here in Olman." He sips his drink and looks at her ready to hear her.

Marney enjoys being asked, "Well, I think it's going to be difficult...but we have to dig deep into this group, or at least an understanding of it. It's a good lead...worth spending time on."

He's watching her. Looking at her hair, her eyes, trailing down her frame. "Because..."

"Well, because of the way the bodies were presented."

He squints, "Go on."

Marney feels a surge of energy, "Well, there is the manner of death for each. Diaz was killed by blunt force trauma to the posterior skull...Noonan a stab to the heart."

"Right. Well wait, how do you know Noonan died from the stab wound to the heart...oh...your brother Liam right?" Mike points at her.

Marney smiles. She likes talking to him. He is intelligent and can stay on her level...even when drinking. "Anyway, both show that the killer was possibly smaller or weaker than the victims. The mutilations all happened postmortem which indicates the killer needed the victims incapacitated in order to complete his or her tasks."

"Her."

"What?" Marney stops.

Mike waves his hand, "I'm betting it's a her."

Marney smiles, "Most likely, the victims were not large men, so I would have to agree with you. But remember, we live in the land of little mexican dudes...never know who's husband is pissed."

"Naw, I'm feeling it's all female." Mike laughs.

"Anyway, the tongues were removed."

"Classic speak no evil type shit." Mike says matter-of-factly.

Marney smiles, "Right...but I'm thinking more of abuse."

"Abuse?"

"Yes, well after reading up on the narcissism stuff...compulsive lying and verbal assaults are MAJOR traits of the disorder. One could remove a tongue to symbolize that the lying is unacceptable and must be stopped." Marney's eyes light up.

"Or so that it will no longer go on in the afterlife."

"Very poetic Mike."

He stops at the sound of his name coming from her mouth. Marney locks eyes with him...then looks away and continues, "The teeth missing from Mr. Noonan could be from the biting, genius by the way...

"Thank you."

"You're welcome. I knew where you were going with that. Kerry Noonan didn't deny it. Her husband was a sick bastard biter. I've seen it before in one particular case. Diaz wasn't a biter." Marney takes a breath.

"And the hands?"

"Well, like you mentioned...a touch-no-more type symbol...same with the genitals."

Mike doesn't flinch, "Right, like no-more-cheating type shit."

"Right." Marney likes how his mind stays on topic, "Both men were known to cheat. Brutal...but betrayal sometimes warrants..."

"Uh?" Mike looks worried but then smiles.

"I meant presents. Sometimes betrayal presents in the genital area with psychos. I've read its more so with sexual abuse...I guess it is abuse though if he's cheating." Marney laughs at her slip up.

Mike chuckles, "Scared of you...but, you're right. When we study profiling...genital mutilations are often linked with betrayal or molestations. But, if you feel cheating warrants castration then we will go with that Furor Jade!"

Marney puts her fingers to her mouth as she lets out a hearty laugh.

Mike cracks up...then looks at her more serious. "Don't cover your smile."

"What?"

"When you laugh...try not to cover your mouth. You have a beautiful smile..." He realizes he's complimented her and tries to cover it up with a welcoming smile for the waitress. "All right, time to grub!"

Marney watches him as he helps the waitress place their food down. *Jeezus he is gorgeous...and big!* Marney watches him with the waitress and sees he is gracious. Not just in size...but in greatness. Mike Taylon is something to see.

He thanks the young girl and looks back to Marney, "Okay friend, let's not talk about scrotums for a few. I'm starving...those pancakes only took me so far today."

"You haven't eaten since our six a.m. feeding?" She is shocked.

"Well, does coffee and danish count? You have some crazy office lady who keeps bringing me junk food." He laughs as he cuts his steak.

Marney smiles, "Oh, you mean our day dispatcher Freda Jackson. Yeah, she's like that.

"Got a fresh mouth on her."

Marney smiles at him, "You have no idea. She likes you right now...wait until you piss her off."

He eyes her, "Marney, I am going to try very hard not to do that."

She likes the sound of her name when he says it and wonders if he is talking about just Freda...or her too. She laughs, "Good plan."

"Okay, so speaking of plans...how do you recommend we proceed with these cases?"

"Well, you're the serial killer expert Mike. What would you suggest because I am trying to figure out how to get to these women in the NSG. The doc is not going to make it easy."

Mike wipes his mouth with his napkin and leans his elbows on the table, "Listen, you are a dynamite detective kid...and I am no expert, I have some ideas but ultimately we both know I am here to babysit your boss mostly. He's a politician, not so much a cop, and I have to bring balance to his job and yours. I like what I've researched on you...and I am very interested...in your err gut and how it says we should proceed.

There isn't a protocol I follow...so you are my guide here." He picks up his fork and knife again and cuts into his dinner.

Marney is flattered and feels she can relax a little more. She knows she's out of her league when it comes to him and to serial killer cases...he's being nice...but she's willing to learn. She is just going to have to take it step by step. "I want to sit in on one of those meetings. I want to get a visual of what happens there and of who shows up."

Mike chews like a gentleman, mouth closed, swallows then speaks, "You know that can't happen right?"

"Yes."

"That would be ideal, but even if you got the necessary paperwork to impose on their little lady meeting...they'd clam up tighter than a humming bird's ass."

Marney smiles at the birdie visual that pops into her mind, "Yup."

"So?"

"So....send someone in?" She furrows her brow.

"Close...but a new member would set the same tone. They'd all be closed lip and focus on the new member's arrival and dysfunction." He takes a sip of whiskey, his water obviously second choice.

Marney bites her lip, "Yeah, you're right. Damn, I need to get to someone who is in the group..."

Mike points his knife in her direction, "Now remember, it has to be trial worthy. Most these serial things end up in court."

"I'm just hoping that happens before anymore bodies turn up."

His eyes glimmer, "You've got a good heart Jade."

Marney smiles. *Yeah, you too Mike.*

# 18. Distraction

Sean looks up from his laptop, "Hey you."

"Hey."

"You okay?"

Marney secures her gun to the nightstand and bends forward kissing Sean. His lips send a surge through her, "Oh yeah."

Sean follows her eyes as she pulls away and begins to disrobe. "Hmmm, is that whiskey?"

"Yup."

"You cheating? Going to other bars instead of mine?" Sean is playful.

"Yup. Meeting with the FBI agent about the case. Apparently, drinks and steak are the appropriate way to discuss a serial killer." Marney heads for her closet.

Sean watches her, "Guess that isn't so bad. Could be worse, like watching Deucen get a haircut."

Marney laughs from inside the closet, "Yeah."

"So have the cases gone public yet...have you all named the killer?" He closes his laptop and puts it on the floor. He turns off the lamp on his nightstand and turns towards Marney's side of the bed waiting for her.

Marney breezes into the bathroom, "No, we're hoping to keep it out of the press for as long as we can. Forever if I had the choice. I'd like to keep Olman the small introvert town it is."

"Marns, there isn't some small part of you that wouldn't want this to get a little attention?"

She turns off the lights, scuffles her tired feet toward the bed, and pulls down the covers on her side. Climbing in she answers him, "Noooo, no, no. High profile cases are high stress. It's hard enough to do good work in this field, what with everyone putting you down and waiting for your big mistakes. I don't need more distractions...or attention." She moves in close to him and smells his lovely scent. Her body reacts quickly which is a little surprising since whiskey usually relaxes her too much.

Sean's face is warm and he looks at her with loving eyes, "I get that...I know I certainly don't want you anymore distracted than you already are."

"I'm sorry sweetie. I really didn't expect this to turn into a serial case so quickly. It's a whole different ball game now."

"That's okay babe...as long as I can still be one of your distractions." He leans in and kisses her deeply. She can feel his intensity coming through and she soon matches his energy, kissing him back with desire.

She bring her hands on the sides of his face and pulls away, "You are my most welcome distraction...my favorite." She kisses him and guides his body to hers. Her body throbs and she's already yearning for him to make love to her...be inside her.

Sean slides his fingers through her hair and moves on top of her spreading her legs so they are on either side of his hips. Faithfully, Sean is ready and warm as always and she's delighted that he is as naked as she, under the sheets. She moves her hands up his back pulling him down to her. His chest feels glorious, his hips amazing...he gently enters her and both release their breath in unison. Always in perfect sync.

*** 

The sunlight peaks through a small opening where the curtains almost come together. Marney stretches her arm over to him...but he isn't there. She lifts her head and sees the bright orange post-it on Sean's pillow.

*Didn't want to wake you. Off to the gym-*
*S*

She smiles and stretches. Her phone buzzes, she exhales long. Marney knows if she rolls over to look at it her day has to begin. She just wants to lay in Sean's spot...smelling his faint cologne on the sheets. Her phone buzzes again. *Ugh!*

She picks up her cell and sees three missed calls from Chris...then she sees the time is 9:42. *Holy shit!* Her head pops up and she looks at her alarm clock. *Fuck....forgot to set it! Fuck, fuck, fuuuuucccckkkk!* She throws back the covers and jumps up, running toward the shower.

Forty minutes later, Marney signs in on the radio telling dispatch that she's at the station. When she walks into the detective's unit Chris claps for her and Mike, sitting at her desk with his feet up, nods showing a sweet southern smile of ghost white teeth.

"Glad you're alive Marns...thanks for calling me back." Chris waves his cell phone at her and she smirks.

"I texted you smart-ass."

Chris looks down at his phone, "Oh..."

Marney looks at Mike and he winks at her, "Long night Jade? Gotta watch that whiskey...it's an ass-kicker." He chuckles and stands up offering her the chair to her own desk.

"Funny. My night was fine thanks. Got better after I got into bed...just tired is all."

Chris is scrolling through his phone, "Yeah...whatevs."

Marney shoots him a look and he laughs silently to himself. Mike walks over and pours himself another cup of coffee. Through the windows to the hallway he sees Freda coming towards the detective's unit with a box in her hands. Spiraling backwards, Mike swoops his cup and body in the opposite direction and walks briskly to one of the back interview rooms, closing the door to escape before Freda tries to feed him more junk. She enters the doorway and her face drops when she doesn't see Mike anywhere. Marney smiles remembering Mike's comment the night before about her. Instead Chris gets up and meets her halfway across the floor to see what she's got in the pink bakery box.

Deucen barges in, "Oh, nice of you to join us Jade. Meeting...conference room three...ten minutes." He jabs his thumb towards the hallway. "Where's Taylon?" Marney jabs her thumb toward the back interview rooms, not pointing to any one room in particular. "Well, bring'em...and Goliath here too." Chris frowns.

Marney nods, wishing she had stopped for coffee on the way in. Dealing with Deucen is always easier with stronge coffee. The detective unit's mediocre blend will have to do.

An hour later, Deucen is briefed, Marney is waking up...finally, Chris is flipping through his notes....and Mike is hinting about pancakes. Another day begins....

***

At four-thirty Marney has about had it with interviewing Kerry Noonan's acquaintances, boss, in-laws and neighbors. She has no family in New Mexico since she and her husband moved here two years ago when she was seventeen. Her alibi checked out as she said, but she still wasn't in the clear...and asking for a lawyer made her look like she knew something more. Marney doesn't think Kerry is a killer, but she may very know who is. Chris and Marney both tried to get more names out of her as to who is in the NSG but her lawyer threw a wrench in that questioning. So far, the case is moving as slow as the Diaz case...the only good lead is that both the wives are in Olman's only NSG group. Weird, yet too coincidental and interesting to ignore.

Marney's phone rings at her desk. She closes a file drawer and reaches for it, "Jade."

"Hey Jade...it's Jade."

"Hi Liam, how ya doing brah." She thinks how nice it is to hear his voice.

"Horny sis...but I'm working on your case instead of being home with Roger."

Marney smiles, "Well, that makes two of us."

"I really hope this shit is done. No more bodies Marns. Find this fucker okay?" Liam flips through some paperwork, Marney can hear him through the phone.

"Trying bud. I really don't want this for our town either. We've all got enough pressure."

"Speaking of...just wanted to give you a heads up that my boss called a meeting for six o'clock. We're ready to go over the coroner's report."

"Six o'clock?" Marney rolls her eyes. "Can't do it in the morning?"

"Tomorrow's Saturday."

"It is? Crap...okay."

"And Marns?"

"Yeah?"

"Call Dad will ya? I'm tired of hearing how he misses you." Liam sounds annoyed.

Marney stops, "Is he okay Liam?"

"Yes...but he's retired...and misses his adult, overly-successful-busy kids. You have to make time...or give him grandkids. I know I'm not." Liam sighs.

"Okay, okay. I've just been super busy and..."

"Marney! It's Dad."

"I know, I know."

"He doesn't ask for much."

"No, I know. You're right. I need some time anyway...you going up Sunday?" She bites her nail. She knows she needs to go up to the cabin and decompress...but Sean has to work this weekend and she really should...

Liam confirms, "Yes. It's chicken and dumplings Sunday."

"Okay. I'll drive up in the afternoon and stay over until Sunday. It'll do him good." She convinces herself.

"Marns, it'll do you good too. Bring that sexy man of yours...so we can drool...and dream." Liam chuckles.

"Liam, I don't drool. I don't have to...and he makes my dreams come true. Now, knock that off or I'll tell Roger you're being bad." She smiles.

"Who do you think I was talking about when I said "we" Marns." Liam laughs harder.

Marney scrunches her nose, "Ew, Liam...you two need help. Can't you just be normal gay...I like normal gay."

"He, heeeee...see you at six."

Marney hangs up her phone and shakes her head. She turns when she feels his energy. Mike Taylon is leaning up against the counter across the room sipping another cup of coffee. She wonders how long he's been there. He smiles and latches onto her gaze.

"Hey."

"Hey there. You got a minute Marney?" He looks around wondering where Chris has gotten off to.

She really doesn't now that she has a six o'clock coroners meeting which she knows her ass-munch boss won't tell her about until twenty minutes before. "Uh..."

"I need to show you something. You're gonna love this."

"Okay, but I've only got-"

"Yeah, until six o'clock...I know."

Marney frowns. She doesn't know if he overheard her entire phone call or is privy to info she is not. "Right, a coroner's meeting already."

"Good. We needed that before the weekend. I'm glad Deucen can take orders." He waves her to follow him and heads towards the door.

Marney secures her gun in her holster and puts her jacket on trying to catch up to him. She gets to the hallway and sees him disappear to the stairwell. Nodding to patrolmen Dawson and Blair, she flips her hair out of her face and heads to the stairway.

She hears him all the way down in the basement level and quickly scuffles down flights of stairs to catch up. Across from the archive files storage area is a boring gray door. Mike is standing with his hand on the knob waiting for her. She comes to the last step, he stares.

"You're gonna love me." He looks serious.

"Huh?" She is confused. *What the fuck?*

"You're gonna love me ya know." He points to his temple in some sort of smart-guy move.

Marney doesn't say anything. She looks up the stairwell and around the room...she swallows and makes eye contact with him. His face is soft...loving almost and he is looking at her hair...her face...her body.

"I-"

"I pulled some strings after our meeting last night."

"Oh, is that what that was?" Marney half-smirks.

Mike frowns, "Well, I heard your frustration and figured we should move on your hunch about this NSG....it really is the only common thread right now."

"Oh?"

"Yes...so try to contain yourself." He opens the door and waits for her to follow.

Marney steps in cautiously. Mike closes the door and locks it, brushing against her back. A surge of sexual tension flows through her and she holds her breath for a moment. He places a hand on her lower back to guide her.

Mike walks past her then and motions with a kid-like grin for her to follow him. Marney is curious...wondering why she isn't more scared. She steps to follow him cautious as to whats going on. He walks through to some floor-to-ceiling shelving that winds around to the left. Marney follows and sees a brighter desk light glowing. When she comes around the shelving she sees on the far end of the room is counter running along the wall with all kinds of electronic equipment and a young guy with headphones on leaning with his elbows near a laptop. Marney is surprised.

Mike places his hands on the guy's shoulders and the guy turns, smiles and takes the headphones off. "Marney, meet Zeek."

"Hi." She is confused. Looks like Zeek is new.

He stands up and shakes her hand, "Hello, Detective Jade. Very nice to meet you."

Mike says, "Anything?"

"Not yet Mike, but I can hear that she's in her car. Sounds like she's headed towards town." Zeek smiles, seeming proud of himself.

Marney gets it, "You guys tapped someone?"

Mike nods, "Yes, Mrs. Kerry Noonan. I noticed that we weren't getting far, but luckily she really likes that brown leather handbag of hers. She takes it into every interview room...and everywhere she goes."

Marney likes what she hears, "You guys bugged her purse?"

"Yep. The little strap part, close to the seam. We need to know a little more about those meetings and what goes on in them. Now, it'll be tough to decipher who and how many go...but it's a start." Mike waves his hand as he speaks.

Marney loves it! Mike just made her job a whole hell of a lot easier. She wants to jump in his arms and hug him long! "How?"

"I pulled some strings with my boss. Pissed yours off, but oh well."

"Deucen gets pissed off if his comb-over flutters in the wind without his permission, he hates not having control." Marney comments.

Mike nods, "Yeah, I got that...it's because he is so out of control with himself internally. So, I let him control where Zeek and I would set up. Told him I needed a private office...this is where he put us." Mike looks around the cold, dreary basement.

"It's fine for me Mike." Zeek is sweet. Marney wonders how long he's been an agent. They must have gotten him right out of college. Probably somebody's kid brother. He can't be more than twenty-five years old.

Marney scans the room, "Yeah, this is actually perfect." She is so pleased to have the help...and that Mike is proving to be such an asset.

"Okay, so Zeek is going to sit on-the-wire for tonight and the weekend, with some assistance from his partner Tracy. Looks like we have to wait a few for that Wednesday meeting." Mike points to a shelf with a few CD cases. "We have some recordings of Mrs. Noonan talking to relatives on the phone about the funeral and the gory details. Only one female friend has talked with her about the NSG meetings. Kerry is pretty distraught but wants to go anyway. Probably to warn the group about us. Zeek will text me if anything important comes up, but you are welcome to listen to those CDs if you need to."

"No, I have enough to do but please keep me in the loop. This is fantastic guys. I'm so happy." Marney smiles wide and is very grateful.

Mike pats his chests, "I think it will help out a lot...besides, your gut tells you something Jadelock...we are going with your gut! Oh, almost forgot, I've had a tail on Jenny Diaz for a few...just in case."

Marney huffs and rolls her eyes. She likes the way Mike hears her...it feels good.

"Okay, let's let Zeek get to it...and we'll go let Chris in on our little secret before that meeting."

Marney pivots on her heel, "Okay great!" She is relieved at the new prospect of progress.

# 19. Same

Chris is beyond ecstatic with Mike's progress and even mentions how he can help Zeek out if need be. Marney is feeling better about heading up to her father's cabin. With Zeek and his colleague listening in, it feels like work is getting done.

The coroner's report on Michael Noonan is very similar to Andres Diaz. Dr. Fine and Jeremy Lockly all but confirm Noonan was killed by the same person, same weapon. The only major difference is the front teeth were knocked out and taken and the body was days older when found. Marney is not happy with Deucen. He pushes, almost the entire meeting, for going public and how it's for their protection and could help with leads. Marney knows it's because he loves the spotlight and being a politician more so than solving crimes. He doesn't care how much more work it will mean for his staff, not to mention all the stupid false public leads that would waste tons of man hours and money. Mike is great and tells Deucen he will let him know when his superiors confirm a need for the public to know but until then, no reporters are to be told of the true details of the deaths. Its bad enough the wives know. Any of them could go to the press...and oddly have not...yet.

Marney drives almost the entire way to her father's cabin, with no music on, just a million thoughts running through her mind. Her mind is swimming with the details of the cases, Sean not being able to join her because of his shifts at the bar, and Mike Taylon. Marney is very impressed with his laid back southern personality in contrast with his perseverance. He has eased her mind with his actions. She likes how he sets things in motion, gets them done...despite Deucen.

Her mind wanders to Mike's smile...his rugged good looks, broad shoulder's and muscular legs in his Levi jeans. For a forty-something year old man, he really has it. She doesn't know exactly what "it" is...but he's got something. He isn't stuffy or prick-like the way some FBI agents can be. The ones she's worked with in the past, for a day or two, were more welcome to leave than stay. Mike....Mike can stay. She wonders what he will be doing for the weekend and imagines him working out in his hotel gym, drinking whiskey and eating pancakes. He seems refreshingly simple...and happy, despite losing his wife "suddenly". She's curious as to what he means by that.

Marney hopes Chris will make it up to the cabin tomorrow. He loves to go fishing with her Dad, but rarely comes up without Sean. Marney's phone beeps:

# Miss you. Wish I could be there.

She pushes a button and speaks into her phone:

## Me too. If it's slow, try to come.

Her phone beeps:

# I always do...(wink, wink)

Marney laughs out loud and puts her phone down. Driving and texting isn't safe and neither is sexting with Sean...when she can't have him after.

Ten minutes later, Marney pulls down her father's long driveway. The gorgeous mountains and full trees all around uplift her and she is able to forget about serial killers for awhile. She pulls Gerda in front of the house and cuts the engine. Old Cody Bear, her dad's great dane, is patiently waiting outside her door wagging his tail swiftly. Marney jumps down and scratches his ears. It's nice to be missed.

"Well hey girl." Asner Jade, Sr., moves slowly across the large porch and stands admiring his only daughter from the top step.

Marney guides Cody Bear out of her path, "Hi Dad. You're looking good!" She thinks how kind retirement has been to him. Climbing the wooden steps she walks into his open arms and feels peaceful, home, accepted and admired. All the same good things her father can expel with just his loving touch. She misses him.

"Arrrrrgh, there's my baby girl." He plants a noisy kiss on top of Marney's head. Asner Sr., makes sure to always give his children the love of two parents...since losing their mother so young. He is a very affectionate father...despite his tough cop exterior.

Marney pulls away to look at him. Sadly, it's been a couple months since she last saw him. She really needs to get to the mountains more often. It always relaxes her. "I like the little facial hair thing ya got going on there Dad." Marney swirls a finger near his almost-entirely white beard. Its close to his skin, trimmed nice.

"Thank you. I'm growing my winter fur."

Marney cracks up, her Dad makes her laugh with his witty comebacks. "Where's Glenda? I brought her Olman wine."

"Oh, she loves that stuff...in the kitchen cooking food she won't let me eat."

"Are you on a diet?" Marney looks at his stomach...same little pouch he's had for years, no bigger...no smaller. Like a little beer belly, except he doesn't drink beer.

Asner rubs his stomach, "No....just making me wait for you guys. I am so glad you came up today...now you can get an entire weekend of rest in."

Marney planned to come up Saturday but she decided she needed to get out of Olman early and away from Deucen's cell phone reach. "Wow, she's making you eat late. Sorry, if I had known I would have left earlier...we had this meeting...."

"Oh? So what's going on down there. Your brother tells me you might have a serial killer on your hands?" He steps down the porch steps and opens her truck door to get her bag.

Marney curses Liam and his big mouth, in her head, "Aw Dad, I don't want to burden you with the details."

He laughs, "Marns, I'm retired, not dead. You can take the cop out of Olman...but.."

"Yah can't take the cop out of the cop...yeah, I know Dad."

"Smart-ass."

"I learned from the best." Marney smiles at him.

"Welp, I didn't teach you anything about serial killers...that I know. That's one thing I didn't come across once in my career."

Marney nods, "Well, Olman has never had a documented one. Surely, you knew of someone though...right?"

Asner huffs his way up the steps with Marney's overnight bag, "I learned about it a little and had friends from other departments who talked about it; but, I never had the FBI come in and have to get involved in one of my cases...well, there was that missing girl...but anyway, you got yourself a once in a lifetime case sweetheart."

"Dad really?"

"What?" He laughs hard. "Honey, you are a great detective. You're gonna smash the bastard...you're making history!"

"Ugh, Dad...it's a horrible way to make history. People are dead. In gross manner I might add." She opens the screen door and smells the orgasmic scent of homemade food. Glenda is a wonderful cook.

He wavers his eyebrows, "But they sucked honey."

"I'm going to kill Liam! You are suppose to be retired, not hearing about bad husband behavior. Hi Glenda!" Marney shoots a look at her father. The subject is no longer up for discussion. Time to decompress.

***

Marney hears the faint sounds of a foreign engine purring up the driveway. Liam and Roger brought the Avalon. It's a little cream-puff next to Gerda. "Gay Luxury" is what Liam calls Rodger's car...and refers to her truck as "Redneck Birth Control". Marney finds this humorous considering he rides a moped to work...which she calls "Mosquito Fury". Liam never thinks this is funny.

Asner, Sr. throws another log into his enormous homemade brick porch fireplace with it's beautiful chimney intertwined through the roof. Marney loves the feel of Glenda's plush blanket around her shoulders and the smokey scent of the fire wafting through her hair. One leg is tucked under a knee and the other dangles down with a toe bracing against the porch floor pushing just enough for the swing to sway back and forth. Marney is so glad she drove up to Reuna.

"Marns, you like Earl Grey tea?" Glenda hands her a cup without waiting for an answer.

"Oh my yes...thank you!"

Glenda sets a cup down where Asner is sitting and has three more on a tray.

"Hola bitches!" Liam waves as he exits the passenger side of Rogers car.

Marney watches her father's face and laughs when he wiggles his nostrils at her. He is the only one crazier then Liam. Her brother Asner,

Jr. has no sense of humor what-so-ever, so her father and brother being comical is refreshing.

"What's this bitches thing?" Asner questions his youngest child as he steps up onto the porch. He reaches out to shake Roger's hand and then reaches to hug Liam.

Liam's voice muffles in his father's neck, "Oh Dad."

"How was the drive up?" Marney shifts her legs farther under her blanket to make room for more seating.

"Nice actually, Liam only sang forty-three of the the forty-five songs we heard." Roger takes a chair next to the fireplace and smiles at Liam. He teases Liam terribly...and Marney loves it.

"See the abuse I put up with Dad?" Liam fans his hands out in his victim-type way.

Asner huffs, "Somehow I think you have that backwards."

"Oh! And speaking of abuse..." Liam ogles Marney.

She frowns, "What?"

Roger smiles, "Oh...your partner is on his way up to go fishing with Asner. Says he has a surprise for you Marns."

Marney smiles, "Oh okay. Will they be here tonight?"

Liam answers, "No, Chris said he will load up in the morning and head up, soooooo if you need anything ya better call him."

"I don't need a thing. Just wondering." Marney sips her tea and snuggles lower in her blanket. She smiles to herself at the thought of Chris bringing Sean up as a surprise. What else could it be?

# 20. Mikey Parts

Her cigarette glows red in the night. The fire is a golden hue under the black star-filled New Mexico sky. The contrast intrigues her. She really loves this part. It's like an endorphin rush after a full-body massage. She sits relaxing by the pit, dragging on her cancer stick, barbequing the bad parts of Michael Noonan...

No longer will he speak terrible words...no longer will he bite her with his animal mouth...no longer will he touch her roughly with his angry, manly hands or cheat of her with his disgusting man parts. No....Michael Noonan can no longer hurt his wife...ever.

Kerry is finally free...

# 21. Bait and Catch

Marney rolls over and feels the cold mountain air on her face through the cabin window. The sun is bright, the smell of smoke from the fire place lingers in her hair and clothing. She smiles and stretches reaching for her phone. *Such great sleep.* Marney blinks until her focus comes in and can't believe it's nine forty in the morning. Rarely does she ever get to sleep in.

She sits up letting her feet muddle around to find the slippers half-sticking out from under the bed. She can hear male voices and laughter coming from the kitchen downstairs and smiles at the thought of seeing Sean. He said he had to work this weekend but must have gotten out of it to come see her with Chris. Pushing her hair out of her face she takes the blanket from her bed and wraps it around her again. Finding a robe is too much trouble right now. All she wants is coffee, fire and Sean's musky morning kisses. She scuffles down the hall and to the stairs...

"Hey Marns!" Mike Taylon looks up from his breakfast and startles the shit out of Marney. He is sitting in the middle of Chris, who is looking all groggy, Liam, Roger and her father.

"Surprise!" Chris shouts poking the air towards her with his fork.

Marney huffs a small laugh and clutches her blanket tighter. This was not the surprise she was counting on. *What the fuck is Mike doing here?*

Chris begins explaining before Marney can even ask. "So Zeek heard Kerry on the wire say that the meeting is Wednesday night and she will be there...so, poor Mike was planning on hanging out at the hotel all weekend. I remembered that he likes to fish so....here we are!"

"Well, the more the merrier." Asner is being sweeter than sweet. He loves company...and fisherman are an even bigger treat.

Glenda agrees, "Yes Mike, we are so glad you could join us. More eggs?"

Mike is watching Marney in her sleepy stupor. He likes her morning look. He can't ascertain her mood though. "Oh wow, yes thank you ma'am."

Liam is finding the whole scene amusing, "Marns, you awake? Need some coffee?"

"Uh, huh." She answers unable to believe Chris brought their FBI case boss up to her parents cabin for the weekend. She wanted to smash his face on the kitchen table in front of them. Mike is cool and all...but our family cabin?

Roger, being the gentleman he is, rises from his chair and offers it to Marney. His swift movements remind her of Mike when she arrived for drinks and he stood in her presence. She shuffles over to the chair and slumps down not sure what to feel...or do with her weekend now. Is she going to have to entertain her new boss....or worse talk about missing penises at every turn?

Anser continues their conversation, "So Mike, you were saying that Abby Wheylin was found not far from her parent's water tank?"

"Well-" Mike tries to answer.

Glenda places a huge plate in front of Mike and a smaller one in front of Marney, "Ok Jade. That's enough of that work talk...eat up."

Marney places her cup down and picks up her fork as she looks at her partner, "Yeah Dad, that's enough work talk." Marney then stabs her sausage imaging it's Chris's face.

***

Marney leans back, resting her elbows against a boulder and looking out over the terrain where her father has rooted himself. It's beautiful in the mountains...and she loves visiting. She doesn't know why she stays away so long. She understands why her father left Olman behind and never returned.

"Hey Marns. We caught enough for dinner....you in?" Mike found her hiding spot and she wants to cringe at the thought of being disturbed. His voice is nice though.

She turns to see that Mike is alone, "Sure, sounds good."

He crouches down next to her, "You mind?" as he points to the ground next to her.

"Go ahead." She pushes over to make room. *Awkward.*

Mike gently places his enormous body down next to her and leans up against the boulder. Marney can hear the bones in his knees crackle and rub, wondering how much cartilage he actually has left. His lovely scent wafts towards her and her body reacts in a way that makes her uncomfortable. Mike smells great....like clean laundry, mature men's cologne and cowboy leather.

"Wow, what a great spot. You come here often?" Mike frowns and Marney smiles. He looks silly, "I know that sounded awful. I mean, is this a favorite spot?"

She laughs even though she wants to be mad. Mad that he is even here, mad that he looks good in the wilderness, mad that he is gorgeous, mad that he smells good, mad that he isn't....Sean. "Yes...and it's fine. You can't be slick every day of the week. It's our day off."

"Yes it is. It's really nice here. Thank you for having me. I know it must be weird...me being on the case and all."

"You mean you being my boss...and hanging with my family?" Marney throws a rock.

Mike turns towards her, "Marney, I am not your boss. I am here to help on a case. Please don't think I am here to grade you or judge you...or make your job more stressful. That's just not me. You just happen to be the detective in charge so I have to work closely with you. And....I can see why you are lead. Your partner is great, but you have a sixth sense it seems...oh, and your boss is a quack!"

Marney starts to laugh again. Mike can make her smile and she likes that. She likes what he is saying. She hates to admit it but she finds she is relaxing more and more around Mike. "So, anything with Zeek?"

"No, nothing interesting...but let's not talk about work. It will be there when we get back. Let's talk about how your dad got this great place."

"He just saved a lot...and kept close to his dreams." She looks at Mike and sees his kind eyes watching her. She looks away. "My mom died when I was little...and dad took his time. He healed, worked, raised us three...and when the time was right he married Glenda, then saved for his second phase in life. This is the result. There is something to be said for good planning."

Mike nodded, "I agree...and proper healing. So many people don't properly heal or get closure after a life-changing event. It's a risk not to, because the baggage is just carried along with the years. I get what you mean by he took his time. He built a great place here to do all his favorite things...and accommodate his family. I admire him."

"Me too."

"So whats your plan Marney?"

"What do you mean?" She looks puzzled.

"Do you have a plan for after police work? I mean you have a long career left but do you have plans beyond that?" He runs the pads of his fingers in the cold dirt.

Marney doesn't know what to say...and realizes she has been living case to case. "Hmmmm, good question." She wants to change the subject.

"Do you like where you live? Would you move after retirement?"

She thinks about it, "Well, I really like it up here...but I like my house too. Most likely I'd have a few escapes." She giggles a little...more out of nervousness. She feels weird not having answers.

Mike smiles, "That sounds great. Play the monopoly game of New Mexico." He laughs, she laughes...then silence.

"You?" Marney switches on him.

"I own property in Texas, spend most my time in New Mexico now...because of the job, so after retirement I really don't know where to land. I like that I have options." He shrugs his shoulders. "You have any future plans with your guy? Any kids?"

Marney almost cringes as he so smoothly changes up on her again, "Not sure. Just enjoying things really. As for kids, that's a tough one. I grew up without a mom...it was real hard." She looks down and moves around a few more rocks she found.

"Oh, so you work a lot and...."

"And yes, I don't think it would be fair to any child or well, anyone." She starts to draw lines in the dirt with a corner of a rock.

"So, you stay comfortably single...and comfortably childless..." Mike says it very lightly. Marney never thought of it that way. He makes sense of her....sense.

"Yes, quite comfortably." She laughs.

"Cool."

"Yeah."

Mike stands up and dusts himself off, "Well, your pops asked me to come find you. So...I'm finding you...and summoning you to dinner before I get in trouble." He reaches down and offers her his hand. Marney takes it, reluctantly...because he is man-beautiful...and just as she thought, feeling his warm skin...made her feel things she shouldn't.

Mike grabs hold and steps back to gently pull her to her feet. She rises and balances herself ignoring her inner woman feelings. He meets her eyes, then lets go of her. He breaks their gaze and continues to dust himself off and Marney does the same.

"Okay, let's go see if we can help Glenda and Asner with dinner."

"Yeah." Marney tries to slow her racing heart.

***

Marney loves the fresh fish dinner. The food is amazing, the wine too, and the conversation completes it all. She feels relaxed...and accepted somehow. A poker game ensues shortly after dessert with real money...and harder drinks. When Mike starts looking more and more attractive to Marney, she excuses herself and heads to bed. She knows her limit...with all things.

# 22. Batya Lehev

She feels his strong hand on her. Again, he's warm and she smiles and nuzzles towards his touch with her cheek. The warmth pulls away and she hears the sounds again. Then the warmth returns to the other side. She turns towards it on her shoulder and this time nuzzles and kisses his touch bringing both her hands up to hold it, only...it slowly pulls away again. Then the sounds...

"Marns!" in a whisper it meets her ears and her eyes fly open. "Marney...Marney?"

She turns to the whisper and startles at the large shadow above her! She reaches for the gun under her pillow. Mike firmly holds her wrist, "Marney?"

"Wha-? What are you doing?" She is confused, and yet sexually elated.

Mike stands in the moonlight, it's dark. *What is he doing in my room?* "Marns...I'm sorry to wake you. There's another body sweetie...are you awake? Do you understand it's me, Mike?"

She blinks again, "Another body?" Her brain is beginning to understand. Mike is trying to wake her up.

"Yeah sorry. We need to head back to Olman. Can you drive?" Mike is still whispering in his lovely, mellow voice.

Marney frowns, "Drive? Yeah, why?"

"Chris is in no shape for driving. We're going to have to head back in your truck okay?"

"Right. Just let me get some clothes." Marney sits up and hops out of bed. Mike spins around quickly and heads for the door. She realizes she has nothing on! *Shit!! Well at least he is decent enough to turn around.* She starts stumbling around in the room trying to find her things.

Mike walks towards the door and whispers, "Okay, I'll meet you downstairs...don't forget your weapon under the pillow." He points towards the bed and then disappears. She hears her door close behind him and is relieved.

Marney runs her fingers through her hair and takes a deep breath. *Fuck, did I kiss his hand? What the hell Marns...what's wrong with you?* She wants to smack her forehead but instead finds her jeans and dresses. *Looks like vaca-time is over.*

Five minutes later Marney makes her way down the steps with her bag, one arm in her blazer, holstering her gun. When she reaches the bottom of the stairs, Mike smiles and comes around the kitchen counter handing her a cup of coffee in her father's blue travel mug. "Ready?" He acts as if nothing happened even though he now knows she is the most beautiful woman he has ever seen naked.

"Uh, yeah." She can't make eye contact yet.

"I left a note. Chris is going to be pissed but he can't even walk so we're just going to let him have the day off. You good to drive or do you need me to?"

Marney likes how gentle but disciplined he is, "No, I'm good...especially with this. Thanks for the brew."

"Sure. Okay, let's roll. Looks like we have a victim of a different gender this time." He breezes by her picking up her bag and winks when she stares in disbelief.

Marney pulls onto the highway and gets Gerda shifted into fourth gear before asking Mike to brief her. He smiles at her, amused at her rugged truck and dishy sleep-look.

"Okay, looks like our John Doe is a Jane Doe this time. Over on your east side. In those newer condos."

"It's ours?" Marney sips the magnificent cup of coffee he made her. The guy is good at many things.

Mike looks at her.

"What?"

"It's ours alright. Tongue removed, hands cut off, and well....you know." Mike squints his eyes and looks out the window for a moment.

Marney watches him, "Are you shittin' me Mike?"

He looks at her and doesn't answer.

"Seriously? Her....hooha is...." Marney frowns.

Mike wipes his hand over his face, "Well, as much as a hooha can be....cut off."

"Fuck."

"Yeah...fuck. Gonna be real hard to keep this out of the papers."

"Not if I can help it."

***

Marney pulls up to the home of Batya Lehev at six thirty-seven in the morning. A little less than an hour after leaving her father's cabin. No traffic on a Sunday morning and good coffee helped the swift trip. Mike hops down out of the truck and Marney cuts the engine. They start their scan and assessments on either side of the road and driveway leading to the residence. Marney is eased to see the scene is already secure and Deucen is nowhere in sight...yet.

As Mike and Marney approach the driveway a tall women, in her forties, short brown hair and in a floral bathrobe is crying hysterically as Officer Dawson waits patiently for her to answer his interview questions. Marney isn't sure of her relationship to the deceased, but the woman is flipping out.

Mike pulls Marney's elbow passed them and they carefully step into the house and follow the crime scene path. Sergeant Blair nods and checks them off the list, then speaks into his shoulder radio that they have both arrived on scene. Marney hears O'Malen's disgusted reply. She knows he is going to give her an earful when she gets to the station.

At first glance, the house is very neat and tidy. There appears to have been no struggle, no robbery or disruption of any sort. That is, until they reach the kitchen. It's a rather large area and on the other side of the median Marney can see a bare foot, attached to a bare leg. She and Mike look and see one mutilated-middle-aged Batya Lehev, lying supine facing the ceiling, eyes open, mouth open, tongue gone, heart stabbed, hands removed lying close by and....vulva area sliced clean off! Marney wants to wince but refuses to show emotion. Mike doesn't turn away or even blink....so she isn't going to either. Besides, feeling things at a crime scene is not what they do. She inhales a deep breath and goes to work.

Since Liam is out of town and not on call, Jeremy Lockly is filling in and meticulously doing his crime scene forensics. He has already confirmed the identity by witness and fingerprints and is on to picking fibers off of Batya's face.

Sergeant Blair comes in and patiently waits. Marney gets as much as she can visually, then gets out of Jeremy's way. Mike motions her over.

"What can you tell us Blair?" Mike points to Marney's pad indicating he wants her to write for him. She readies her pencil.

Blair readjusts his cover under his arm and takes a deep breath, "Okay, this is one Batya Lehev, age forty-three, partner to Ms. MaryBeth Hoffman...err outside, age forty-two. They've been together eleven years, residing in this house for six. Batya works for Olman Electric, has for seventeen years. MaryBeth is a fifth grade teacher at Sevenia Elementary school. She's been at her job for nineteen years. MaryBeth says they both went to bed around eleven after a day out shopping, nothing different or out of the ordinary. MaryBeth needed a drink, says around midnight, Batya went to the kitchen for her, MaryBeth fell asleep, wakes up around two-thirty, goes looking for Batya, who had not returned. Says she thought she might find her on her computer but instead almost trips over her here in the kitchen. That's it...calls 911."

"Hmmmm...." Marney's thinking.

"That's about all I can get right now. She's starting to lose it." Sergeant Blair shrugs his shoulders which tells Marney that MaryBeth needs some time now...the trauma is setting in and her hysterics are taking over. Normal spouse behavior at a scene. When they don't lose it and act all weird or calm...that's when they need to be taken to the station for hours of interviewing.

Mike smiles, "No, that's great Sarge, thank you. Where is MaryBeth now?"

"She's sitting outside, we gave her some water. I have to go check-in with my officers along the perimeter, the neighbors are starting wake up and I think one of them called the news van. So, if you need me I'll be dealing with that outside." Blair excuses himself and leaves.

Mike looks down at Marney, "Welp? Looks like we have one question for MaryBeth then."

"Yup...NSG connection?"

"Bingo."

# 23. Makes Three

Four hours later Marney is answering her phone and typing away at her computer. Mike sits across from her at Chris's desk with his feet up watching her. He has a passive, light smile on his face. Marney isn't excited to be working on a Sunday, but she realizes it's much easier without all the distractions of a full station. The quiet helps counteract the stress of another murder. Deucen is out dealing with the press in his dark gray suit and pink tie that makes him look fat. It's his church look. Marney has already gotten phone calls from both Chris and Liam, hangover ridden of course, but on their way in. She told them to forget it, they weren't going to be much help, but they insisted. With three bodies now, things are even more intense. Deucen wants all the women from the NSG brought in and interrogated until someone cracks or brings a good lead. Mike told Deucen that would mess up the entire wire tap...that none of the women would go to the meeting, out of fear...or protection. He has to wait until the Wednesday meeting. Marney is afraid more bodies will surface in three days but Mike says its a risk they must take. The coincidence is too great. Someone in the group knows something. Deucen threw a three-year-olds tantrum and Mike told him to get out of the office and do his job. Marney is secretly elated with Mike.

He sits watching her still, connecting all of Chris's paperclips together in the top drawer, "You like your job a lot huh Marns?"

Marney looks at him, he's not watching her but instead spinning the new necklace he has formed, which is sure to piss of her partner, "You're really calm Mike."

"What's to get upset over?"

"That's a little insensitive don't you think? MaryBeth just lost her lover of eleven years to a violent and unfair death."

Mike locks eyes with her, "True. Unfair?"

Marney is surprised but doesn't show it, "Well, her life was taken from her...it's kinda unjust...keeps me working, but still unjust."

"Everyone dies Marney. What's fair or unfair? If it's our time...we must go." Mike just stares at her. He's acting strange. As if his boredom has erased his heart. Marney knows he has one. He tends to be very caring at moments. She wonders whats different about this moment, wonders if he would say that about his dead wife.

"Mike, you okay?"

"Yeah, hey what do you say we go interview Ms. Hoffman a little more, cut her lose, and grab some lunch? Maybe whiskey and a steak?" Mike waves his eyebrows at her. What a difference from this morning when he was trying to wake her. *Does he not care that we have a serial killer on the loose?*

Marney shakes her head, "I don't know, I have a ton of work to do."

"I'll tell ya what, let's go grab some food, make some inquiries with Batya's co-workers and neighbors, and see what we can dig up. Liam isn't going to get far with Jeremy Lockly already claiming the body and Chris is in no shape to be working. If he wants, I can send him to the neighbors, but I really think he's going to have to cut his day short...if you know what I mean." Mike has it all worked out in his head. He knows there isn't much you can do about a dead body on a Sunday. Oddly, at times he seems to not want to waste his time and is putting a lot of confidence in Zeek and the wire tap.

Marney misses Sean, "I'm sorry, I can't. I need to finish up here and head home. I'll be in early tomorrow though and work on some leads. I'm curious as to what Batya's employer will say about her...and anyone else for that matter. Oh, and I've got to call my Dad and explain."

Mike smiles, "Right. Okay. I'm gonna head out then. See ya."

Marney watches him pop out of the seat and disappear. *Weird.*

# 24. Ringa Ding

Marney waits by the bar for a few minutes. No Sean in sight. She finds this strange, he said he's working four days straight. She wants to surprise him.

After what seemed like another seven minutes or so she decides to see if he is in the men's room or out back. The big wooden door to the restroom creaks at it's hinges. Empty. She walks further down the hall. Silence. She reaches the double doors to the back parking lot and quietly opens one. Finally, she hears the beautiful, deep voice she longs for. Sean is in a conversation on his cell.

"Yeah man, I'll be there no problem. You get a hold of top? He clear the pass for AZ?" Sean is speaking military, very low and confusing. Marney doesn't recognize any of what he has said. She hears another male voice coming through the little cell.

Sean nods his head, "No brotha, it's ringa ding mutha fucka time, you know what I mean? Body count is already three now man, it's article 7...you know what I'm saying cuckoo?"

Marney is more confounded by Sean's military jargon. He always speaks so clear and respectful to her...and is he by any means talking about her case?

Sean continues, "No...okay. I'll be there. What? Aw, no man, my hammer is good...she's real good. Okay, out." Sean hangs up and stares out into the night, one hand in his pocket, the cell in his other, resting against his lips. Marney isn't sure at what point she should make her presence known. Hearing him talk so oddly unnerves her.

She watches her lover. He is tall, muscular and confident. Very attractive. He's always been quiet and reserved. This time it makes her a little uncomfortable...and she can't quite figure out why. Probably because she has no idea of what he is up to.

She steps further out passed the dumpster, "Hey."

"Oh hey baby!" He turns and comes to her. "How are you?" His eyes go from "business" to "tender" in a nano-second.

Marney loves his face, "I'm okay...and you?"

He kisses her...lingering a few breaths, just enough to ignite her body...in the way he does. "Hungry, can I get you dinner?"

Marney watches his face...nothing. Sean has the most peaceful features. From the neck down he is all ex-military, disciplined and...gorgeous. From the neck up he is blue-eye, baby-face tenderness. Nothing...nothing but love. Marney can't look at him without feeling it.

"Yeah, that'd be great thanks."

"Great. Let's go see what Albert's got going in the kitchen. I'm sorry you're weekend was cut short, but I'm glad to see you." Sean lovingly trails his hand down Marney's spine and rests it on the small of her back, guiding her back inside the doors. As, they walk down the hall he glances her way and catches her eye. She smiles at him because that's what he does to her.

When they reach the bar, they round the corner and she looks up and sees him. Mike Taylon is looking at her from across the room. *Fuck, I turned him down for lunch and said I was going home. Fuck, fuck, fuck! Wait? Did this fucker follow me?*

Mike nods and musters a half-smile Sean doesn't catch as he guides her to her stool and heads behind the bar to help Cherie with the crowd that formed while he was outside. Mike tips his glass to Marney. She smiles. He looks at Sean long, up then down, back and up again. Marney knows he has figured out who he is...and the man-comparison has begun. Only thing worse to her than to woman sizing each other up...is two men! It always seems to end with "I can kick his ass" type talk.

Mike is leaning on the bar talking with some old geezers, but his eyes are on Sean. He's bigger, older too. He is Texas, rugged...with a lifetime behind his eyes, Sean is masculine, edgy...with a sweet face. Both are stunning. Marney exhales. *Shit.*

Mike looks at her again. She can't tell what he's up to. He shakes hands with the men and excuses himself heading towards Marney. Sean walks into the kitchen.

He smiles at Marney scuffing his boots to the stool next to her, "Well, hello there Detective Jade. Long time no see."

"So what brings you here?" She is calm and smooth.

"Well, I hear this is Olman's little cop bar."

She smiles, "Are you sure?" She wants to accuse him of following her...he is FBI after all. Her eyes lock with his and she remembers his touch from this morning when he tried to wake her. He was gentle, and warm...

"Well, that's what your boss says." He smirks. Marney realizes he isn't following her and feels silly.

"Oh, did he want to meet here?"

Mike smiles at her, "Unfortunately. So is that your man?" He nods towards the kitchen. Before Marney can answer, Sean comes through the kitchen doors and sees her. He has two plates with fish, fries, and vegetables. He delivers them with his endearing smile.

"Here ya go babe, want a Seagrams to go with?"

Marney looks at Mike, he's watching Sean care for her. She feels flush, "Yeah, that'd be great. Sean, this is Mike Taylon."

Sean smiles and sticks his hand out, "Oh hey, nice to meet you...Sean Faherty."

"Likewise." Mike meets his hand.

"You two are working the...well, the case?" Sean's voice is low. Mike looks at Marney and then back at Sean.

Mike smiles, "It's nice to put a face with the name. Jade has told me good things about you." He lies.

Sean looks lovingly at Marney, "Oh wow...well, she's something. My better half...if you will."

Marney feels awkward, "Yes." They both look at her. "I'll definitely have a whiskey on the rocks." She wanted to shift to any other type of conversation...*killers, douche bosses, fucking smurfs...*

Sean points at her, "You got it. Oh hey Mike, can I call you Mike?"

"Of course."

"Can I interest you in this fish plate...or another beer at all?" Sean goes right into work mode. Marney looks uneasily up at Mike noticing he's drinking a beer when she knows he is so much more fond of whiskey. She wonders if he will mention their drinking night before at her father's poker game she has yet to tell Sean about.

"Oh no, but thanks. I just had lunch and I'm going to keep to the easy stuff here while I meet with Deucen."

Sean smiles, "Sure thing, and good luck with that."

"Yeah." Mike huffs a laugh and stares at Marney while Sean makes her drink.

Marney feels strange around Mike. She can't quite figure out why...but, she is uneasy as to why she is worried about how he feels. She looks passed Mike and sees her boss walk in the door. Cherie smiles at him and he walks to her on the other end of the bar. Mike watches him, then looks down at Marney inquisitively.

She smirks, "Yeah, that's a thing."

"Hmmm...interesting."

"Not really, but for them I guess it is. Has been for years now." Marney picks up her knife and fork.

Mike sips his beer, then nods when Deucen acknowledges him. "Well, that wasn't in his file."

"There's a lot not in his file Mike."

"Well, ya could've mentioned it...and that you like steak and whiskey so much." His eyes dance and he smiles at her.

"Oh, that wasn't in my file? What I prefer to eat, who I'm with...where I go on weekends?" She's being sarcastic.

Mike sips his beer again, "Well, some of it is."

Marney shoots him a look. He smiles wider, teasing her and places his hand on her shoulder to say goodbye, "See ya tomorrow Detective Jade...enjoy." Mike raises his beer to Sean to say goodbye. Sean walks towards Marney to eat with her.

"Nice meeting you Sean. Have a good evening."

Sean waves, "You too Mike, pleasure."

Marney watches Mikes walk away and head to a back booth where Deucen is standing, removing his jacket. She's content with not being a part of whatever it is they are meeting about.

# 25. Uneasy

Marney's eyes open before the light even enters the bedroom windows. She can't sleep. It's five o'clock in the morning and she's been up since three. Sean purrs softly next to her, his heat radiating like a furnace. She enjoyed their night of good food, catching up and amazing sex but, something is bothering her and she can't quite figure it out. Mike and the whole "bumping into her" thing felt odd. She doesn't know why just yet, but her mind keeps rolling over it in her head.

Marney sighs and rolls over. The strange phone call Sean had with his buddy, who she assumed was his old military friend he called Grill....Antione Grilliam, weighs on her mind. Sean never talks indepth about his past. She gives him that space so in turn, she has her own. They talk as much as they want about things and then leave it at that. It's just a thing between them, and its worked for years...until now. For the first time, she wants to ask him questions. She wants to know why it sounds like he is going to pick up his friend...the friend he calls cuckoo...which she knows means sniper in military terms. Its not like Sean to keep things from her, and it isn't like him to get involved in any of her cases more than just being a sounding board and support for her.

Marney flips the covers back and gets out of bed. She doesn't care that it's early. She's got a killer to catch.

***

Two and a half hours later, Mike strolls into the detectives unit. Freshly showered, shaved, and smelling divine. Marney looks up from her computer and makes eyes contact.

Mike smiles his sweet smile, "Good morning Marney. How are we today?"

"Weeee are fine Mike. How was your meeting last night?"

"Bearable; well, for the most part...your boss is so fucking focused on naming this damn serial killer for his "public persona" when he should be more focused on getting his employees what they need to solve the case." Mike flops down in Chris's chair and starts to dial the phone.

Marney can see the familiar frustration, in Mike, one often gets when dealing with Terry Deucen. He is a politician through and through, first and a cop last. And not the good kind of cop.

"Yo bud, how we doing?" Mike speaks to Zeek in a college-buddy type of way that Marney likes. "Oh really? Okay, well let's grab some lunch and we can line it up." Mike looks at Marney and smiles his charming, gorgeous-white-teeth grin. She looks back at her screen and continues her report. "Right....see you outside." Mike hangs up and stands.

Marney is curious, "Everything okay?"

"Yeah, looks like our Kerry Noonan is going to have lunch today with Dr. Cordova...an unscheduled type of lunch."

"Really? So no therapy appointment, but lunch?"

Mike nods, "Sounds to Zeek, more like a "we need to talk now" kind of lunch."

"Ooh, alright then." Marney smiles.

Mike moves his head towards the door, "So lets go get pancakes and work this out with Zeek...after we can visit Bahtya's work."

Marney feels conflicted, "Well, I'm waiting for Chris. Meet you there?"

"Yeah...okay. See ya in a few."

Marney updates a very annoyed, flustered Chris. He is not happy with this third murder interfering with his weekend...Marney smiles, it's more that he is not happy that he was in no condition to affectively help on the case...and Mike knew that. Marney listens to Chris bitch and moan, which he usually doesn't do unless he is mad at himself, then catches him up to speed. He feels better after getting interview reports from some of the officers which helps them know where to start after breakfast. Marney knows she'll be listening to the same sort of banter from her brother about mid-day. Both Chris and Liam hate feeling left out or behind in their work. Poker and too much alcohol can do that though.

Marney watches Mike and Zeek almost outdo Chris when it comes to breakfast food. She isn't as hungry as she thought she would be and attributed it to her uneasiness. After arranging for Zeek to get some sleep, Mike plans to sit on the wire during Kerry and Dr. Cordova's lunch, and Marney and Chris will dig more into Batya Lehev's co-workers. If Kerry Noonan takes her purse into the restaurant with Dr. Cordova at lunch, everything will go smoothly and there might be some good intel by the evening.

Chris pulls into Olman Electric and parks facing the building. It appears business as usual, but he wants to sit for fifteen minutes to get a feel for the activity. It's just a "Chris Thing" as Marney calls it. She reaches in her pocket to see if Sean has texted her cell. Nothing. She wonders if today is the day he is picking up his friend. Her stomach feels funny.

"Yo Marns, what's up? You keep watching the phone. That's not like you...you hate that thing." Chris touches her arm.

"Well, that's because it's usually fuckin' Deucen calling me all damn day."

Chris laughs, "You waiting on Deucen to call?"

"No. Hey, Sean say anything to you about this weekend?"

Chris shakes his head, "Naw, just that he wished he had gone. He loves fishing with your dad yaknow...and being with you Marns." He touches her cheek teasingly and she moves her head away and smirks.

"You guys getting together at all soon?"

"Why?" Chris is curious.

"Oh...well, it's just I feel guilty working all the time and him not having any free time. I was bummed Cherie made him work all weekend and he couldn't come to the cabin."

Chris suggests, "Well, you could always try again this coming weekend. I think Sean is off no?"

"I'll have to ask. We could plan another poker game. I'm sure my father would be more than happy. We could bring a few more people."

Chris agrees, "Yeah, sounds good. I can bring Mike again, you and Sean got anyone you would invite?"

Marney tries, "I'm not sure. Who do you think we should bring?"

"I don't know Marns, it's your life." Chris snickers and Marney wants to slap him. *Damn it.*

"It sounds great to me though. I love going up to Reuna."

Marney wonders if she should just outright ask Chris about Sean's buddy. Chris moves to get out of the car. She decides to hold off. If anyone is good at figuring out lines of questioning better than her, it's Chris. She doesn't want to raise suspicion.

***

Back at the station, Marney and Chris get ready for a meeting with Deucen and Mike. She and Chris didn't get far at Batya's work. Over eleven employees were interviewed, two being her bosses, and most were more concerned about the details of her death than if they liked her or noticed anything different about her lately. Most confirmed she was a lesbian, and most likely the male part in the relationship from what she looked and acted like. Marney noticed some discrimination issues with Batya's sexual orientation and her Indian ethnicity, but the company seemed proactive about putting it to rest or getting rid of employees involved in complaints by Batya. Other than that, she seemed an exemplary employee who kept her life private and her mouth shut. Chris and Marney both agreed, not one co-worker was worth asking down to the station for further questioning. Marney didn't want to have to tell Deucen this today at the meeting and listen to his grumbling. These murders were just running into walls with the outside world. Marney hopes to hear good news from Mike regarding the Noonan/Cordova lunch. The NSG is really the most solid lead so far.

Chris continues drafting up his reports and Marney is searching through her desk drawers for a pen that actually has ink in it.

"Well guys, guess that record for solving cases the quickest has gone to the shitter huh?" Jimmy Hoss chews on the stirrer to his coffee and smiles wide. Marney's not in the mood for his banter. He is a notch lower than Leeana Kazib when it comes to hating Marney and Chris's success. She doesn't even look up at Jimmy and instead bends lower to the bottom drawer.

Joe Radden comes up behind Jimmy, "Better watch out. We're coming up on your flank now." Joe opens his mouth again to sass and is cut off.

"Gentleman, don't you have some pizza store fronts to shake down for meth? I don't remember either of you working a serial case in your short careers...so move on before I make your careers even shorter." Mike Taylon's voice sounds like heavenly music to Marney. She secretly smiles to herself until she looks across and sees Chris's goofy grin. She can't help but chortle.

Jimmy and Joe move on without another word and Mike locks eyes with Marney. Her stomach flips a little because his look is intense. She hasn't seen him all day so she has no idea where he's at with the case. He points at her...then at Chris. "Can I talk to the two of you for a moment?" He doesn't wait for an answer, "Room four."

Chris and Marney both get up and follow Mike to an interview room. They look at each other, Chris points to her and mouths that she's in trouble. She squints at him and mouths back "bite me". Then they both smile at each other swiftly.

Mike closes the door and pulls out a chair to sit, "Okay, the lunch with Kerry Noonan and Dr. Cordova was brief...and boring. It was therapy sweet "how are you feeling honey" type shit. Cordova trying to shrink Noonan's brain over her dead husband. Encouraging her to continue with the group and more private sessions. If you need anything...blah, blah, blah. The interesting part was Mrs. Noonan admitting she had often times dreamt of Michael being hurt or getting "bit" back, but that she never thought he would end up murdered. The chick is freaked out and I can't ascertain if either of them were knowledgable about anything more than what we already know."

Marney asks, "So, what are you thinking?"

"I'm thinking we continue to listen in and definitely hit that meeting with a few ears since there could be numerous ladies showing up on Wednesday." Mike leans back in his chair.

Chris admits, "We didn't get far at Batya's job either. I was hoping for something there but, it seems her work ethic was stellar."

"Oh really? Well, I didn't think you would. This NSG is where it's at, I'd almost bet money on it. We just have to be careful how we proceed. I don't want to scare any intel away you know?"

"Yeah. Well, what's this meeting about with Deucen?" Marney has a ton of work to do.

"Fluffing balls really." Mike smirks.

"Really? So no Dr. Fine or Jeremy Lockly info?" Marney asks.

Mike shakes his head, "Naw, not yet. Tomorrow maybe. I spent last night holding Deucen's hand through how he needs to do press releases and news appearances. Fucker was prepared to go with some "Olman Slasher" type shit. I squashed that and refocused him, reminding him that this is our case and we're going to take it slow with the media. Olman is already in an uproar over three murders inside a month. People aren't stupid and they don't need to be frightened. He needs to stay away from this case being about him in front of the camera...and creating more drama. It makes our jobs harder."

Marney watches his face. She likes what he's saying and how the faint little crows feet appear around his eyes when he enunciates his words. He's really taken a lot of pressure off of her when it comes to her boss and she is enjoying her job more. "So, how are we going to play this media-wise?"

Chris chimes in, "Yeah, I'm kinda getting tired of saying "no comment" all the time."

Mike laughs, "Well bud, you are doing great...and sorry, but you know the rules, you can't comment on this case."

"I know, I know."

"All right, so lets go update Deucen and get you guys home for the night. I've got a date with the gym." Mike stands and stretches, Marney catches a glimpse of his sculpted stomach. She likes that he takes care of himself...it's admirable.

Chris stands and pulls out Marney's chair before she is ready, "Come on sparkles, get yo glitter ass moving."

She wants to smack him but decides to follow Mike instead.

# 26. Blader

Marney walks groggy out into Sean's kitchen and sits at his counter. He smiles at her and pushes a plate of food, a cup of coffee, and the newspaper towards her.

"Your going to want to read this sweetie." He has a tiny smile for her as he points the the article on the front page of The Olman Times.

"The Olman Blader right?" She looks into his languid blue eyes wishing they had made love this morning. Sean didn't get in until two-thirty, and mentioned he didn't want to wake her. Odd, since he wakes her most every other time.

"No, just "The Blader". I find it amusing because if you read it too fast, your mind sees bladder." He sips his coffee.

She laughs, "Yeah, Deucen fought last night with Mike at the meeting about it. I'm glad they went with "The Blader". Some of the shit Deucen was throwing down was just ludicrous."

"Like what babe?"

Marney loves when he addresses her like that...and with his soft, deep morning voice. "Oh, it was comical. He had dicer, avenger, Olman Revenger-type crap. I mean he really just wants to make this thing as big as it can be. Like People magazine big...he is such a-"

Sean laughs, "Sounds like Deucen...all about him, nothing about keeping people calm and families protected."

"Yeah, well...Mike put a stop to it fairly quickly in the meeting. We have to release the serial killer information now and put a name to him or her. I'm glad he took Olman out of the title. Mike told Deucen that he couldn't name the killer with Olman in front of it because it couldn't be established just yet that this is only happening in Olman."

"And Deucen bought that?" Sean raises his eyebrows.

"Yeah, if you can believe it. That's how much he isn't paying attention to what this is really about. I mean, we have a serious killer on the loose!"

"Sounds like this Mike guy is a pretty cool dude."

Marney nods, "He knows what he's doing."

"Well, so do you Marns." Sean touches her hand.

"I don't know Sean, this is big, I'm learning a lot...about doing multiple cases at once, and keeping things quiet...it's intense." She watches him. He's freshly showered and smells amazing. She attempts to concentrate on eating her breakfast.

"It's just because it's new to you right now. You have a lot of experience with solving cases...but this is your first serial-killer- high-profile-in-your-face-not-enough-time, kind of case. You'll be fine." He interlaces his fingers in hers.

She gives him her bedroom eyes, "I have enough time right now..." His flattery is getting him everywhere and she wants to forget about The Blader until she gets to the office.

"I have all day...so you finish up your food and I'll be waiting for you in the bedroom." He stands and nibbles at her neck before trotting away. Marney puts her fork down and runs after him.

***

"The Blader? Seriously Jade?" Leeana breezes by Marney's desk with a danish from Freda Jackson's pink bakery box.

Marney doesn't even look up. She is getting good at ignoring all the jealous detectives in her unit...Chris, not so much.

"Kazib, we don't name'em, we just catch'em girl!" Chris sings it more than says it. He walks towards Leeana, forcing her to stop and go around him as he makes a path to his desk from interview room two. "I think there are some old ladies in the lobby here you could arrest if you need something better to do."

Marney shakes her head at Chris's relentless teasing. Between him and Mike, she never has to say a word to her nemeses.

"Sup Marns..."

"You're in a good mood today...you get some?" She jokes.

He slumps in his chair, "I actually didn't, instead I went to the gym with Mike Taylon."

"Really?" *And thats better than sex?*

"Yeah, you know he is a really nice guy. I learn from him every time I'm around him. And, I feel great today...not sore like I thought. He knows a lot of shit about a lot of shit." Chris leans back flexing his biceps at Marney.

She's curious, "Why is that?"

"Oh, well Mike does one set of everything, as many reps as his body will allow. It's weird Marns, but I feel like I got a full body workout in under an hour!"

She raises her eyebrows, "Wow, sounds like it. It's good you feel good." Marney feels conflicted about Chris's time with Mike outside of work. First the cabin, now working out...she doesn't know if she is uncomfortable with it because he is their superior or because of envy. "So, how'd the interview go?"

Chris looks over at the room he just came from. Officer Chan, a rookie, is escorting MaryBeth Hoffman to the lobby. She's in tears. "Oh, she's a hot mess."

"What do you mean? New information mess?"

"No, three-days-into-her-lover-being-dead kind of mess. Well, there was the cheating, the lying, and the manipulating messy stuff." Chris nods and blinks slow matter-of-factly.

Marney bites the side of her lip, "Fuck, you mean Batya right? She was the cheater?"

"Yup, for the last three years now...that's why MaryBeth is in Dr. Cordova's fuckin' "fix me" group." Chris flexes his forearms and examines them. "I'm telling ya Marns, some dude is pissed. He is just wiping people out. Err, cheaters out I mean."

"Hmmm..." Marney thinks in her head, *or some woman.* "I think we are going to need to start putting tails on all the members of the NSG tomorrow. I don't care if we need more man-power. Maybe Mike would approve it."

Mike strolls in, "Approve what?"

Marney tries, "Hey, we were just brain-storming. Do you think the police academy would let us use some of the new recruits for surveillance? Could we put tails on those women when they leave the meeting tomorrow night?" Marney looks him up and down. He looks somehow bigger to her. She blinks, trying to rid herself of the distracting thought.

He nods, "Good idea! Already have my boss working on the paperwork...Deucen is bitching about budgeting and unmarked vehicles being used but I'm all over it." Mike smiles at Marney. She feels a little late with her idea but, understands why Mike has been in a holding pattern now. *Why didn't he say something?*

"I didn't have enough approval yet." Mike nonchalantly mentions. "In case you were wondering if I've been sitting with my thumb up my ass."

Chris laughs out loud and gets up, "Freda have anymore of those damn bear claw danishes? I'm flippin' starving!"

Mike follows him, "It's the reps man, I'm telling you. Ya have to double up on your food intake...and by food, I mean food." They both depart the unit, leaving Marney staring at the doors.

# 27. Gone

Marney checks her phone again. Sean hasn't texted her all day. Strange for him. He usually checks in every few hours. She decides to send him a third message, maybe his phone battery is dead. Sean usually never let's little mistakes like that happen, not even for her. Rarely, does he forget anything...which is why it's so unusual not to hear from him.

*Did he forget me today?* Marney climbs up into Gerda and starts the engine. Reaching over to put her cell on the seat she hears a knock at her window. Startled she instinctively reaches for her leg gun and notices Mike standing at her window. It's odd he is tall enough to look right in. She rolls the glass down, cringing at the hideous screeching sound the old window makes. He raises his hands so she sees them.

"Are you trying to get shot?" She jokes.

He locks eyes with her and smiles sweetly, "You want to get some dinner Marns?"

She almost says yes, "I've got something I have to do."

"Oh, okay...after?" His eyebrows furrow and she fights the urge to reach out of the window and touch his face. His skin is smooth and cowboy-tan.

"Uh..." She goes blank.

"Just text me when your done and let me know. I wanted to get with you about the NSG tomorrow."

She nods, "Okay...let ya know." She smiles and puts the truck in gear.

He pats her door and waves, "Great." Stepping back he puts his hands in his pockets and walks away.

Marney feels a little down about not saying yes right away. She wants to drop by Sean's work and check to see if his phone is working. She backs out and heads towards the bar.

Ten minutes later Marney pulls into Daytone's and parks in her usual spot towards the back. Her phone has a text message from Mike:

# Your brother is looking for you. MT

She texts back:

# TU

She cuts the engine and scans the parking lot while dialing Liam. Sean's green Scout is nowhere in sight. *What the fuck?*

Liam picks up on the second ring, "Jade." He sounds busy.

"Hi Liam."

"Hey Marns, how are ya?" His voice lifts.

She smiles, "Heard you called for me?"

"Yeah, just want to tell you Doc Fine is almost done with Batya Lehev so I set up a meeting tomorrow to go over cause of death and pathologies."

"Oh good."

"Your boss said first thing so eight-thirty, okay?"

Marney wonders if Deucen is planning to do another press release by noon, "Okay, I'll be there. Anything big Liam?"

"Well, her fuckin' genitals were removed...that's kinda big Marney. I mean I didn't know that was possible on a woman." Liam kind of laughs uncomfortably.

Marney jokes, "There's a lot about women you don't know little brother. And you taught me that they call that "mutilated" when a chics stuff is removed."

"Oh, har har har Marney, you're hysterical. All the reports say "mutilated" but with the way the skin is severed clean off like that...yucko!"

She chuckles, "Come on, it can't be worse than missing man-parts right?"

Liam asks, "Ugh, what a waste of lovely man-parts. Who does that?"

"A psycho killer...who wants trophies." Her voice is smooth. It makes sense.

"You guys need to get going on this one. I'm getting tired of seeing mangled corpses Marney. Can't we just have a normal elderly guy with heart failure or a fat woman with a stroke?"

She laughs, "Trying. Get me a print...some sweat...DNA...something huh? I really need a little something."

Liam admits, "I don't know...whoever this is, is quite clever. Covers their tracks well...wears gloves...doesn't even leave a hair behind."

"I know. Believe me, we are on it. It's the only case I *am* on. Deucen made it priority...of course. For weeks now." Marney bites the inside of her lip.

"I know, I know. Just want it over. You should see the fuckin' people...and damn reporters that keep coming here...soon we will need a lobby and airport seating."

She huffs, "Yeah, we have it too...and the phones don't stop. We've actually had to bring in two more dispatchers from the 911 center and place them up front. I have to sneak in and out of the detective's unit and sign-in via phone instead of radio. There are tons of freaks listening in."

Liam chuckles, "Yeah, and the killer is probably one of them."

"Oh, I'm sure Li...this shit is reals." She jokes trying to keep things light. It's a skill needed when it comes to cop stress.

"K-well I'll see ya in the morning. Give kisses to Sean for me!" Liam laughs.

Marney smirks, "Funny...actually, have you heard from Sean?" Sean's always been good about contacting everyone at least once a week to touch base. It's just how he is with her family and their friends.

"Marney, did you really lose track of yo man?"

She denies, "No, just thinking there is phone trouble or something."

Liam teases, "Good. Don't lose track of yo man gurl...someone ull snatch those buns up right quick!"

"Nice...just lovely Liam." He cracks up laughing...and hangs up leaving Marney sighing.

***

The place is dead. Cherie's regulars don't stroll in until dinner time. *Probably when they wake up.* Marney's always thought it unnatural that Cherie could pay her business bills with just her regulars. *Alcohol, sex and religion...never goes out of style.*

Marney walks up to the bar as Cherie turns around, "Hey, what happened to your boyfriend today?" Cherie looks past Marney towards the door, not really making eye-contact. She has a huge yellow and purple black eye and Marney fights the urge to ask her what happened with hers.

"Uh, thought he was here Cherie. What the fuck?" Marney points to her eye hoping to hell it's not a present from Deucen.

"Oh that, got between a couple of old hags here the other night...something about their mother's will." Cherie waves her hand and laughs it off.

Marney frowns, "Jeez, sorry to hear that."

"Oh, no biggie. Part of the job. Lucky Sean can clear this bar in one jump...or else my twins might be looking just as purple." Cherie points to her breasts. Marney doesn't look down. She is in no way interested in talking about Cherie's presents paid for by the douchebag.

"Oh wow, he didn't mention that. Anyway, hope that heals up real quick. Looks painful."

"Naw, looks worse than it is."

"So you haven't seen Sean today?" Marney is growing more and more concerned. She wonders if today was the day he was to "be there" for whatever thing he hadn't told her about yet. She wishes she had pressed him. In seven years, Sean has never not been where he was suppose to be.

Cherie uses a washcloth to clean the bar, "Nope. He didn't even call. Not like him at all. I even checked the schedule thinking he was off...but it says he is working the next three in a row."

Marney could tell Cherie wasn't real angry, Sean's been the best thing for her business. But, she did seem concerned. "He's only called out two times in the last eight years."

Marney knows its true. Both times were for her. "Hmmm, right."

"Guess he hasn't called you either?" Cherie eyeballs her, just waiting for something to gossip about. It's the trait Marney can't really stomach when it comes to Cherie Daytone. She feels gossips should never own bars. Or breathe.

Marney lies, "Well, I've been so busy on this damn case I-" Marney's cell beeps and she sees it's Mike. "Tell ya what, I'll have Sean call you okay?" She backs up looking at her phone and decides to go look for Sean at his house.

"Oh alright honey. See ya."

Marney heads back to Gerda. She checks her text message:

# Meet at Retreat? MT

Marney rolls her eyes:

**Can't just yet. Let ya know soon. MJ**

Mike texts back:

# K. See you at 6:30. MT

Marney sighs. *Geez, persistent much?* She starts up the truck and heads to Sean's house. She thinks how she needs to be finding a killer...not her boyfriend. She tries to run the conversation over in her head again. The one Sean had with "Cuckoo". *What the fuck could they be up to?* She wishes she had confronted him about it. Sean never talks about his military days unless she asks...and even then he has always been really light about it. She knows there are big secrets there...he just never needed to share. She figured his past was his past. Now she wishes she had been more involved. Maybe his past wasn't really in the past...maybe it was just on hold.

She pulls up, his truck is gone. None of the neighbors are out, but she notices the trash cans are. *He put out the trash cans.* He must be home or has recently been. She knows they were not out when she left that morning. Maybe his truck is at the garage.

Marney jumps down and slams her door. She's getting annoyed. The walkway looks untouched, the porch, the furniture...she uses her key to let herself in. No lights, no food smells, no cologne...nothing. She wants to call out to him but something tells her not to. She starts a visual perimeter search...

# 28. I'm Sorry

Marney makes it to the bedroom...where they were making love only eleven hours before. She sees it and immediately her heart hurts. The paper, folded three ways, not even in an envelope very simply has M written on the outside.

She slowly opens it, her hands shaking:

*Dear Marney,*

*I am so sorry. Don't wait. You know why...*

*I've always loved you,*

*S*

Marney slides to the floor, her hair falls into her face. She stares at the beautiful handwriting on the page as tears form and blurr everything. There is no question...just a knowing. He is gone.

Her heart begins it's torturous break.

# 29. Abandonment

Marney bursts through the door of conference room three. All eyes are on her. Doc Fine doesn't skip a beat and keeps on rambling about the corpse of Batya Lehev. Marney takes the first chair available and slumps down not caring she is eighteen minutes late. Everyone but Doc Fine stares at her, dumbfounded. Marney Jade is never late.

Her hair is not brushed, her clothes are the same as the day before, and her mascara is sitting in the bags below her eyes rather than up under her lashes where it should be. Marney is fourteen hours, three minutes and twenty-one seconds into full blown heartache. The abandonment almost couples the loss of her mother at age twelve...a trigger she doesn't need right now.

She hears mumbling for what seems like days; then, "So in conclusion, it's the same killer by modus operandi and therefore, in my opinion, can be added to "The Blader" case file. Any questions?" Doc Fine points to Deucen, no doubt, to stroke ego and then makes his way around the table. Marney pretends to scribble notes on the little yellow pad of paper in front of her, pulling her hair behind her ear with her other fingers. Chris pushes his cup of coffee toward her and she takes it without eye contact. It's the only thing she has had at all and drinks it completely down to the bottom of the cup.

Moments later everyone begins to stand and push their chairs out startling Marney who attempts to get up and gracefully do the same. She nods here and there without eye contact, but maneuvers around everyone to get through to the door. In the hallway she realizes she has no idea where she is going and begins to slow her steps. She can't remember what it is she is doing. Suddenly, she feels a strong arm around her waist and a force pulling her to walk quickly forward. She scares and looks over making out his beautiful broad chest. He is holding her up and forcing her towards the stairwell. She looks up and sees his strong jaw line, he is looking straight ahead, very seriously.

She looks forward too and sees the gray stairwell door coming at her face but, just before she hits it he pushes it open forcing both their bodies through the door. She smells him then, his scent is a wondrous man-scent mixed with leather and musk. Her nostrils are overwhelmed with his cleanliness and her senses ignite almost waking her out of her excruciating pain. She looks down and sees stairs! Then her head flips back and she sees the ceiling come into view over her as he lifts her into his arms and briskly runs down the stairwell with her tucked to his chest. She feels safe now. His shirt is unbuttoned and Marney rolls her eyes open to see thick, sculpted pecs sliding against the inside of his shirt. She reaches her hand up and into his neck opening and feels the heat of his skin running down her palm. His chest hair is soft and curls a little around her fingers. He clears another flight of steps and walks to the basement door, flinging it open with his foot. The fluorescent lights hurt Marney's eyes and she buries her face now into his neck inhaling a lungful of him. She wants to open her mouth to his skin and kiss it. Her face vibrates when the sound of his deep voice comes through his neck.

"Zeek, gives us a ten would ya?" Mike nods his head toward the door.

"Sure thing."

Marney hears footsteps disappear. Suddenly, she is hoisted to her feet and pushed against the cold cement wall. She picks her head up and squints to see the mammoth frame in front of her. Her knees feel weak but she tries to straighten them. His large hands cup her shoulders and press them gently back against the wall. He tucks his head down to find her gaze. Marney stares and the blurring fades. Mike is piercing his eyes into her and waiting. He is breathing heavily, but no words come.

She smiles and blinks slow again feeling drunk, not with substance, but sleeplessness. She is so tired she wants to slide down the wall to sit on the floor and just...sleep. He says nothing, watching, waiting.

Marney tries to lift her head again. Her heart hurts so bad it feels like she's broke inside. Pain, not physical, but shear excruciating heartache shoots down her body. She would cry if she had anything left, but it is taking all her strength just to try to bring her eyes up to look at Mike. He stares into her like he knows...like he is familiar with how time has stopped. Her head drops again and her eyelids burn when they close. They feel so hot and fevered...they burn! She inhales trying to muster the energy to look at him again...sweet, sweet, beautiful Mike Taylon.

Quickly, she lifts her head up and against the cold wall. He has her braced by her shoulders and watches her still. She looks at him, and he her. He frees one shoulder and brings his hand up wiping the hair out of her face. He is so gentle. She loves how his palm feels against her cheek. She turns to his hand and kisses it closing her eyes to the glorious feel of his strength. He moves it and pushes her hair farther behind her, cupping her slender neck in his hand. She brings her eyes up again and he stares. Somehow, for just a fleeting moment, he has erased the pain. She feels his energy, it's so intense, almost like the sun on her skin. Her eyes trail down his face, his neck, his chest...trim waist, bulge, thick thighs and long legs. She brings them back up and sees he is still piercing through her with his gorgeous blue eyes. She steps forward fast and before thinking, she has her lips to his! He grabs her quick and pulls her body into his, plunging his tongue into her mouth tenderly and passionately. Marney's body ignites and she grasps at his back pressing in to feel him. Mike turns his head the to deepen the kiss and she feels his large hands wrap around her back. She feels she has never been closer to another than this moment. It feels so...

Mike brings his hands up to her shoulders again and pushes to break the kiss! "I-, oh Marney...I'm sorry." He whispers his apology and she feels confused, her lips still searching for his. The pain is back like a familiar cut from glass. He felt so good...and he took it all away for just a second.

She looks up into his eyes, he feels bad and she sees that. His eyes look down into her, over her face, her hair. He runs his thumb along her cheek and she wants him. She reaches for him and he steps back taking her hands and placing them together in front of her chest. His face shows torment and his breathing is erratic.

"I'm sorry...I just wanted to see if you were okay...I didn-"

"No, I'm not okay...I'm sorry. I need to just-" She stands straight and takes her hands from his. She runs them down her shirt and tries to smooth it. She runs her hands then over her face and opens her eyes wide trying to wake up. Breathing in deep, and then out again, she tries to compose herself. "I just need to get my fucking shit together here. Today is a big day." She looks over at Zeek's huge wire-tap set up...thankful that he is not in his chair.

Mike is staring at her, one hand on his hip the other hand leaning against the wall. "I didn't mean to uh...look I just know..." He stops to gather his thoughts. It's not like him to stumble on his words.

Marney is sobering from her emotional break and is a bit annoyed with how attracted she is to him. Something feels so right. Her stomach starts to swirl with the realization that she just fucking kissed her boss! *Holy Shit!!*

"Okay, let's just regroup here. Why don't you go home and get cleaned up, get some food, get a few hours sleep...I'll take care of Deucen. Come back an hour before we listen in on the tap, I'll fill you in on the day and then we can sit in on the NSG. With you, me, Chris and Zeek we should be able to get a good spread on the many voices in that room. Okay?"

"And this?" She circles her finger in between their bodies. He takes his hand off the wall and tries to step back another step. Mike is way too comfortable in Marney's personal space.

He has such a serious face, "We'll talk about this another time."

"I'm-"

"Me too. No worries. Sometimes shit happens." He half smiles to make her feel better but more out of shock at himself. He didn't know she had such an affect on him, he damn near got a full blown erection from just the feel of her tongue. He is playing it down but his heart is racing. The woman stirs him. Deeply.

She smiles, "Right...thanks. I'll be back in a few hours."

Mike steps aside and lets her by him. He waits until he hears the door open and shut, then places his head against the wall. *Fuck.*

# 30. Luke Rance

The doorbell rings...then again...and again. Marney unholsters her firearm from the nightstand pocket and jumps out of bed. She fights the nausea she feels and quietly patters her bare feet to the door, slowing up as she gets near to the peep hole. She prepares to get on her tipy-toes but hears his familiar tone.

"Marney it's Mike." His voice is deep and smooth.

Marney lowers her gun and takes a deep breath. She unlocks the door, opens it, and walks towards the kitchen.

Mike steps in and sees her mound of tussled hair, a long gray t-shirt, a gun, and what seems like a mile of gorgeous legs that end in two bare ass cheeks her underwear is not covering. He looks away reluctantly and shuts the door locking it. Marney walks a little faster, then even faster, until she is in a full trot to the kitchen sink where she throws up, projectile, down into the garbage disposal. Mike winces feeling bad for her. He takes a seat at the pub chair and places his elbows on the counter. He wants to go over, hold her hair back and help her as she's heaving into the sink...but, he thinks he should keep his distance...especially after what happened at the station earlier...and the fact that her underwear is not doing it's job well. Marney runs the water to clean away the soup she tried to eat before falling asleep. It looks the same as when it went in. She washes her mouth, her hands, and her face. Leaning against the counter she buries her face in a towel and tries to catch her breath.

Mike looks her up and down. He thinks she is so beautiful. No bra, perfect skin...her thighs peeking out from beneath her t-shirt. He gets up and walks around the counter. He removes the coffee pot from the coffee maker and bends towards her to rinse it in the sink she just yacked in. She watches him with her eyes half closed. He fills the pot with water, pours it in the coffeemaker, and places it on the burner. He reaches up into the closest cabinet and finds coffee grounds and a

148

filter. Placing the filter in, he looks over at her then looks back to scoop in the grounds. He pushes the filter tray in and pushes the on button. Resting his hands on the counter he slides his eyes up her body and to her face again. Marney is watching him. She knows he has never been to her house before...yet he seems to know where things are. Then again, she could just be very predictable. She likes that he is so capable, comfortable in his own skin. And in her house.

"Feeling better or worse?" He says it low and gentle.

She smiles and huffs, "Trying to feel something."

He opens another cabinet and gets two coffee mugs down, "Let me guess...your pregnant and he's not sure that's what he wants...so he bailed." Mike is harsh...but, logical.

She laughs, rather fake, and throws the towel aside, "Well, that would be a hoot."

"I was reaching huh?"

She walks around to the counter and takes a seat, "Yeah. I'm just all wrecked. I'm not pregnant...and he just up and left with no explanation...told me not to look for him...and that he is sorry."

Mike lifts his eyebrows, "Really?" He wants to ask more but knows Sean is a military man, he will research it more when he gets the chance.

"Really. I don't want to talk about it. The confusion almost outweighs the hurt-"

"Listen. You don't have to say a word until you want to. When the confusion fades, I'll be here...to listen, if you need."

She shoots him a look, he smiles lovingly at her. She wonders if getting up and walking over to wrap her arms around him would be a horrible mistake. She feels the need to be held by him.

Mike turns to pour two cups of coffee, then hands her one as he stretches across the counter to move closer to her. He sips his and studies her face. She locks eyes with him and sips the black heaven that actually makes her feel less nauseated for a moment. She blinks slow, remembering how magnificent he kisses. Her eyes trail down to his lips that are now fevered from the hot coffee. His face falls to a look of sadness.

"I know you feel angry, abandoned, and confused. The "why" is never going to come Marney. Even if he returns right now...you would still need the "why". It's brutal...and I am sorry." His eyes are compassionate and she loves to look at him.

"You know?"

"I know. Wish I didn't...but I know."

"What happened Mike?"

He stares at her for what seems like minutes. He sips his coffee again, watches her, and decides to trust her, "I watched another man kill my wife...as if she meant nothing."

Marney feels deep pain for him suddenly, she knows she cares deeply for him now, "What?"

"I watched a criminal take my wife's life because I had ruined his." Mike placed his cup down and began tapping on the handle. Marney's breath catches in her throat. The guilt this man must feel would kill a weaker person. Suddenly her "why" about Sean seems insignificant to his. A revenge killing holds a little more weight than a disappearing boyfriend. "It's going to take you time." He speaks from true knowing.

She nods.

He continues, "I'm sorry if I complicated things today, I-"

"No, that was me Mike. I just needed to..." She searches for the words. "Feel, less...numb."

"Yeah." He forces a smile and tries to prepare how he is going to tell her what he came over to tell her. He clears his throat and changes the subject to ease her into it, "So, were you able to sleep some?"

She nods and sips the coffee again. She fights the urge to question him further about his wife. "Took a hot shower and was asleep before my head hit the pillow."

He gazes into her eyes, "Good. Because I'm going to exhaust you." She looks at him wondering if he is telling her he is going to blow off the wire tap and instead come around the counter, take her in his arms, and make love to her until she forgets Sean exists. Her stomach does flips and she feels nervous...she waits.

"Uh-"

"I'm here to pick you up, lead detective."

She frowns in confusion.

"We just got another one Marns." Her eyebrows raise, she can't believe what he's saying. *Another one? Fuck!*

*\*\*\**

Mike pulls up to the scene and parks. Marney gets out and scans the area. She is super late on this one but in her defense, Mike was trying to console her with coffee and she thought she had time before going to the station to sit on the wire for the NSG. She didn't know that another body had surfaced. Mike had already been to the scene and left Liam in charge. Looking around, Marney is secretly happy she had gotten some sleep, it's going to be a long night.

"Looks like a decent neighborhood." She doesn't get a creepy vibe from the looks of the surrounding apartments. The cars in the parking lot were of middle class status and the neighbors staring behind the crime tape seem to be properly dressed and concerned.

Mike shrugs, "Yeah, it's okay...except for the dead body part."

Marney smiles at him and he smiles back. She likes working with Mike, even if they are after a deranged psychopath.

Unfortunately, the news cameras are in place as are the three newscasters planted in front of them. Two uniformed officers come out and escort Mike and Marney into the scene holding off the approaching media. They fire off questions about how many bodies are inside, is it The Blader's work, and will there be any comments tonight. Mike puts his arm around Marney to block any photos, they make their way through the apartment sidewalk maze and up one flight of steps. Marney nods to fellow law enforcement and shows her badge to Sgt.

Blair who nods and checks her name off his list. There are twice as many people on scene as the three previous crime scenes, no doubt due to the publicity of the case now.

Marney squints her eyes as the flash photography is lighting up the small apartment and Deucen is heading towards the door. He looks disgusted as usual.

"Nice of you to join us Jade."

Mike steps beside her, "She was following orders Terry, take it easy."

Deucen ignores Mike's reply, "How are we with the surveillance and recruits back at the station?"

Mike finds his question humorous since it was he who complained about budgeting and cars for the extra men. Mike had to pull strings with his own higher ups to get the NSG bugged and the extra man-power to tail the ladies when they leave the meeting. He really wants to help Zeek out but the body takes precedence. Luckily, Chris is assisting Zeek and Tracey, and he and Marney can work the crime scene. "Everything is set up back at the station and Marney and I will take care of things here. You better go deal with the press outside. They're getting antsy."

Marney eyes Mike and thinks how clever he is to get rid of Deucen like that. She watches her boss straighten his posture and fix his zip-up police jacket and matching hat, looking the part, as usual, for his camera time. She turns her head to look into the living room and sees her brother and two other cops roll the body.

"Yes, yes...I will take care of the press. I expect a full report on my desk in the morning." Deucen nods to others in the room and bee lines for the door.

"Right." Mike shakes his head and smiles at Marney. "Shall we?" He hands her a set of gloves.

"I'm going in partner."

"I'm right behind you." Mike snaps his glove and sees Marney chuckle. He would do anything to make her smile.

***

Luke Rance was a forty-three year old white male, who owned a local insurance agency which he had run for sixteen years, owned it for the last four. His neighbors describe him as single, athletic, and somewhat of a player. They point out his BMW in the parking lot, which is silver and the cheapest leased model one can purchase. He has never been married and they say he is known to entertain numerous girls throughout a week, but never all at once. There doesn't seem to be a specific one they would call a girlfriend.

The scene is bloodier than the others' since The Blader stabbed Luke Rance dead in the heart, kicked his body over, broke his jaw, cut off his hands and of course, removed his penis and scrotum. This time the tongue wasn't removed. The hands were severed in the same fashion and left behind, and the genitals were nowhere in sight. After doing the damage postmortem, it appears as if the killer again kicked the body over, prone, and let the heart bleed out all over the cream colored carpet. Marney notices it looking a little more severe. The dark blood on the light carpet, gives it an gruesome contrast. Liam estimates the time of death around lunchtime, which correlates with Mr. Rance's pattern of eating at home every day, twelve-thirty to one-thirty. The call came in at one-thirteen that "a round person with a black sheet over them came out of the apartment carrying something long in one hand and a bag in the other." This coming from a ninty-two year old female who is the mother of a resident, and happen to be looking out the window waiting for her daughter to get home from work, to have lunch with her. She thought it appeared odd and called the police. The woman is old and has no idea what "The Blader" is, or much else of what's going on. Mike thinks her statement is helpful, but getting her down to the station for an interview is proving difficult since she is afraid to leave the house. Her daughter says she has a touch of agoraphobia, and doesn't leave the residence often. She says she will try to bring her mother in, but the woman doesn't stay up passed nine and will usually only go out if she can stop at church.

Marney and Mike search the apartment along with the other officers. Luke Rance was a player and loved to take photos of himself with his lady friends. Marney logs all of the nasty photos in as evidence and knows for sure it will only be a matter of time before one of the women in the photos turns out to be in the NSG. Other items were logged too, like his laptop and briefcase. Marney has to try and figure out Rance's patterns and some sort of motive. Mike told her most likely he liked to punch ladies in the face since his jaw was caved in. Looks like a pretty big hit with the butt or hilt of a weapon. With his heart stabbed, Mr. Rance is most likely in the broken hearts club as well. Meaning, he did the heart-breaking. It all seems so symbolic, yet again. Marney is tiring of it.

After a few hours, Marney is ready to head back to the station. The neighbors have all returned home and the news vans left shortly after the body. A fourth dead body to add to the count. All Marney wants to do is solve this damn case...and head to her dad's cabin. She knows she needs the mountain air to heal.

Mike drives slowly back to Olmanson P.D., "So a round person with a black sheet over them carrying something long in one hand and a bag in the other." He squints a little at the road, thinking how incredibly unusual the words sound.

"Interesting huh? She's ninty-two." Marney writes on a pad with the interior car light on.

Mike nods, "It's not much...but it's something. More than the other bodies. This time there was a witness. What do you think round means?"

"Well, old people are like kids so round probably means short and fat...not sure about the black sheet thought."

"Yeah, but that would explain why there is never any DNA at the scenes and no real witnesses." He frowns. "Whoever is doing this, knows their forensics. Maybe it's like a black surgical outfit...or something HAZMAT-like?"

Marney nods and smiles, "Hmmm, might be someone closely linked to crime scenes...or law enforcement. I hope we can get grandma down to the station tomorrow...maybe she'll enjoy drawing with crayons. Just hope she remembers more."

"Or at all..." Mike smiles and parks in his spot at the P.D.

"Ooh yeah, your right...it could be bad."

"Let's go see how Zeek and Chris made out with the NSG tonight."

"Yes, let's!" Marney is feeling better even though she has tons more work to do...but she likes not thinking about Sean...and working alongside Mike. He is a welcome distraction.

# 31. Whispers

"Are you fucking kidding me?" Mike runs his hand through his thick hair and slouches against the counter. Zeek and Chris stand with headphones around their necks looking like scolded neighborhood rejects.

Marney has a sinking feeling in the pit of her stomach mixed with a little disbelief.

Zeek, being his calm, nerd-type self, speaks again. A little more monotone, "We tried Mike, we really did. I know my equipment is working. We could hear them moving chairs, and pouring coffee which was almost too loud...fuck, we could even hear Dr. Cordova or whoever, with a goddamn dry erase marker going to town on a white board in the room! But, their voices, their voices were all fucking whispers!"

Chris nods to corroborate what Zeek is telling Mike. He comments, "Mike, someone must have tipped off those women...I mean it wasn't like the bug on Noonan's purse was knocked off or broken, the shit was working loud and clear. The whole fucking group was just whispering! Except for when someone was using the damn markers. Occasionally, there was a cough or a chair screeching. It was nuts. Boring as shit...and nuts."

"Alright, so we've got some smart or tipped off ladies in this group. Do you think they saw the tails...what's the word on the LOC?" Mike sounds annoyed, but not at Zeek and Chris. It really isn't their fault. He moves on.

Zeek answers, "Recruit 2039 called in, confirmed the meeting was held at St. Francis Church on Twinnings Road...in the basement with an entrance around back. The meeting was only forty-five minutes long and none seem to have noticed their tails. We've got nine women total. I'll have a list of residences in a few. I was just heading upstairs to meet up with 2039 who is en route to this location. They had to run tags and try to identify some of the women."

Marney attempts to refocus, "Okay, lets all head up to the D unit, get some coffee, and start planning a strategy for these nine residences. At least we've got some new leads to work with. Lots of interviews ahead. It's not a total loss guys. You did good!" She reaches for her partner and rubs his bicep. Chris looks like a pledge on the first night of a college hazing.

"Yeah, let's just get our head in a new game...I'm interested in who the fuck tipped off this group though!" Mike walks towards the door with Zeek and Chris in tow, not really wanting an answer. Marney looks on and smirks as she sees the three of them with their heads slightly hung. She finds it humorous that these *three* men thought those *nine* women would make this case easy. There are already four bodies. There is no easy.

\*\*\*

Marney bites into a stale, vanilla-pecan cookie and sips coffee. She watches Mike, who seems to be negotiating with his higher-ups on the phone. He has a grace about him. His movements are attractive...even in the depths of stress. She feels he is very good at his job.

When the door opens and Chris and Zeek enter, there seems to be a hungry look in Chris's eyes. He's holding lined papers stapled together and wrinkled...as if it had been through a lot.

"Marney! Look at this. Look at number six on this list!" Chris shoves the list at her.

Marney puts her coffee down and wipes her mouth with a napkin. She starts at the top and see's a handwritten list of names. The names are written a second time down the page but, with addresses. Her eyes skim over it and stop at number six. *Shit.*

1. Angel Islata
2. Juanita Diaz

3. Susan Cordova

4. Vizi Malone

5. Kerry Noonan

6. Cherie Daytone

7. Maryann Hoffman

8. Julia Newton

9. Gail Saunders

Marney looks at Chris, then to Zeek. Crap! Is Cherie Daytone really in the NSG? She looks at Mike, who is pacing back and forth on his cell, and tries to catch his gaze. He's looking down at the floor, one hand on his hip. Marney waves at him, across the room, trying to get his attention. Mike is slouching, staring down, taking in information. Marney waves again with no luck. She looks down at her desk and grabs the pecan cookie. She takes it and heaves it at Mike hitting him in the chest. It bounces off to the floor and he lifts his eyes to her, frowning. Marney gives him the throat-cut signal for fear he is talking to Deucen. Mike stops talking mid-sentence and tells whoever is on the line he will call them back and hangs up.

"Yeah Marns?"

"You need to see this."

Mike comes to her and takes the list. He reads it and looks at her waiting.

"Number six Mike." Marney points to the page.

He looks again, then at Chris and Zeek. Chris nods. "Why does this name look familiar guys?"

Marney takes the list back so she has it when Mike flips out, "Cherie Daytone is Terry Deucen's mistress Mike."

Mike takes off abruptly and heads out the door with Chris and Zeek in tow. Marney sinks down into her chair. This case just got ten times more complicated.

# 32. Big Brother

Mike pulls up and parks in front of Marney's house. She wants to invite him in, but doesn't want to interrupt his ranting about Deucen.

"If that fucker even tries to step foot in the station while we are on this Blader case, I will have him permanently suspended! And Marney, I'm telling you, if I find out that he told his mistress about this case or our wire tonight, he is so fucking fired! I will bring his ass up on obstruction charges!"

Marney smiles at him, more out of admiration than anything, "Mike?"

Mike doesn't hear her, "I am so fucking infuriated with the political shit-storm this could bring down on us, not to mention the poor victims and..."

"Mike?"

"Yeah?"

"When you suspended Deucen, did you ask him why his mistress was in a narcissistic recovery group?" She looks at him.

Mike is quiet, he looks off as if trying to remember, "Yeah, he said something about her Harley boyfriend...or something like that. Honestly Marns, I'm so disgusted with him I just want him to clear out. I told him if he speaks to the press or takes any calls...he's fired."

"Boyfriend?"

"My superiors are coming in to investigate him while you and I catch this killer." Mike runs his hand through his hair, resting them behind his head.

Marney frowns, "What boyfriend? Sean never mentioned Cherie had a boyfriend."

"Deucen said she lives with some guy. Damn, this is a fucking nightmare scandal waiting to happen Marney."

Marney quiets a moment then puts her hands to Mike's face to get him to look at her, "Mike, what if Cherie doesn't have a boyfriend?

What if....what if Cherie is telling Deucen about all the women in the group and..."

"And what Marns? Killing their abusers?" Mike looks into her eyes searching.

Marney lets him go and sits back, "Well...nothing is normal with the abnormal."

"True." Mike exhales. "And Deucen certainly is not normal."

"No, he certainly is not." Marney looks at her house and then back at Mike. She knows there is nothing more they can do tonight. "Would you like to come in?"

Mike smiles at her.

"What? Is that a yes?"

He looks down at the steering wheel, "It's more like an I'd-love-too but, I'm going to pass."

She smiles, "Really? After the day we've had? I mean I threw up in front of you and all...I've got beer."

"Yeah, you did...and beer sounds great right now." Mike chuckles and notices how nice it is to decompress for a moment. The stress of everything is as thick as a fog. "You blow chunks quite nicely, I might add." He remembers the curves of her ass cheeks poking out from under the bottom of her t-shirt.

Marney looks at him, his strong features and gorgeous, manly face and chest. She reaches over and touches his hand, "And you kissed me..."

"Yeah, I did...wayyyyy before the chunks blowing part I might add. Which sadly, is why I am going to take a rain check on the invite." He cants his head to the side apologetically.

"because of the kiss I mean..."

Marney takes her hand away slowly, "Really? Why?" She knows why but, needs to hear him say it.

Mike reaches in, knowing she's hurt. He runs his hand along her cheek to her ear and pulls her close to him, "Because Detective Jade...you are another man's woman."

Marney stares at him, oddly hoping he will ignore what he himself has just said, and kiss her again. She didn't know he saw her that way. Is this why he has been close and then distant? Does he want her but want to respect her situation...err other man? She sits back against the seat. Could tall, put-together, methodical Mike Taylon, FBI agent...be torn? Marney smirks. How foolish she must look. Of course he is going to decline. He's been through enough pain, he sees hers. He doesn't want to add to it. He's too intelligent, too perfect, too respectful...to complicate her already complicated life, any further.

"Marney?"

"I heard you Mike...its-"

He reaches out with his arms and pulls her close again. She can feel the heat of his skin. She can smell his lovely scent of men's shampoo and lightly splashed aftershave. He whispers, "Please don't think you are not wanted Marns...nothing could be further from the truth. I'm just trying to be-"

"Smart about it...I know. Responsible and agent-like right? I get it Mike. It's good. Thank you." She hears herself whispering it in the quiet car space. He can feel her breath on his skin and his arousal is desperately trying to convince him to change his mind. Marney can see it in his eyes and wants to respect him. She pulls away and turns to get out of the car.

His heart hurts, "See you tomorrow?"

"Yup. See you tomorrow...and hey, don't let Deucen out of your sight okay?" She bends down to the window and tries to smile at him. She doesn't want to be alone. She doesn't want to go inside and hurt.

"Already got a tail on him...in fact I think I'm going to go back to the station and have him brought in for questioning. Get some rest."

"Yes sir." She taps the door and waves, pivoting to walk to her dark, lonely, empty castle.

Marney waves again as she approaches her doorway and Mike drives off. She turns and instinctively slows. She sees the glow of his red cigarette in the dark, followed by the stench and then his old spice cologne. She doesn't have to reach for her gun because she knows exactly who he is.

"Hello Junior."

"Hey Marns. How do you always know where I am?" Asner's deep voice bounces off the roof of her porch.

She digs out her keys, "You know you could get shot sitting in the dark like that Asner."

He laughs, "You wouldn't shoot me now sis, would you?"

Marney unlocks her door and hears her brother's knees crunch as he stands from her porch swing to follow her. She already noticed the suitcase leaning against the stucco wall and knew her brother had come to stay with her as he does every six months or so. "Nope. I don't shoot people I know. So, guess ya got some time off from the oil rig...or did the girlfriend throw you out?" Marney opens the door wide and turns the lights on.

Asner scuffs his feet, grabs the handle to his suitcase, then pulls it in to the house. She smiles at him noticing how tall he is. He bends to kiss her cheek and she hugs him close. Stepping back, she takes a good look at him. He looks well. Tired, but well. "Ah, a little of both I guess. I got time off and she went on vacation with her girls, so I decided to visit you, Liam, and Dad. You know, my yearly thing."

"Well, that's cool. How long?"

"Couple weeks."

"Couple weeks...as in two? Three?"

"Uh, two. Just enough time to miss home, then I'll go back for a week, spend some nookie time with Shania and head back to the rig." He turns and wheels his suitcase farther into the foyer.

Marney takes a quick scan outside, shuts the door, then locks it and turns the lights out. "You want some tea?"

"Yeah, you got that Earl Gray one?"

"Yup, comin' up. You know where to put your stuff right?" She points down the other hall.

Asner turns and continues on to the spare room, "Yep, still a non-smoking room?" He jokes.

"Sorry, brotha. That is still a non-smoking, jizz-free kinda pad." Marney knows how to joke along with him. She hears him laugh while he opens the closet doors, knowing he hates her rules, but he respectfully follows them. She puts the teapot on and heads to her bedroom to change into pajamas. It's been a hell of a day and tomorrow doesn't look to be any better...well, except she won't have Deucen on her ass anymore.

Marney breezes into her bedroom and her footing slows. She looks around, feeling empty inside. Her bed is still made, except for the corner flipped down from where she climbed out earlier when Mike was at the door. She feels sad looking around and realizing Sean is gone. Totally gone. *Don't wait...you know....* She walks into her closet and flings her shoes off at the wall one at a time. They hit and fall to the carpet. *Why?* She pulls her jacket off and throws that down, her shirt and bra, then the rest of her clothes as well. *Why?* She knows her brother will be in the kitchen soon. She refuses to be a victim and pushes it all aside. Mike pops into her head as she pulls her sweatpants on. She wants to be angry at him too but, she can't. All she can think of is how wonderful he is to her. How visually attractive he is, and how the internal parts of him are even better...and how much she finds herself respecting him. Marney pulls on a shirt and slipper socks, then heads towards the teapot that is already whistling. She welcomes her brother's visit. Anything to push away the pain of desertion Sean has left.

"Marn-ay! You want me to turn the burner off?" Asner's voice echos through to her bedroom.

"Coming...coming." She trots out to the kitchen to find Asner at the counter with a newspaper. Marney knows he must have brought it because she reads the news on her laptop and doesn't get the paper delivered anymore.

Asner watches her fly around the median to the stove. "I could get that Marns."

She turns the burner off and moves the teapot to a cold one, the pesky whistling ceases, "Oh I've got it. I'm a little slow though, especially after this day." She smiles and squints her eyes.

Asner watches her take out two coffee mugs and tea bags, "Yeah, what's this shit I'm reading here about a serial killer? Dad says you are crazy busy...what with three, four bodies now?"

"You know I can't talk about the case with you Asner."

He scoffs, "I'm not asking you anything you can't answer."

"What's it say there then?"

"Fourth body found."

She points, "Then there's your answer." She serves him his tea and a spoon.

"Jeez, aren't we testy?" He puts the paper down.

"I'm not really. I just know you. You always try to get me to share too much with you. I could get in a lot of trouble...the fucking FBI is here on this one." Marney comes around and takes a seat at the bar stool next to Asner.

"I'm not going to get you in trouble Marns. It's interesting that's all. First time serial stuff in Olman huh?"

"Yes."

"Pretty gory then?"

"Ass-ner!"

He squints as he sips his tea, more from her calling him "ass" then from burning his tongue. He hates when she calls him that. "Marney, it says in the paper that *The Blader* takes the genitals and leaves the hands?"

Marney's eyes get wide, "What!" She grabs the paper and reads the front page article she had not gotten to earlier in the day. Shaking her head, "Fucking Deucen. I can't believe what an idiot my boss is!" She thinks how Mike is going to go ape-shit on Deucen once he finds out such confidential information has been given to the press. Not good.

"So I'm assuming, since The Blader is named *The BLADER*...you are hoping to find a murder weapon at some point...like a big fucking knife right?" Asner smiles. He doesn't let up.

"Well, that would be great...but as serial killers go, this one isn't leaving behind many clues...they do that so they can keep killing without getting caught Asner." She's being sarcastic with him because she knows he just wants to keep siphoning information from her.

"Okay..." Asner sips his tea and burns his mouth again. Marney laughs, he has always been stubborn and hard-headed.

"I'm not telling you-"

"One more question."

"What!"

"Are the hands sawed off or cut clean through?" He stops and watches her.

Marney looks at her brother, impressed by his question. "Why?"

"Are they sawed Marns or chopped clean off?"

She can't believe he is asking such a great question...how would he know to ask that. She decides to elaborate...if she doesn't, Liam will. "Held out and cut with one swipe...why?"

Asner nods and looks straight ahead...his mind going. He doesn't say anything.

Marney frowns...waiting.

"What time do you go into the office tomorrow?"

"I asked you why, Asner."

"Eight then? Okay, well after showers, you and I are going to make a little visit to my old dojo sweets." He widens his eyes at her and smiles.

"I have to go in and work...the FBI is here, remember?"

Asner nods, "You are going to want to go with me Marns."

"I don't have time to take you to visit to your old master Asner....what's his name?" She sips her tea.

"His name is Master Joon Lee...and you are going to want to take a minute to go with me."

"Why? Oh, wait...that name is familiar."

"Because I might be able to help you find your killer."

Marney stares at her brother trying to figure him out...and what he's saying, in his obscure way.

He stands up, takes his tea and paper and starts to walk to his room. "Get some sleep sis, you're about to get an education on knives, swords, blades and how they can be used to dismember a body part with one swift movement...I would almost put money on your killer being a trained martial artist. I bet your witness probably couldn't see the killer either...because of some sort of uniform right?"

Marney stares after her brother who shakes his ass at her as he disappears down the hall. She's shocked at what he just said and feels bad for being evasive and sarcastic with him. *What a smart little dingas.*

# 33. Vera

Marney parks along Main Street in the little historic part of Olman. Asner is still trying to fix the handle to the passenger side window when Marney turns off the engine. Asner loves the truck and tries to fix things on it every time he visits. She doesn't have the heart to tell him that the handle is not fixable and that she is months overdue for a visit to the junk yard to find a new one.

She looks around. The Fighting Venom's school, which she always felt was a pretty dramatic business name, appears to be closed. She reaches over and pokes her brother in the ear making him flinch and jerk his head. Asner frowns at her, totally pissed off from being interrupted from his project. She points out the window then looks back at him for a reaction. Asner's hands let go of the handle as his eyes tell the story of disbelief. She can tell he was not ready to see his old dojo closed down.

Asner steps up on the curb and stares at the storefront. Although the sign is still intact, the windows show dirt and then an empty shell of a place inside. Marney steps up, scans the area and then peeks in. She suddenly remembers the case last year involving this place. It was Detective Kappre's case, but he retired a few months ago. An intense case, attempted murders, martial art rivalries, poisonings, shootings and even death. Marney remembers Kappre didn't have a partner...or rather wouldn't really work with one. He and Deucen did not get along either. But, that's no surprise.

"Unbelievable!" Asner has both of his hands holding his head, his eyes the size of saucers.

"So, this is where you wanted to bring me?"

Asner looks to be holding his breath, "Well, I wanted to introduce you to my Master...ask him some questions about his weapon collection."

That perked up Marney's ears, "Weapon collection? You know that the owner was shot last year right As?"

"What! Master Lee was shot Marns?" Asner's hands moved from his head to in front of his mouth.

Marney feels bad for him. He didn't know. She wonders if she should have a slower delivery. "Yeah brotha, I'm sorry. I heard about the case at the station...a little in the papers and on the news too." She stops there, not wanting to mention how his master was considered a real asshole around town.

"Who the fuck shot him?"

"An old woman from what I remember. Self-defense. She was protecting her granddaughter and her boyfriend...some kind of kidnapping...revenge sort of debacle."

Asner turns and leans up against the front of the store, "What the hell...why didn't I hear about this?" Asner was turning a few different shades of gray.

Marney tried to be soft, "You left As, you've been gone...and I didn't know this was your school man, I'm sorry...I would've-"

"Nah, I know. I just can't believe all that happened and I never got wind of it...not even Dad mentioned anything."

"It's been years since you trained. He probably didn't think you really had a part in any of it anymore. You know he doesn't talk a lot about the stuff in our lives from when Mom was alive. He just let's it go. Probably doesn't want us to remember the tough times." Marney defends her father.

Asner nods, "Yeah, you're right. I just can't believe Master Lee is gone."

"Well, how well did you know him?"

"Why?"

"Because he was into some deep shit from what I remember, I don't want you to be super wounded over this. I can follow-up on this another day."

"Aw no, I want to know. I mean I didn't know him personally, just training-wise. Still, he was my teacher. I looked up to him. Obeyed and learned what he instructed."

"Well, I hope you only took the good stuff...cause he was a real tough one from what I understand."

Asner's eyes are sad, "Really? What about his son...uh, Neeko?"

Marney shakes her head a little, "Don't know much about him."

"Can we read the case file...at the station?"

"Are you high? You know I can't do that with you, but you can research the newspaper articles." Marney is trying to be helpful but, brother or no, she can't share case files. "I will peruse the file and share what I can okay?"

Asner walks away. He walks all the way down the block and steps off the curb, past Gerda and crosses the road. Marney frowns and starts to follow him. He hops up on the opposite curb and walks to Vera's Diner. He turns back to see where she is and enters the front when he sees she is following him.

Inside the diner smells of fish and chips. There are two patrons at opposite ends of the counter, a television is playing a morning talk show, and Vera is at the far end of the place taking an order from an older couple in a booth seat. Marney watches as Asner takes a seat at the counter with his back to the door. This drives her nuts since she has to sit next to him...and she hates having her back to the door.

"You okay?" She sits down on the stool next to him.

"Yeah, just need some breakfast...and a few answers."

"You know these people?"

Asner nods slightly, "I used to."

"So you trust them?" Marney whispers.

"Well, as with all things sis, you take what you want and leave the rest."

Vera comes around the side and rips the order off her pad and sticks it to a cute, little merry-go-round figurine. She spins it around and the paper moves to the opposite side which stops back in the kitchen. A little old guy peeks out from the opening and takes the order. Vera sticks her pencil into her up-do and lifts her eyes to Asner and Marney. She smiles and takes the pencil back out of her hair while walking towards them.

"Hey folks...well, if it isn't Asner Jade, how the hell are ya?" She stops and leans far to one hip.

Asner smiles, "Doing well thanks...uh, could I order a coffee, your big breakfast pancake special and..." He points to Marney.

"Oh, I'll have the same please." Marney smiles at Vera who is writing but looking at Marney's hair, face, neck and body. The kind of look that strikes Marney as photogenic. The woman probably never forgets a face.

"Alrighty. I'll put that in and be right back with your coffees." She turns and is gone.

Marney watches her brother. He's quiet and hanging his eyes on the television show but, Marney can tell he isn't paying attention to the talk show host or the guest. Asner has his hands folded in front of him with his right thumb scraping the left one. Asner always finger fidgeted as a kid, when he was upset. She decides to let him be. Men cave. Marney knows it because she does it herself...ever more comfortable on her male side than anything. She looks at her watch. *Man, Mike is going to be pissed I'm so late.*

Vera returns with two coffee cups and a pot of coffee. She asks the older gentleman on the left corner if he needs a refill and he declines. She pours both cups without really looking. This fascinates Marney.

"So what can you tell us about that Venom school down a ways Vera?" Asner digs right in.

"What do you need to know?"

"Is it true Master Lee was shot?"

She makes eye contact, "That is true. Shot dead."

Marney can see Asner blink slow, trying to think of the next question. "Do you know why?"

"Well, he kidnapped Old Kiki Palemana's grand-daughter, Kai and her boyfriend Eli. He owns that martial art gym right there." Vera points a spoon out the window, across the street. Asner doesn't turn to look, but Marney does. She looks back at her brother and wonders if he knows of the place.

"Kidnapped?"

"Yup...well, more like held them hostage at gun or knife point, can't remember which, with some of his body guard students. Made them walk from a burial site back to the house, tried to force them to hand over some sort of family artifact or something. Kiki was waiting for them when they arrived and blew him away with her 12 gauge."

"Jeezus why?" Asner stirs his coffee.

Vera smirks, "Oh honey, that man tortured that family for years. Just took time to trickle down to Kiki. She's a no nonsense type old gal. Some sort of master rivalry between the two schools I guess. Kiki's grand kids just got caught up in the middle and she was protecting her own. I would have done the same thing."

Asner stares at her.

"I'm sorry if I sound harsh. Your cop friend here should be able to help you out more with the details. I only hear the gossip and read whats in the papers or on the tube. As just a pair of eyes around here, that school across the way, the MMA one, turned this town around and protects us. That venom one only brought fear and crime to our world. Things changed when Eli James moved in. We all sleep a little better now."

Marney has to know, "How did you know I was a cop ma'am?"

Vera turns to Marney, "You were in the background of a crime scene shot on the news last night...with a tall, good-looking fella. He lifted the crime tape up for you and you both went under it with your little police windbreaker-type jackets on."

Marney smiles.

"Sorry, I never forget a face."

"No, that's quite alright. I was worried I looked too much the part is all." Marney laughs trying to lighten the mood. Asner is looking drawn.

"Oh no sweetie, you as pretty as a model. You don't look the part but I'm sure you work it very well. How close are ya to finding that serial killer anyway?" Vera places the coffee pot down and wipes her hands on her apron.

"We are trying everything we can ma'am. Actually, we were looking for this Master Lee guy...didn't realize he was dead. I mean it wasn't my case so...I didn't put two-and-two together."

Vera steps to turn away, "Well, I can tell you that Joon Lee is not your serial killer, and that crazy black-haired girl Jet isn't either...she's dead too."

Marney smiles and nods wishing she knew more about Detective Kappre's case. "So-"

Asner softly interrupts, "And the son, Neeko? What happened to him?"

Vera was set to walk away but stops, "He was up for charges for his father's bad choices...for quite some time actually, while his pops was missing. Last I heard, they deported him and about twenty-three hidden supposed family members hiding out over in the basement of that dojo. Sent them all right back to China. Our town has been so quiet since. Crime has gone down and we are all getting back to feeling safe. If you're interested in training...you should see that Eli James or his three main instructors. They know what they're doing over there. Run a real tight ship from what I hear. We get the most respectful, honest people come in here from that Cave gym. I haven't heard one bad thing about them."

Asner finally speaks, "We were actually looking to speak with someone from the Venom school about purchasing some of Master Lee's vintage weaponry."

Marney looks at her brother with some surprise. She was unaware they were doing that.

Vera started to walk away, "Don't know nothing about any weapons...but I do know your breakfast is about ready. I'll go get it."

Marney leans in, "As- why would we need to talk to someone about martial art weapons?"

"Liam told me about how the hands were severed from the bodies...how the cuts were from a double-sided blade...one body part cut one way, another cut the other."

Marney exhaled, wanting to choke her little brother Liam...and his big mouth. "We are still-"

Asner turned and looked at his sister finally, "There is only one kind of knife...err sword, I know of that works like that on the body...and the last guy I knew to have it is dead."

Marney's eyes enlarged a bit, "What do you mean sword?"

Asner sighed, "You have a lot to learn about a few things Marney. The first thing you're going to want to do is read up on that Kappre guy's case. I'm going to go see Dad and enjoy myself. You find where Master Lee's Kris sword is...you'll find your serial killer."

"Kris sword?" Marney frowns.

"Yeah...k-r-i-s...Kris Sword."

# 34. Angles

Marney was on hour three of her research. She's been interrupted four times already, so now has the door locked to interview room two. She wants a damn uninterrupted few hours to go over Detective Kappre's last case...and then all the information she can dig up on this Kris sword.

*Asner is too fucking smart for his own good some times.* She wants to punch Liam for talking about the case too much with her older brother but, on the other hand, she's really happy to have this new information. She wouldn't be this far today if it weren't for his surprise visit...and Liam's big mouth. She's fascinated by the photos of the severed body parts of her victims and how they match up with the cuts and severed body parts of pictures she printed off of the internet of Kris sword wounds. The similarities are remarkable!

Marney's stomach tightens as she sees Mike, through the little window, coming toward her room. He knocks softly and then tries to enter, finding resistance from the locked door. She pushes her chair out and reaches to unlock the door. She turns back to the table to take her seat.

"Hey Marns, what's shakin?" He smiles his sweet smile and she tries not to allow herself to get too unbalanced with her attraction to him.

"Hi Mike, sorry I had to lock the door. So many distractions and I just need to research this angle of the case."

"What angle?"

"I'm not ready to share yet, but trust me, if it keeps lining up the way it has...you'll be really happy with me." She ruffles through a few more pages.

Mike closes the door and leans against it, "Okay...I'm already really happy with you...and with your work."

She looks up at him and then back down at her laptop, "Thanks, didn't seem that way when you were rejecting me in your car last night." She wishes she hadn't said it as soon as it comes out.

Mike shifts his weight and lowers his voice, "Is that what you think that was?" His eyebrows furrow and his eyes turn sad.

"I don't know what it was...what this is...it's whatever-"

Mike leans in on the table, his broad shoulders and lovely scent causing Marney some beguilement. "Now, now...when a woman says "whatever" there needs to be a discussion." She looks into his eyes and her body reacts without even a touch. She finds it fascinating that she can get such a reaction from Mike's energy and closeness, Sean was able to do the same but, not as rapidly. Marney squeezes her eyes. She just wants to forget about men...and focus on this case.

"We did have a discussion. You made it clear, I get it. I need to get back to what I'm doing."

Mike bends his knees and leans even closer, "Marney, please don't think I don't want you." She looks at him and then away. She finds it hard to handle Mike's intense glare. "Nothing could be further from the truth. I'm protecting you-"

"Yeah Mike? Yeah? Well...well, maybe I don't want to be protected! Did you think of that? Maybe I-" She shuts down, angry at herself. Not sure what she wants...*ugh!*

"What Marns?" He reaches in and runs his fingers along her hand, trying to coax her to continue.

Marney feels vulnerable. Something keeps making her stop when she starts to express herself to him. She can't put her finger on it...she just hurts. Her heart hurts. She abruptly stands up, "I've got to work Mike...I've only got so much energy today, and I need to put it toward this case. Where are we with Deucen?"

Mike stands slowly, towering over her. He wants so badly to take her in his arms and kiss her. He wants to feel her plump, wet lips beneath his again and explore how slow and passionate she is. Marney

Jade may not be able to express herself fully with words but, damn can she send a clear message with her affection. He still feels her from their basement kiss...and can't get it out of his mind!

Marney looks down, instead of up at him, and steps around him to get through the door to the coffee she is using as an excuse to end their intense interaction. Mike composes himself, "Uh, well...Deucen has some real problems with his mistress there..."

Mike follows Marney out of the interview room, not sure if she is really listening.

"What does that mean? She's in the NSG because of him?" Marney begins to make herself a small cup of coffee. Mike stands watching her, not sure how to handle her.

"I'm sure she would deny that, got a real son-of-a-bitch old man at home, might make Terry look like an angel you know? But, after spending hours upon hours with Deucen, I'm convinced he is not the man for this job. He has hugely compromised this case with his ability to run his mouth at that bar with Ms. Daytone. Chris has been interviewing the other women, so have Zeek and few others, and there is no doubt that Cherie Daytone was the one who told those woman that the meeting was wired! Deucen won't admit it...but the only way Cherie could have told the others is from him! I have plans to have my own little discussion with miss booby bar owner there." Mike leans against the counter and crosses his arms over his chest. Marney looks at him and sees he is pursing his lips in anger.

"You couldn't have known Mike. He's a first class dick. Always has been. More concerned with how he looks than protecting his employees...or his girl for that matter. I work with him because he was the one put in the position, doesn't mean I respect him. Can't tell you how many times he's crossed the line with sexual harassment, almost getting me killed, and taking credit for work he didn't do. Oh, and then there's his poor wife. I'm not even going there." She stirs her coffee. "No one blames you Mike. Deucen's a douche."

Mike smiles at her, "Marns, my bosses have me as acting Chief *and* overseeing this case."

"Well, you never know. You may like leaving the bureau and stepping up into small town law enforcement." She teases.

"Fuck that. I'm too close to retirement to shift gears now. You can have it." He chuckles, happy that she is teasing him.

Marney smiles, "Not the job for me. I'm a cop...not a politician."

"I hear ya. Hey, I'll let you get back to it. Let's get together later and talk about your uh....angle?"

She looks up at him as he walks away backwards, "My angle? Oh, you mean of the case-"

"No, your other angles. The case isn't going anywhere. My hotel, seven o'clock...steak and whiskey?" He points at her but doesn't wait for an answer. He turns and heads out the door. Marney doesn't know if she is ready to talk about her angles. *Did he just invite me out after rejecting me yesterday?*

# 35. Indonesia

Marney decides she needs to get a hold of Detective Rick Kappre and pick his brain about his former case. The case file is intense, and although very complete, she wants to talk with him directly and see how similar his opinion is to the case facts. Marney knows that cops have to write only the facts of what they research but often, there is so much more thats helpful. Gut stuff. She could never explain how much casework she has solved based on her intuition. And, by the intensity of his notes, she feels Kappre could really help her.

She picks up the phone and dials his number. After the fourth ring, Marney prepares to leave a message but, a young woman's voice comes across, "Hello?"

"Hello, is Rick Kappre available?"

"Who's this?"

"My name is Detective Marney Jade of the Olmanson Police Department ma'am."

"Oh...did you know my Dad?"

Marney gets a sinking feeling, "Uh, yes ma'am. I worked with him in the detective's unit here, for the last year, before his retirement. I'm sorry, may I ask who I am speaking with?"

"I'm Rickie Kappre...my Dad is not well." Rickie's tiny voice is nasally, as if she's been crying.

Marney feels bad, "Oh, I'm sorry to hear that Rickie. Should I call back another time?"

"It won't matter Detective Jade, my Dad is in his last days of lung cancer ma'am...hospice. He's in and out, and no longer speaks. It spread through his body...to his brain...he doesn't formulate words." Rickie stops and there is silence.

"Oh wow. Oh, I am so sorry Ms. Kappre...we didn't know. We just thought..."

Rickie huffs a tiny laugh, "He tried being retired...even went to Bermuda for a time, but without his work...and without my mother...he just, well-"

"I've heard that sometimes when workaholics retire, they have a difficult time adjusting." Marney smacks her forehead, cursing herself for saying something so stupid. "I mean, he was a phenomenal detective."

Rickie agreed, "Yeah, my Dad and I talked about that. It's like the cancer stayed where it should while he was too busy to let it get him...but once he had too much time to think-" She stops talking again and Marney can sense she's choking back tears, trying to catch her breath.

"Well Rickie, is there anything I can do...or the department can do? Anything you need?" Marney decides she'll just study the case file and leave this poor family be.

Rickie sounds gracious, "Aw, thank you Ms. Jade but we're all set. My Dad made sure of it. I'll head back to Berkeley next semester...after-"

"Oh I see, yes...okay. Well, please let us know if..."

"I will ma'am, thank you. And I'm sure my Dad thanks you all too. He loved his career there. It was a positive in his life." Rickie sniffles.

Marney blinks slow, "That's really nice to hear. Take care of you Rickie...and call if you need to. I'm so sorry."

"Thank you. Goodbye."

Marney rubs her face in her hands. *That sucked!* Looking down at the mess of papers in front of her, she suddenly feels the pangs of hurt again as she thinks of Sean. She knows it's such a present death, the way Rick Kappre's illness is also a present death. It lingers thick in the air.

She scoops all the papers and photos together and closes the file pushing it to the side. Pulling her laptop to her she types in *"kris sword"* and begins a further journey on this mysterious weapon, her brother is so adamant about.

***

An hour later, Marney is astonished with what she's learned about this little dagger. It's between the size of a sword and knife, more like the length of a human forearm. It's origin is Indonesia but is also indigenous to Thailand, Singapore, China, Malaysia and the Philippines, where it is known as Kalis. The Kris sword is distinctive with it's wavy blade, like ocean waves down either side, but some also have straight blades. Asner mentioned that the wavy cuts, Liam told him about, around the genitals and such is why he knew it was the Kris sword. There's no other like it.

Marney rubs her eyes and looks at the clock. It's almost time for her to meet Mike, which she's not so sure she should do. She continues on to study more about this interesting dagger. The pictures of the Kris show it's a three-part weapon. The handle is often called a *"hulu"* or *"hilt"* and can be meticulously carved with art using materials such as metals, precious woods, gold or ivory. The most interesting part is the blade, which is referred to as the *"bilah"*. Since the blade is so sharp and a double-sided type, this weapon often comes with a beautifully designed and colored *"warangka"*, better known as a sheath, which covers the deathly sharp angles of the blade. Marney raises her eyebrows as she reads the part about how this dagger was the "preferred weapon of execution" in Indonesia and that it was usually used as a secondary weapon if one lost their spear. *How do you fucking lose a spear?*

Marney can feel her edginess coming on and knows she's way too hungry to work effectively anymore. She continues on, despite her ravenous appetite, typing her notes, documenting how the blades of the Kris were believed to have either good luck or bad luck for those who believed in its essence, presence, and possession of magical powers. Marney chortles to herself thinking how it has only had bad luck for those in Olman. The one area that seems unusual, is how the historical value of this particular type of knife can yield thousands of dollars in worth. This makes her think back to when Vera mentioned all the immigrants that lived below that closed dojo and of Master Lee's belongings. Where could all the artifacts have gone, if he really had as many as Asner thought? And did those immigrants bring such weapons over? Maybe that's how he got such things...smuggling goods along with illegals? She has so much more to research. But, first things first, food.

As Marney cleans up and locks up her case work, she contemplates over whether she should ditch the Mike idea or go. She knows she has to work with him, she knows he is honorable and wants to keep their relationship professional, not only for her, but out of respect for Sean as well. Marney slams her other drawer, holsters her weapon, and pushes in her chair. She feels agitated. *What about my respect? What about what I want and need? Fuck Sean...he's not coming back...and what about Mike? What about his needs?*

Moments later Marney starts up Gerda with a roar and heads home. Mike will understand when she doesn't show up.

# 36. Big Mike

Marney pulls in to The Palms hotel. She was heading home but found herself turning the truck around and somehow ended up at Mike's hotel...early.

She marches in the front, stumbling when the automatic glass doors do not open as quickly as she is moving. At the front desk she abruptly says "Michael Taylon's room?" and walks off when she gets the number, 323, from the young desk manager. She rounds over to the Retreat Bar & Grill and stands inside just long enough to see he isn't there yet. This makes her decide she is going to go straight to his room and take what she wants! She's going to respect her own wishes this time...if he doesn't like her, he can tell her now!

Four minutes and a too-slow-of-an-elevator-door-thirty-seconds later, Marney arrives on the third floor. She looks left, then right, scurries down the hall to the end and finds room 323. With her stomach in her throat she knocks on the door and steps back so he can see her through the peep hole she knows he will check. She can feel his heavy foot steps come toward the door, then after a pause, the lock on the door is reversed. As the door opens she can smell his freshly showered scent. From the floor she runs her gaze up his sizable feet, sculpted shins and knees to his tightly tucked white hotel towel. His stomach is mounds of abdominal muscles she was unaware existed and they run up into large salt-n-pepper-haired pecs that seemed to stretch for days into hugely defined shoulder deltoids. His neck is wider than the button-up shirts from work show, and ends in his gorgeous face with the blue eyes she longs to see each day, and just realized. His face is that of mild surprise, eyebrows raising. Before he can get her name out in question form, Marney steps in, kicks the door shut and pushes him against the wall. He looks down at her with complete adoration and as he slides his hands along her jaw, Marney brings her lips up meeting his with intensity. She parts his lips and sinks her tongue into his mouth with a desire she has been suppressing since the moment she locked eyes with him that first day they met. Mike accepts her graciously, slowly exhaling elation, almost not believing she is here in his arms. Marney flings her blazer off of her arms so it falls to the floor, her gun strap follows it with a thud. He moves his head to the opposite side, further deepening their kiss. She unbuttons her jeans and wiggles them off along with her boots, leg knife, socks, and panties. Reaching for the bottom of her shirt she pulls it up and to her head but, pauses not wanting to break their fiery kiss. His tongue is gentle and exquisite. He is a master at kissing and she wonders if everything will be this good. Her excitement blazes inside her as she realizes he has not rejected her, not pushed her away...rather, draws her in with each smooth, slow flick of his tongue. His hands run through her hair and massage her sweetly. He inhales her deep...and long.

Reluctantly, he pulls away so she can complete her undressing and marvels at her beautiful-almost-naked body in front of him. She's more breathtaking than he imagined! He watches her eyes as she reaches backwards to unclasp her bra. Her eyes are dilated and hungry, her mind is set. He sees her creamy skin, her perfect round breasts and large, pink nipples. He loves how they match the color of her lips. Her stomach is smooth and flat curving inward at the sides where her fabulous hips meet and show a flat abdomen. His eyes rest on her splendid mound of pubic hair that matches the exact color of her long flowing locks. Her strands rest on the sides of each breasts. He feels intense desire for her, something he hasn't felt with anyone before. He simply can't believe she is here, standing in front of him...wanting him as he wants her.

Marney steps close and takes his mouth again. He pulses with arousal and arches towards her. He's tried to hide his feelings for her, reject her nicely, talk himself out of it, but he can no longer rationalize being away from her. He hasn't told her but, his heart aches for her when she's not in his sight. He misses her when he stays at his hotel at night and knows she is home alone. He feels her pain, knowing she has been left and abandoned by her lover...and all he can think about is how grateful he is that she's here...in his arms.

She reaches for his waist and tugs at his towel. It falls to the floor and she steps into him to feel his body against hers. He is warm, and exquisite, his erection glorious against her stomach. Mike sinks his tongue down into her wet mouth and she accepts him. His body yearns with more want for her every moment that passes. Marney runs her hands up his broad back. He wraps her in his arms and feels her soft, fevered skin. Marney feels herself aching for him, just his kiss is creating a moisture that is silken against her thighs. She runs her nails along his back and around to his ribs and stomach. Mike moans slowly into her mouth and she can feel his manhood pulsate against her. He likes how she does that. Needing to see him, she breaks gently from their kiss. Looking deeply at him she knows she wants this. Something feels so right...even if it's all wrong tomorrow, she won't give up the opportunity to have a memory of this moment. Mike smiles at her and caresses her face. His touch is magnificent. Marney stares at him not understanding the magnetism they share but, welcoming it's intensity. Mike knows this could all go wrong in the morning...he knows he could potentially lose his job on the case, yet he doesn't care because experiencing these precious moments with Marney is the most profound risk he has taken in years.

She runs her fingernails gently down his chest. He loves how she touches him! He moans softly again. As she reaches his stomach she presses her palms to him to feel the crevasses and curves of his muscles. He kisses her, looks at her, then kisses her again. He can't get enough of how gentle she is, yet firm. Marney watches his eyes. She loves to watch him. Her hands linger only slightly and then begin to slowly fall lower. His breath catches in his throat and when she gently engulfs him in her hands he closes his eyes with the pleasure of her touch. He exhales slowly. She can't believe the size of him and looks down. *Oh my...Mike...wow.* She brings her eyes back up and he opens his to find her. He is unsure, vulnerable in her hold.

She whispers, "I want you..."

"Are you sure?" He leans against her forehead, whispering back.

"I want you Mike...I'm sure."

"I-"

"I want you...now Michael. Even if only tonight...I want you..." Marney is soft but firm. She reaches one hand lower, and caresses his testicles while the other hand reaches higher to pull his head to her. Their lips meet with fierce passion and there is no turning back.

Mike picks Marney up in his arms and walks over to the large king size bed across the room. She wraps her arms and legs around him in an intense grip and her body pulses with want for him. This tall, handsome...genuine man. Mike is huge and as his weight comes down on top of her she lets out a sigh of pleasure. He reacts to her and lifts himself up to enter her. She is so willing and ready, as he slides within her she realizes their fit is perfection! Marney pulls him into her and they both moan in unison at the dire pleasure of feeling each other for the very first time. Mike's body reacts with every synapse as he slowly thrusts forward. Marney opens to him and squeezes his ample size in each breathtaking movement. Their rhythm is flawless. Her body tingles in every pleasurable way and her eyes roll back beyond her eyelids. Mike kisses her again as he heightens their rhythmic motions. He giving and she receiving. Both in perfect timing, perfect unison. She can hardly believe how astonishing this feels and pulls him in deeper and deeper...trying to control her respirations, knowing that it's he who takes her breath away. Mike pulls her arms up and over her head, deepening the kiss that he hopes will never end. He feels her accepting him in her perfect body. Caressing and cradling him...wanting him as he had only dreamed of.

He moves slowly with a passion he has never before experienced and feels his heart igniting for this woman...as he makes love to her...fully and completely. He is scared for what he feels for her, for what it could mean...for how she may not understand it. This risk is great, for she may have love for another. He breathes into her and then breaks free of the kiss, so he can look at her. His mind overpowering his heart for the moment. Marney opens her eyes and searches for him, he is there...he is so present. She brings her hands to his face and pulls him close, "You...feel...so...right..."

Mike reacts with intense, deeper thrusts and picks up speed. She is magnificent, she meets him each time and stays so perfectly in his timing. He wraps his hands in her long, brown hair and holds her head so he can support his weight on his forearms. He watches her face writhe with pleasure every time he moves forward...putting pressure on her most endearing area with his pelvic bone. Not too much...just enough, letting her expressions guide him. She wraps her hands around his back, pulling him to her, letting her hands lower with each rhythmic thrust until she finds his toned buttocks. She holds him here, pulling him to her. Mike moans and presses his lips down onto hers. Again Marney feels surges of pleasure as his size is exquisite. He is an adept, masterful lover, with experience that creates perfection. Marney has never felt such precise, soul-emphasizing pleasure. She feels she is losing control of her body and he is taking over. She reaches up with one hand to grab his hair, unsure if she can hold on much longer.

Mike releases from their kiss, taking her queues, "Are you?" His breath labored, he knows she is because her body is one with his...and he is so...

Marney tries to answer but instead can only moan breathlessly. She nods against his forehead. Mike loves her vulnerability and takes charge even more of their rhythm. They move and breathe together....deeper...he flicks his pelvis creating even more friction and pleasure...deepening...and                    deepening.              She receiving...deepening...deepening... Marney pulls him in tight one last time and she can hold on no longer...Mike thrusts long and takes her...and himself over the edge of ecstasy...

Never to be the same again-

# 37. Next Day

Marney awakens to his glorious caress along her neck, down her shoulder and arm, to her waist. She feels safe in his arms and doesn't want to move...ever. Her heart beat increases with the finality of what they've done...he her boss, she his lead detective. She didn't want to think of it this way.

She stretches and arches her body to him, pleasantly surprised at how ready he is for her. He moves away slowly whispering an apology. She moves in closer with a smile. Reaching back to run her hand lovingly through his hair. He hugs her close, then runs his palm down her stomach. She decides she is delighted that she doesn't regret anything! Being with Mike exceeded all her expectations.

Marney whispers into the room, "I kinda wish we hadn't waited so long...that was amazing."

Mike moans in agreement placing a kiss in her soft hair. He pauses a moment then decides to tell her what he knows will alter their sweet moment, "Your phone has been beeping nonstop Marns. You may want to check it. If it were the station, mine would be going off too...so I'm kinda thinking it's personal sweetie." He secretly hopes its a wrong number.

"Oh shit! My brother...crap, crap, crap!" Marney jumps out of bed and runs to her pile of clothes, looking for her blazer.

Mike leans up on one arm to watch her. He smiles at how beautiful she is, rummaging around naked on the floor. She has no idea how desirable she is in any situation.

Marney dials and stands up pacing. Mike follows her with his eyes.

"Asner! Hey, it's me I uh-" She pauses then throws her head back in relief. "You're at Liam's?...Okay. Yeah, I got tied up on this case and fell asleep! I'll be home soon. You need your stuff to go to Dad's?"

Marney finally relaxes enough to look at Mike. She smiles at him and marvels at how sexy he looks relaxing in bed with his arm behind his head watching her. She points to the bathroom and mouths to him that she needs to take a shower. He nods and smiles at her with total adoration.

"Okay, I'll run home and let you in...sorry As, I should have left you a key somewhere." Marney shrugs at Mike and he smiles wider. He consumed her time and she forgot about her brother. He is enjoying this. "I'll come get you from Liam's okay?"

Mike sits up, stretches, then stands up to turn the shower on for her. Marney stares at his glorious body. He is a behemoth of a man and every inch of him is pleasurable to look at, not to mention, brings pleasure. Her body starts to yearn for him again, just by the sight of him. She hangs up and watches him approach her. He comes to her and gently runs his hands down her arms. She instinctively reaches up to kiss him and realizes she really doesn't want to go anywhere.

Mike breaks free of there contact, "I'll get your shower going for you." His voice is gruff and low.

"No, you'll be in my shower..." She interlaces her fingers with his and pulls him towards the bathroom. He follows willingly.

*** 

Marney pushes through the detective unit doors, a little late for work, but she's here. Chris looks up and says hey. Everyone else goes about their work. It's super busy for some reason and she feels she better get to it...if she can concentrate.

She looks around for him but he is not near. He is either dealing with chief bullshit upstairs or wire tap bullshit downstairs. She just wants him in her arms. *Argh, this is nuts...we're in the middle of a murder case...what's wrong with you!* Marney gets to her desk to see a pile of messages, more file folders, and some sort of headphone set.

"What's this about?" She picks up the headphones and inspects the wires.

Chris looks over, "Oh sorry, I left those there. My bad." He holds his hand up for her to throw them at her but, she walks them around the desk to him instead. "Hey, you see Mike yet?"

Marney's body waves with desire at the sound of his name, "No why?"

"Uh, Zeek's looking for him."

Marney knows this means he is upstairs dealing with Deucen's crap. Poor Mike. Probably has to sit in Deucen's fart-smelling office and meet with the higher-ups from, not just his agency, but our town as well. She slumps in her chair and unlocks her desk. Detective Kappre's file is in her top drawer, she remembers she was suppose to update Mike on her new knowledge. "Hey Chris, whatcha up to today brah?"

"Gotta interview Cherie Daytone again...oh, and two other potential asshole husbands of two of the chicks in the NSG. Why? You want in?" Chris sips his coffee reminding Marney that she needs one if she is going to be able to work and shake off her fabulously breathtaking night with Mike.

"I would but I've got a lead to follow up on for the possible murder weapon. I was hoping we could get together again...you know, be partners." She smiles, knowing Chris is doing a great job with his new wire tap abilities. She misses her partner.

Chris sniffs jokingly and wipes an invisible tear, "You is tow tweet Ms. Marney!"

She stands up and throws a pencil at his head. He ducks and she laughs her way over to the coffee. Leann Kozub turns and almost runs into Marney spilling hot coffee on her own hand. "Ah, fuck Jadelock! Watch where your going would ya?"

Marney stops, hands up, and backs away, going around Leann. Not even her evil temper can get to Marney. She feels too good today. She makes her cup and tries to get her mind off of her brave initiation the night before. She smiles remembering how Mike couldn't reject her again...how gentle and sweet he was. Her body reacts as she sees his amazing physique in her mind, she yearns for him yet again and it's only been three hours since she was in the shower with him. She shakes it off and heads back to her desk, hoping she can get her head in the game. It's hard to concentrate knowing he is in the same building as her...she wants him.

The door to the detective unit opens and Zeek breezes in walking in his fast-paced nerd motion. "Blader Case meeting in thirty guys." Zeek doesn't slow down or stop, he is obviously on his way down to his basement office. He's gone out of the other side of the room before Marney can take a second sip of coffee. Figures, her lead will have to wait.

She scoots her chair in and opens Detective Kappre's case file again. Looking at the mounds of paperwork and pictures, she takes a deep breath. *If I can't interview Kappre....who can I interview?* She thinks, turning to the list of individuals involved in the case. She knows from reading over the pages and pages of reports, that the main crux of the case was a beef between two martial art masters, one American and one Chinese, both trained by the same grandmaster over in China. It's a pretty sad story from how it appears to have escalated...love triangles, leaving to America, the bad one following the good one, harassment, threats, just ugliness...

There is one guy on the interview lists over and over...some Eli James guy. He owns the MMA dojo across from Vera's Diner. Marney thinks he may be someone to talk to since he is in almost every incident and seems to be a pretty upstanding guy from what Kappre reports. He may know something that could help her or at least give her more information on weapons. She figures she will start with him, after the meeting, and after she sees Mike.

Forty minutes later Chris stands up to stretch, "Okay there pretty lady, let's do this."

Marney looks up and sees they are already ten minutes late, "Oh yeah, almost forgot." She picks up her things, takes the last sip of cold coffee, and follows Chris out the door.

Upon entering the stuffy conference room, she peeks around Chris and sees Mike's already glaring at her. He's looking for her the same way she is for him. In the "you're mine" way. Her body does some weird fluttery thing and she tries to ignore it. He winks at her quickly and stops what he's saying to the group to address them, "Nice of you two to join us."

Marney takes a seat and doesn't answer, she leaves this sort of stuff up to Chris. He answers right on queue, "Sorry all, deep in it...but, we're here."

There are about seven others around the table. Mike has had to bring in more staff for the case now that Deucen is suspended and the body count is rising. Marney can tell the dude in a suit is from Mike's agency and then she recognizes another women from Internal Affairs, no doubt here for Deucen. She looks over and sees Zeek in his disorganized pile of papers receiving unwanted attention from her brother Liam, which she finds amusing. As serious as everything is, she feels happier. Ready to jump in and work harder. Her eyes trail down the table and up to the blue eyes of the man she made love to hours ago. He is in his element, answering tough questions, giving orders respectfully, working on a better strategy than the day before. She watches his mannerisms, his hand gestures. Marney is enamored with the man. She realizes she has been for quite some time...and didn't even know it.

# 38. Eli James

Marney didn't get any new information from the meeting but, seeing Mike was worth the hour. The changes on the case don't affect her or her part of the investigations so she decides to go with her plan of questioning this James guy.

She jumps up into Gerda and heads towards the historic part of Olman again. Marney scans the area. She notices this time that it's actually a pretty little section of town. Historic street lamps, classic signs and lettering, calm colors. It's a cleaner part of Olman and appears to be well cared for by the business owners. She passes by the new Children's Museum. A bus load of children are squealing and laughing while waiting to go inside. Marney smiles at what a cool field trip that must be for them. She's heard amazing things about the museum and how it really encompasses the businesses and residents of Olman. She thinks how genius it is for someone to create such a treasure in the city.

Marney drives a little ways more and sees the MMA dojo called "The Cave". It too, is very well kept and gives the town a mature, serene look. The sign overhead is artistically crafted, and she can't help but stare at the cave-like entryway. She parks and jumps down out of the truck. The lights are on inside the dojo, but there aren't many cars parked in front. Marney hopes the place is open.

When she reaches the door she sees that the hours are from eleven to eight, so she has just made it in time to open. As she enters, she feels a strong awareness of peace. There is a beautiful arced entrance, is smells of fresh wood and the sound of a waterfall is nearby. Marney stops abruptly, not sure of what to do since there are shoes lined up along the outside of the wall entrance. The place is immaculate and very welcoming. She looks around and is startled when she turns and finds a large Hispanic gentleman staring at her. She didn't hear him approach from the back and makes a mental note that bare feet can be very stealth-like.

"May I help you ma'am?" He smiles politely with his hands interlaced near his waste. He has crazy, just-woke-up type hair that is black except for the blonde tips. Attractive, yet odd.

Marney presents her neck badge, "Hello, is Eli James available? Detective Marney Jade from Olmanson Police Department. I need a word."

He steps closer and offers his hand, "Nate Corel, Detective." Marney shakes hands. "Most call me Nasty. Welcome to The Cave. You just missed Master James."

Marney smirks, "Really." Unsure she believes him.

"Yes, but I'm sure he wouldn't mind if I told you he is with his wife at Vera's, getting a little breakfast." Nasty points out the window to the diner across the street.

Marney doesn't turn, she knows where he is referring. She decides his mature look is one of honesty and feels bad for immediately thinking he was trying to get rid of her. She thinks back to what Kappre reported about the tight nit family here and decides she likes them. "Oh, okay. Well...thank you mister...uh Nasty is it?" Marney crinkles her nose at the sound of his nickname, hoping she remembered it correctly.

"Yes, and you're welcome. Come back anytime." Nasty bows slightly and returns to wherever he came from.

Marney looks over the gorgeous space once more and turns to go. Even if for just a moment, she thinks how most people would benefit from the wonderful energy in this place. She certainly feels it.


Marney steps into Vera's Diner and a few patrons look her way. Vera is carrying a tray and nods as she passes by. "Anywhere you'd like detective."

"Oh...okay." Marney didn't recall telling her she was a detective. She smiles but Vera is already gone. The diner is busy. She scans the room making a mental picture of the thirty three tables, eight booths, and thirteen customers. Her eyes stop over on a handsome couple toward the back, early twenties, both looking her way. The male stands up and is beyond gorgeous, Marney can't help but gawk at him. He begins to make his way toward her and Marney can't decide if his face, his body, or his walk is sexier. He stops short of entering her personal space and offers his hand.

"Hello ma'am, are you looking for me?"

"And you are?" She shakes his hand already knowing who he is from the embroidery on his black martial art pants that says "Master James" down the leg.

He smiles almost distracting her with his perfect teeth, "Eli James, pleasure. I saw you come from my dojo." He glances toward his place of business.

Marney is pretty sure it wasn't just his keen eye, but probably a text from his loyal student. "Detective Marney Jade. I was hoping to ask you a few questions if you have a moment?"

"Yes of course detective. Please, join us." He steps aside and Marney walks to the occupied booth where he was sitting. She looks over Kaileigh James, who she is aware is his wife from Rick Kappre's notes on the case from last year. The girl has a warm smile and is, if she dare say, even more dishy than her husband. Marney slows and turns towards Eli who towers over her. "Kai, this is Detective Jade. She was hoping to ask a few questions. Detective this is my wife, Kaileigh James."

Marney notices Mrs. James reaches forward and to shake her hand. "Oh wow, welcome detective. Please take my seat. I have to run so it's all yours. It's nice to meet you."

Eli moves swiftly around Marney and helps his wife out of the booth and to her feet. Marney notices an enormous pregnancy belly come out from under the table as she stands. She steps aside and watches how he is instinctively protective of his wife. They kiss sweetly and she tells him not to fuss. He motions for Marney to make herself comfortable and says he will be right back. The guy doesn't miss a beat as he walks his wife to the door, speaks with her as if the world doesn't exist when she is near, and again kisses her lovingly holding her face. Marney can't help but yearn for Mike. She sees now why Vera said these people changed the town for the better. If there were more folks like them, she would be out of a job.

Eli returns to the table, "I apologize ma'am. With a week to go, she just needs a little help here and there."

"Wow, a week? Congratulations. Boy or girl?"

"Son. We are so grateful and excited." His face is that of a man in complete elation.

Marney smiles, "That's wonderful Mr. James. I wish you both the best." She has no idea where that came from but, she meant it.

"Thank you, thank you...now how can I help you?" He sips coffee from a mug and points to offer to get Marney one.

She puts a hand up, "Oh no thank you. Already had a cup earlier. Well, the questions I have involve that closed gym...err dojo down a ways." She watches him.

He nods, "Sure."

"I've read up on Detective Rick Kappre's case from last year...quite a time for you all." She didn't really formulate a question.

"Yes. It was actually quite a few years time for us actually...glad its over."

"Right, well I'm looking for a collection of weaponry from a Master Joon Lee?"

She watches him but he doesn't really react. He is studying her face. "Okay."

"Do you know of such a collection?"

"I was aware that Master Lee had a large collection of weapons and artifacts yes." Eli sits back against the booth, confident in his response.

Marney nods, "Okay. Now, do you have any idea where that collection is?"

"No ma'am, I'm sorry I don't."

"Would you know of what type of weapons were in that collection?"

"No, not specifically detective. I heard about the items through talk amongst the students." Eli waves his hand towards the windows closest to his dojo.

Marney is confused, "Your students?"

"Former students of Master Lee...the ones I would accept into my training program. Many of his students needed a place to train when he...well, when they no longer had a dojo." He takes another sip of coffee. "I'm not sure how to help you detective."

She doesn't want to let on to too much but she has no one else to ask at this juncture, "Are you familiar with the Kris Sword?"

Eli smirks somewhat. Marney can't believe how unequivocally attractive he is. She sits up and watches him. "Yes."

"How familiar Mr. James?"

"It's a very serious weapon."

"Serious enough to testify about?"

His smile fades, "I'm not an expert ma'am."

"I hear you are. Your pants say Master James, do they not?" She waits.

"I'm confident with the weapon...what exactly are you asking here?" Eli raises his hand to Vera and motions that he needs the check. Marney can tell she is losing him.

"I'm looking for information on the Kris Sword, Mr. James. Detective Kappre is not able to help me...so you're all I've got at this point. Can you tell me if Master Lee owned one?" She softens her eyes knowing she is sharing too much.

"Is this about The Blader case?" Eli feels weird prying but, if he is going to be asked to testify on a weapon that was one of hundreds he learned, he needs to know more.

Marney nods, "It is...and I have a hunch. Now, I know that doesn't hold shit in court but, in my life, in my line of work Mr. James...it's solved me almost every case."

He exhales, "Look. I've had a hell of an experience with Master Lee and his whole existence. It didn't start with me and it didn't end with me...but ma'am, I've got a family to protect, not to mention a town I care very much about. I can try and help you...this evasive questioning doesn't fly with me though."

Marney is enamored with how sweet the guy is even though he is being firm. She respects the "killem'-with-kindness-approach" he uses. She feels bad, "I'm not trying to be difficult. Its-"

"I understand you have to do your job. I have to do mine too." He stops.

"No, no, no I understand. Okay, do you have any Kris Swords in your possession?"

His voice is deep, "No."

"Have you ever?"

"Only when I was training...even then they were not mine."

"Who's were they?"

He is reluctant, "My master's."

"Where would you say they are now?"

"I don't know."

She wonders if he is lying, "You don't have your master's belongings?" She knows she read it in the report.

"I do have a lot of his belongings. I do not have his weapons."

"Do you know, generally, where his weapons are at this time?"

"Yes."

"Do you also have a collection of weaponry Mr. James?'

"No."

"You do not?"

He is still even toned and looks towards Vera wondering why she hasn't brought his check, "I only have training weapons at my place of business...no Kris Swords."

"And at home?"

"No."

"Why not?"

"I have no need to bring these weapons to my home."

"So you yourself don't have a collection?" She is curious.

"No."

"Why not?"

"No need."

"What do you mean?"

"I don't feel the need to collect numerous material items. Weapons, trophies, awards or plaques are not a huge interest of mine. I value a photograph more and hang those around my dojo. The weapons I do have are for training purposes and the use of my students. I'm sorry, I don't have Kris swords."

Marney is impressed, "What about protection?"

Eli smiles, "What about it?"

"You don't have any weapons in your home for protection?"

Eli chuckles deep in his chest.

"You're laughing Mr. James?"

"I have my wife detective. I am more protected than you could understand." He smiles, thinking of his "gifted" wife.

Marney frowns, her confusion evident.

He asks, "Detective, am I on trial here?"

"No sir, not at all. Just trying to understand some things. You said you know, *generally*, where your master's weapons are yes?"

He exhales trying not to lose patience. "I don't know exactly where his weapon collection is ma'am...but, I do know they are not in Olman."

"How do you mean?"

"Because they are in China, where he is. Where in China, I have no idea. I have not yet visited with him there."

Marney searches his face. Now she gets it. He isn't hiding or being difficult...he's being truthful. She smiles, "So your master is in China now, with his belongings, is that what you're saying?"

"Yes."

"Ok, good. Now, back to Master Lee, what do you think happened to his collection?" She interlaces her fingers, interested in his ideas.

Eli raises his eyebrows and rubs his forehead, "Detective, I couldn't even speculate. The guy had so much going on, most of it illegal, I wouldn't even know where you would begin. Have you tried searching the dojo?"

Marney hangs her head for a moment then looks up and smiles, "I have to have reason, probable cause...to do that."

"Yes, I'm aware of that detective. If you look into it you will see that my associates, my black belts, and I have called your station this year on numerous occasions regarding that building, and the activity in it."

"For what reason?"

"Well, for one, there is some type of light that is on in the basement area of that space. We can see it from time to time when we're here, in the diner, mostly at night. It's not always on, just some days. Then, there was a gray Charger that would park there in the back from time to time." Eli pauses but, there's more.

Marney sits up, "Gray Charger?" She knows this can't be good. "Like under cover?" The only cop in Olman with a gray Charger is Deucen.

"Exactly, like under cover. I thought it was you guys until I got a call from your, what's his name....Terry something...said you all appreciate the calls but, it's under control. We stopped calling thinking there was under cover activity going on there. We don't want to interfere, but we are very concerned." Eli smiles as Vera hands him the check and apologizes for taking so long. She tells him she'll see him later and touches his shoulder. She nods to Marney and rushes off.

Marney's heart if racing. She is not happy about Deucen being anywhere near all the illegal issues with Master Lee. She always knew he was difficult but, to be difficult, a cheater, a narcissist and a possible serial killer...well, she just might put a bullet in him herself! "Is there more Mr. James?"

"Just one last thing."

"What's that?"

"The cleaning lady." Eli picks up his check.

"The cleaning lady?"

"Yeah. I don't understand why the cleaning lady goes in and out of the place still. It's closed...and a mess still. She shows up to clean yet, the place never improves. A little odd don't you think detective?" Eli stands up. He towers over her. He puts his hand out and his energy hits her like a wall...it's either that or the realization that the guy has been trying to protect his town, calling in strange activity, and the whole time Deucen has been squashing it at the dispatcher level!

Marney shakes his hand, "Mr. James, it was a pleasure to meet you. Thank you for your time...I do apologize for being abrupt."

Eli smiles sweetly, "Detective Jade, I understand you are just trying to do your job...I'm trying the same. Please tell Asner I said hello and that my door is open if he ever wants to train again."

Marney is shocked that he knows who she is. And even more so, her brother Asner. He nods and walks away waving to the older gentlemen seated along the counter and to the cook in the back. The screen door slams as he exits. Marney watches him cross the street to the gold mine of a business he's created. He opens the front door and a young boy with his mother approach. Eli holds the door and greets them. The little boy bows so respectfully and he nods back. Marney smiles and realizes there are some really decent people in Olman.

# 39. Senior

Marney's cell buzzes in her pocket but she chooses to ignore it. Since Eli James insists there is activity at that old dojo, she figures it's her duty to check it out before heading back to the precinct.

She turns towards the back of the building, the front shows the same vacant, dusty storefront it did when she and Asner peeked in the other day. The rear is empty, no cars, no dumpsters. Every door is locked, even the door to the basement entry down the cement steps. There is a metal fire escape ladder up to the roof but she decides thats a little too much snooping right now. There are no signs, no numbers, it's like the place is non-existant. *Weird.*

Marney looks around. The set of buildings behind are much taller. She sees that the roof of the large end unit is a great place to camp out and do surveillance. She makes a mental note. Her phone buzzes again...and again. Damn. She takes one last look around and sees small rectangular basement windows that match the ones from the front of the store. She wonders if this is where the light is seen by Eli James and his instructors when they are dining at Vera's. She thinks of Deucen and how sneaky the bastard is. She can't believe the balls on the guy for intercepting the calls from Eli James each time he reported the activity at Master Lee's old dojo. Sounds like Deucen has something to hide.

She rubs her hands together to get rid of the dust. Her phone goes off again. She decides it's time to get back to Gerda and find out whats going on with Mike. Sounds like he is eager to find her, it must be him blowing up her phone. She hates to admit it but she misses him too. She reaches in her blazer to get her phone and sees there are twelve missed calls! Her heart drops. The number is not Mike's but rather Asner's, Liam's, and sadly Glenda. It can only mean one thing...her father is in trouble.

***

Marney fights back tears as Glenda tells her they're in the emergency room waiting to hear from the doctors. She says in a quivering voice, that her father collapsed in the river while fishing and Asner Jr. pulled him out with Liam. It doesn't look good. They did CPR on him until the ambulance came and the EMTs took over. Marney holds her mouth trying not to make a sound. This can't be happening! Glenda goes silent, unable to say more.

"I'll be there in an hour Glenda. I'm leaving now!" Marney hangs up and starts driving. Serial killer or not, her Dad is her hero...and she has to get to him. She starts up Gerda and punches it towards Reune. *Is this really happening?*

*** 

It's been seven days and still no response from him. Asner Jade, Sr. lies in his hospital bed, peaceful look on his face, machines beeping away, tubes everywhere...lifeless.

Marney's eyes watch the lines move across the screens that show her father's heart still beats. She holds his warm, aged hand in her own as another tear falls to the blanket. It's like her head weighs fifty pounds and decides lying there with his hand to her cheek for another hour won't bother anyone. She feels completely helpless. There is nothing they can do...there is nothing she can do. A heart attack in the middle of fishing...and too much time without oxygen to the brain...equals silence. Marney looks up at her father's face, his white hair, his eyebrows, eyelashes, cheeks, a week's worth of overgrown facial hair...his chest rising and falling to the timing of the machine that gives him false life. *What's the fucking point!* She sits up and back in her chair, releasing his limp grasp. Marney throws her head back and stares at the ceiling trying to hold back another set of tears.

She purses her lips. Angry. Angry at it all. Losing her mother, stuffing it all away, fighting twice for every accomplishment in law enforcement, having to prove herself over and over. She squeezes her eyes tight. *Fuuuuuuck!* She fights back tears...tears for the victims of the serial killer, tears for the abandonment Sean left, tears for missing Mike, tears for never giving her father grandchildren, tears for....*ah, knock it off Jade! Get off your victim horse!*

She shakes her head to rid herself of the bullshit and leans forward again. Her elbows on her knees, she watches her father. He's gone, she knows it. His life has ended. He moved on and now they all must. She kisses his hand and stands smoothing her clothing. It's time to let Glenda know she can pull the plug. By day three it was a done deal, now it's just cruel. She bends to kiss her father one last time, "Thank you Daddy. You did good...time to fly. I love you infinity...tell Mom we're all okay." She takes a look at him for the last time and as she turns to go, Marney can feel her heart break like it has never before.

# 40. Six Weeks

Marney packs up the last of her things...well, her father's things. The things he wanted her to have. Glenda tried to get her to take more but she wouldn't have it. Marney just didn't feel right removing her father's belongings from his home.

The weeks after his funeral had been brutal. His home, although tranquil, was tough to stay in. She tried to rest, and she tried to go back to work, nothing felt right. Mike had come up to see her each weekend and for the funeral, but with her and Liam gone from the case, he had even more to do. The good news was the serial killer had gone into hiding. No more gruesome killings for the time being. This is good. Marney feels guilt for not being there on the case that she is supposedly lead detective on. She finds it very interesting that the killings stopped once Deucen was given his "leave of absence" as the papers describe it.

She pulls into her garage and sighs at the thought of having to unload all the boxes in the bed of her truck. She just wants to crawl under her blankets and forget everything from the last month. She hasn't been feeling so good...aside of losing her father and going through the torture of his absence, she just feels unbalanced.

She lays her head on her steering wheel and attempts to summon the energy to get out of the truck. *Tap, tap, tap.* Marney jolts and looks out the window! Mike raises his hands in surrender and smiles lovingly. She sighs with relief that it's him, slowly removing her hand from her weapon and rolling down the window. Mike opens her door for her instead and she slides down into his arms. He lifts and cradles her.

"I missed you sweetheart. So glad you're home." His warm breath caresses her neck and she buries her face in his chest saying nothing. Mike locks her door and slams it closed with his foot. He turns and carries her into the house she's been missing from for over a month.

The sun is already setting spreading golden light inside the hall as the door opens. Once inside, Mike locks the door and turns on the porch lights. He doesn't bother turning on the foyer lights and leaves her luggage and belongings in her truck for the new camera system to babysit. He installed her new security system while she was away. He feels terrible for all that Marney has gone through and wants to take care of her...and, he has a funny feeling Deucen isn't as far away as he hoped.

"Need anything from the kitchen?" He's still holding her in his arms.

Marney declines, shaking her head and snuggling into his neck. She missed his smell, his warmth...his body, definitely his body. Mike continues on and takes her to her bedroom. The fading sunlight lays beautifully across her bed. It's obvious no one has slept in it for quite some time. He's never seen her bedroom, not even when he had Zeek come and install the security system. He looks around, quite impressed with her taste and serene décor.

Mike gently sets Marney onto her bed, she molds to it like a rag doll. When he tries to move to leave and make her tea she grabs him close again. He relents and allows her to pull him down to her so he can stretch out along her body. He feels her and begins to stir inside. He's missed her so much, his chest aches.

"Please stay with me."

"Of course." He runs his hand along her face. "I thought I'd make you some tea."

"No...please don't leave."

"I won't Marns. I'm here."

"Thank you...and thank you for coming to the funeral...and to Reune as much as you could. It means a lot Mike."

He sighs, "I wish I could have been there more."

"You were great. It was a horrible time...but you were great."

Mike kisses her forehead. His heart goes out to the slender, pain-ridden, tough-as-nails woman in his arms. He can't believe all that she endures and wants only happiness for her now. What he feels for her is deeper than anything he has felt before. He has no way of telling her...and now isn't the time anyway. All he can do is hold her. And stay.

"I mean it Mike. I can't thank you enough...for holding down the case, for cutting Liam and I loose so we could get through this and keeping me in the loop with everything...and then showing up for the funeral and helping out so much. I-" She stops to choke back tears. He places his finger to her mouth.

"Rest now. There is plenty of time for thanks later. It was the least I could do. I am so sorry for your loss Marns."

She looks up at him and runs her palm down his face. His eyes lock with hers and she can't help but take his lips onto hers. He is reluctant, unsure but she pulls him in to deepen the kiss. Slowly she parts his lips and sinks into his gloriously warm mouth. Mike's body stirs, immediately at her intensity, and he wraps his arm around her with a longing he has suppressed for weeks. Marney feels a hunger deep within. Her heart aches, yet her body yearns for this man...and the love affair they had started and put on hold.

Marney feels a fire burning deep inside. She reaches for him with her hands and finds his rippled stomach, warm and taut under his clothing. She runs her hands along his ribs and around to his broad back, he's familiar and she pulls him to her breasts. Mike runs his hands up her spine and then down along it to her waist. He has missed the feel of her curves, the softness of her skin. To him she is just...exquisite.

Marney brings her hands around and up his neck to run her fingers through his hair. He moans into her mouth and kisses her deeper, his longing now evident through his jeans. She releases from his fevered lips looking at him in the darkening room.

"Make love to me...I've missed you...missed us. Please take all this pain away. Make love to me."

Mike kisses her gently...and did exactly as asked.

# 41. Storm

Mike's cell dings with another text. He's in the middle of a conference call with his agency and IA. Tracy Wegman, the assigned agent from Internal Affairs, is restlessly sitting across from him frowning at who keeps texting him. He knows it's Marney but there's no way he can answer her right now. They've got a shit storm on their hands with Wegman's partner losing the tail on Deucen. Mike is not pleased and realizes that just because IA is a higher authority, and may get better pay, doesn't mean they are more effective! He's pissed he didn't go with his gut and put his own people on Deucen as well. Losing this fucker at this stage of the case is a big boo boo. One he is not taking the flack for.

His phone beeps again....and again. Tracy is in the middle of her excuses and shoots Mike another dirty look. He ignores her and pushes a button on his phone without looking. A horrible feeling runs through his chest and he hopes that Marney is okay. She doesn't usually text him this much. It's killing him inside to have to ignore her. He misses her.

A knock at the office door forces he and Tracy to look over. The day dispatcher, Freda Jackson, pokes her head in the door and whispers, "Mike...you need to take that call." Freda points to his phone and quickly leaves.

Mike picks up his cell then speaks to the phone on his desk that's on speaker, "Uh, sir...I have to excuse myself for an emergency call. Please continue."

Tracy gives him a look of even more contempt, he doesn't care. They're in this mess because of her and her incompetent sidekick. Mike leaves the room to find a side office where he can return Marney's call in private. He sees he's missed seven texts from her and three calls. *Shit.*

She picks up on the first ring. "Mike!"

"Hey Marns whu-?"

"Mike, I need a search warrant for the old Fighting Venom dojo ASAP!" Marney is driving way too fast from what he can hear.

"Well..."

"Well what?"

"That's gonna be a problem."

Marney rolls her eyes. This is not what she wants to hear, she has been watching from Vera's diner all morning and finally sees a light on in the basement window of the closed down school. "Come on Mike. I need you to do this for me."

He squeezes his eyes shut in frustration, "I know babe, I would, believe me but, I'm right in the middle of a shit storm-"

"Mike! I'm on my way to you. I can brief you...but I really need to get into that place today. I can crack this case!" She is breathing heavy, trying to shift gears, drive and talk on the cell at the same time. She has that old gut feeling again.

He puts his fist to his forehead, "Marns...we lost Deucen."

Marney takes her foot off the gas...*not good.* "You what?"

"Deucen is MIA." He knows he shouldn't be telling anyone, but he trusts her.

"You gotta be fucking kidding me..."

Mike pauses a moment, "And Marns...that's not the worst of it."

"Oh great, there's more?" She decides to pull Gerda over.

"Deucen owns that building...he purchased it last year after the previous owner died."

Marney rubs her hand over her face. Her probable cause to search the place is looking less and less useful. Deucen has too many crooked friends and could hold up the paperwork.

"One last thing."

"Great."

"Cherie Daytone's bar is closed down. No one showed up to open it...and we can't find her either."

# 42. Daydream

Marney makes a u-turn and heads back toward's the diner. There is no need to go to the station if the search warrant is a no-go. She turns left and pulls the truck around the back of the pharmacy and parks. She checks her firearm and the magazine out of habit. Placing it back in her holster, she makes sure her blazer covers it and her badge is tucked away. Pulling the rubber band out of her hair, she runs her hands through her scalp and tussles her hair to make it look messy and less cop-like. She wants to blend in while she crosses the street and heads around the back of the strip of stores the Fighting Venom School is in. Marney doesn't think she'll find the gray Charger but, Deucen has been known to be a fucking idiot before. Mike is super pissed at her, especially since she just hung up. He has enough on his plate. She'll just take care of this on her own. Marney inhales slowly and wishes her partner was with her. She sure misses Chris. The case has taken everyone in a different direction...without enough backup.

She takes a look around. The quiet little town is still moving slow and steady. People nod and say hello when they pass, it's refreshing. Olman is historic enough to look great, but modern enough to have cameras at the intersections. She is fine with being on camera and walks at a relaxed pace. If she should disappear, she would hope Mike would pull the camera shots and see her in the crosswalks. She's pretty sure he picked up on where she was heading...search warrant or not.

Mike did mention the day squad was looking for Deucen and Cherie, as were the surrounding cities. He even has the border patrol and airport staff on alert. He's covering all areas, requesting coverage from surrounding districts, putting out fires, and following protocol as a good boss must. She really wishes he could get her the paperwork she needs though...nothing would feel better than solving this case today.

After crossing a second street, she walks at a nice pace and passes the back alley for the strip of stores the building is in. She looks to the right and looks quickly left than right again. None of the vehicles are familiar. Deucen's Dodge Charger, nor Cherie's Nissan Sentra, are parked in the back. She walks farther, to the next set of buildings, and moves unseen down an adjacent alley to a ladder that leads to the roof of a hardware store diagonal to her target building. She scans the area and decides to perch up on the roof and just do a little more surveillance.

Marney trots softly across the roof to the far corner and lays on her stomach. Reaching in her pocket she pulls out her mini binoculars and a piece of gum. She settles in and decides to just watch for awhile. From her angle she can see the rear of the martial art school. The back door is an obnoxious faded yellow color and then there is the stairwell going down into the basement. There is another doorway but the railing and lower door is painted black. Marney wonders if this is the basement area Eli James was referring too. It looks to be the only one and Marney is pretty sure there is light coming from down there. Eli had mentioned, some days a light can be seen from the diner as night comes in but, she is certain she saw it go on today. That's a sure indication that there is activity in the building. But, now that it's near noon, the sun is proving difficult. She's got to give Eli credit, he notices things others would just pass off as normal. He has a keen eye for his home town.

She decides to sit and wait. The sun is blazing...as soon as Mike texts her that he has the warrant, she can enter the building. She's decided, with or without backup...she's going in.

*** 

Two hours and thirteen minutes pass. Marney has texted Mike at least four more times. He isn't answering and it's a little alarming. She decides to adjust her legs again so that she doesn't lose circulation. What could be taking him so long?

Marney takes a deep breath. Ironically, this has been the stillest she has been all day...and she starts to think about how her day started...intensely, in the shower with Mike.

Marney smiles a little. She lowers her binoculars and lays her head sideways on her forearm to rest her neck muscles a moment. The sight of Mike's body comes into her mind and she can't help but feel a quiver of arousal inside. The way his back spans out, the muscles so defined, she wants to touch him. She remembers what her hands looked like slowly washing him, the steam rising up to the skylight. His skin glistening under the hot water, turning her on without his even knowing it. She likes how her arms fit around his waist and her palms fit flush across his stomach. The sound of his deep breathing in and out comforts her as she lay her ear to his back. She didn't realize she was embracing him so intently until he touched her arms to loosen them. Mike turns to her and bends to kiss her, resting his hands along her jawline. His soft, warm tongue meets hers and a surge of passion runs through her. The smell of fresh linens, hotel water, and men's sandlewood soap swarm her senses. She instinctively reaches up to enclose her arms around his neck. Mike deepens the kiss as she closes the space between them and the feel of his body wet against hers sends her pulsing for him. She pulls her body up and into his arms to feel him engulf her with his embrace. She loves how this man touches her! He's strong, but...kind. Running her hands through his wet hair she presses harder into the kiss. Mike moans into her mouth and she can tell he is as aroused as she.

Marney moves her sore neck up and looks down at the school again. Nothing. The sun is too hot, she doesn't care, she just wants to be right about this hunch. Still no text from him. *Damn...*

After she's satisfied with her visual, Marney decides to move her head to the opposite side and stretch her neck out that way. Staring off again she realizes the visual of her and Mike in the shower is deeply impressed in her mind and she enjoys the daydreaming too much. A wave of passion moves through her as she remembers how he placed her against the shower wall and she clung to him with one arm, bracing herself with the other on the handicap railing that was so conveniently placed under her rear. The leverage gave her enough balance to relax, yet pull him toward her. She kissed him hard then and he understood what he should do...and he did.

When Mike thrust into her, Marney threw her head back and exhaled. She couldn't believe how perfectly he fit her, the pleasure indescribable. Never before had she had such gratifying shower sex. He somehow found a way to balance himself so he could yet again, pull her arms up over her head, to remind her it is okay to let go...and trust. Only then did he break their kiss so he could trail his mouth down her neck and to her primed eager breasts. This simple delight sent a jolt of electricity through her body and she felt she was losing control too quickly. Instinctively, Mike took over and taunted and teased her with his pelvic moves. Marney began to softly moan. He smiled as he covered her mouth with his own again and took her vocal queues as a guide to pick up his pace and stay in sync with her body. Marney moved her arms down to brace against his strong body...she felt herself getting weaker. He felt her getting close and placed his arms along side of her holding the railing to secure her from falling. She loved how he thought about her safety. His mind, a unit with his body, his body one with hers. Marney broke the kiss so she could look at him. His eyes burned with want for her...he felt so damn good. She could no longer hold on, her head slung back and her body began its decent off the cliff. Mike thrust deep one last time and jumped the cliff with her...

A footstep scuffed behind her and she cursed herself for daydreaming. She tried to flip over...

blackness-

# 43. Nude

Slithers of light, dim light, show through the little openings that are her eyelids. *Fuck my head is sore...* Marney can smell musty water, she can feel moisture, a dampness. She tries to move but everything hurts so bad. *Why does my body hurt so fucking much?* Her shoulders, her wrists...her ankles. *Oh no! Oh fuck!* Marney takes a deep breath in and feels her heart racing almost out of her chest. She can't breathe well and flares her nostrils...realizing that she has duct tape over her mouth! *Oh shit, oh shit, oh shit!* Her eyes open wide, her breathing erratic. She wiggles and wrangles but cannot break free! Her eyes come into focus at the moment she realizes she is nude and hanging! She is hanging from her feet, rope tied tightly around her ankles...and it hurts so bad. *Fuck!* Marney's breathing is out of control, her head is moving all around, she's trying to understand what she sees. The entire room is upside down. *Oh no, noooo, no, no, noooooo, no, no, nooooo! I can't get free! My hands, my hands are...what is it? Oh fuck. It's duct tape! Oh my god, oh my god....*

Marney's head feels as if it's going to explode. Her body is cold and... completely naked! Humiliatingly naked. She feels like her body is dislocating at every joint and knows she has been hanging for quite some time. *Shit, I must have been knocked out.* She frantically moves around, looks up, over and behind her...flailing like a fish. She tries to make a sound. Her panic is taking over and she can't seem to find her voice She would hyperventilate if she could breathe! Sticking her tongue up and to the edge of the tape she begins to rip it away from her lips creating a small tunnel. She takes a breath in using both her nostrils and lips. *Marney get a hold of yourself!* The room is...wet, damp bricks, dark bricks that glisten with water in a disgustingly dim bulb of light. She looks toward the light but it hurts her eyes. It's just one light bulb in...a very large, creepy basement room.

Marney feels exposed, frantic...and chilled! My gun! My phone! Where are my fucking clothes! She takes a deep breath, tries to slow her heaving chest. *Control yourself Marns...* She moves her hands, but they are tucked behind her and duct taped. *I fucking hate duct tape!* Marney remembers in the police academy when she learned about killers, she was taught that ninety-one percent of perpetrators who used duct tape on their victims, kill them. It was a statistic but, one that stuck in her head. This makes her breathing excel. She squeezes her eyes shut and tries to compose herself. Mike flashes through her mind and she realizes she has to get herself together. He knows in general where she is...kind of. *But, I don't even know where the hell I am!* Marney stifles her breathing and tries to get control of her emotions. When she can, she tries to make sounds through the tape that covers her entire mouth and half of her nose openings. She moans through her nasal passage. She gets a little louder...then louder...

"Don't do that."

Marney's head snaps toward the distant female voice. Pure darkness. She can smell the stench of a freshly lit cigarette. She hates the scent of nicotine and carcinogens but, for a moment finds it more appealing than the moldy basement. *Who is this freak.* The voice is aged, far off in the room. Marney eases her breathing and squints her eyes trying to calm. She's terrified and knows she's going to die. She decides it must be with self-respect. *Not giving this bitch the satisfaction of seeing me beg.* Easing her heart and her breath, she calms. Squinting once more, Marney can see the glow of red way across the wet, musty-smelling room. Her death room.

In a muffled voice, Marney questions, "Is their a reason why I'm naked?"

"Wasn't my choice."

Now Marney knows she isn't working alone, "Oh, so it's not you that gets pleasure in seeing a bare ass chic?"

"Watch yourself detective. You aren't in control enough here to go pissing me off."

"True. But, seeing as I am at such a disadvantage-"

"You were at a disadvantage when you decided to climb up on the roof, all by your lonesome, and spy on me. You should have minded your own business." The woman takes a drag of her cigarette and Marney hears the faint squeak of the inhalation.

"I was looking for someone else." Marney moves and winces, everything hurts.

"Ahhh, not much of a liar are you?"

Marney takes a chance, "So, how does someone of your...stature...hang someone from a ceiling?" She decides she needs to anger this woman enough to get her to come out of the darkness...or enough to get her to shoot her and end this torture. "and duct tape-"

"Jade, let's knock off the grab-ass. We both know what your trying to do." A chair moves across the floor and foot steps come closer. "Why don't we get down to the good stuff. You play detective in your last moments, I answer the burning questions you have, and when this is all over, your death will be the only tragedy on my list."

Marney closes her eyes at the shear panic that radiates through her system. Mike, her brothers, Chris, Glenda, even Sean flash through her mind. She regrets her impatience for backup, she regrets going this alone, she regrets getting side-tracked with thoughts of mind-blowing sex with Mike...she regrets not having children. So many regrets... "So the other murders aren't a tragedy to you?"

"Ah, good. Now your getting it."

"You're a fucking psychopath."

The voice chuckles, "No, my husband was a psychopath sweetheart...I am merely a sociopath...with a few extra skills. Type B personality I guess you'd say."

"Sociopaths don't kill." Marney baits her.

"I wasn't always a killer Detective Jade. For most my life I was just your average abused wife. Then...I got tired of it. Tired of assholes getting away with being assholes."

Marney feels like every bone has dislocated in her small frame. She wonders if she can anger The Blader enough to take the pain away faster. Her mind begins to settle into her impending doom. "Fucking tired..." She huffs.

"You don't have to use such language with me."

Marney hears her feet scuff along as she walks, still distant in the room. "You'll have to forgive my ignorance Blader, I deal with this crazy shit every day. I cope by cursing...it's better than alcohol or drugs."

"Such a stupid title...oh, and the alcohol thing isn't quite true. You shouldn't be doing that anyway. In your condition." Marney has no idea what that means and wonders if telling her she's crazy would infuriate her more. "I'm going to feel bad about you and your baby dying. I don't often feel bad...but, two for the price of one is-"

"Fuck you, you crazy bitch."

"Not crazy...just type B." The chair pulls out again and Marney hears the sound of bones popping as the woman sits down.

Marney realizes she is not going to come over and into view. "Okay lady, why the mutilations?"

"Ah, now we're getting somewhere. I didn't take you for one to go straight for the goods but, it's a valid question. Heard you were smart...believed it up until today. Really wish you would have stayed on your side of town Jade." She lights another cigarette. From what Marney can hear, she uses an old type of flip lighter. The kind that have to be filled with fluid and make a neat sound when the lid is flipped back into place. "The simplest answer is this...they cheat, lie, and hit, they pay."

"Right." Marney is not impressed...but, it does go with one of her theories.

"And the removal of the hands?"

"Come on. I had to leave the prints. It would have taken you pendejos months to identify them if I hadn't...dental records aren't always quick."

"Still doesn't explain the hands being slashed off. Nice left swing by the way."

"I'm glad you caught on that I'm a lefty. Doesn't really matter does it?"

Marney winces in pain, "So, let me guess, they touch or hit they lose their hands right?"

"Cheaters are cheaters Detective."

"Same thing with the tongues then..."

The woman huffs showing attitude, "The only thing I despise worse than a cheater is an abuser that leaves scars with the tongue. Words hurt forever."

"Oh, instead of with the fists?" Marney is annoyed at the elementary discussion.

"Well, the hands get removed when there is unjust touching of any kind. Up to you idiots to figure out whats what."

Marney hears a thud on some sort of metal and thinks the woman may be sitting at a metal table...perhaps with a weapon. She takes a chance, "Is that the sword you used? Will I have the pleasure of being hit in the head with the butt of it first...or will you keep me alive through the slicing?"

The Blader lowers her voice, "Again, you should be very careful with how you speak to me detective."

Marney ignores her, "How many more questions do I get?"

"As long as I am entertained Jade, you stay alive, although with being hour three of hanging there...I'm betting you would rather die sooner than later."

Marney feels her heart racing again and clenches her body to push the anxiety away. She feels so close to hyperventilating and curses her fear of death. *At least I will see Mom and Dad.* "Yeah...and I'm naked...why?" A shiver runs through her and the cold temperature affects her a little more than the embarrassment of being nude.

"I told you...that wasn't my choice."

"Well, it wasn't fucking mine either...your victims all got to keep there clothes."

"Temper, temper detective. I guess you just pissed of the wrong-"

Marney waits but her voice stops. *Damn, she almost said it. Who the hell have I pissed off lately-* She takes a chance, "So, it's Deucen who hung me here."

"You don't think I want to stare at your skinny ass do you?"

She didn't confirm it, but she didn't deny either. Now to see how well she knows him. "What a degenerate asshole, douchebag ginger." Marney mumbles the words. She could never stand him and regrets keeping her mouth shut about him all these years. He should have been fired after the first two weeks of chauvinisticly harassing her at work.

"Ginger? What the hell does that mean?"

Marney hears the four legs of the chair slide out. She finds it interesting that this woman picked the more sensitive word of her four-slang assault. Means there is a personal relationship between the two. "Gingers have no soul...haven't you ever heard that?"

"What did you say?"

Marney can tell she is getting to her. "Gingers...you know, redheads. The soul-less children?" She hates saying it, especially since her brother has red hair but, she has to keep baiting this hag. "He's probably on his way back here to do unspeakable things to my lifeless body right?"

After a long pause, the old voice sounds in the room, "You should watch what you say Jadelock. A tongue is a very easy organ to lose."

Marney knows now there is an intimate relationship between this woman and Terry Deucen. It's not Cherie...the voice is older...and she knows Cherie's annoying voice. The sounds of Deucen banging her in his truck in the woods those many years ago still haunts her. "So nephew or son?"

"We are needing a change in this line of questioning. I'm getting bored."

"Okay, your footprints?"

"Nope."

Marney flinches in pain but makes no sound, "I realize that...how were you able to erase them?"

"I guess I'm just good." The woman chuckles.

Marney is alarmed at how she can be so angered one minute and then laugh the next. "Well, we've established that Blader...four bodies and counting..."

"You don't have to flatter or validate me Mija."

"So there are more?"

"Don't worry your pretty little head about that now. It won't matter much."

"So, here's the big question then." Marney moves on, "Why?"

"Why?"

"Yeah why? What did three men and a lesbian woman ever do to you?"

The Blader takes a moment, "It's never been about what they did to me."

"Okay, then your whatever-he-is...Deucen." Marney is hoping she screws up again.

"Not even close. Look, some people just have to go."

Marney rolls her eyes in the dark, "So, you feel you are ridding Olman of bad people?"

"Hmmm...not just Olman."

"Oh, so you are doing woman a solid by eliminating what...cheaters? And what the fuck is the eye-slicing about...and the broken jaw...busted teeth?" Marney wishes this was all being recorded...and suddenly realizes why she is naked. She hopes her death will mean something.

"Broken jaw was about hitting. Men should not hit women because women are not as physically matched. Eyes should not look at other women in an unsavory way. Porn is for couples to watch together, not apart...you know about the teeth, biting is never acceptable...it's all very simple really." The voice stops and takes a drag of the cigarette making Marney's head throb even louder. She feels as if every ounce of her blood has pooled to her head.

"Stupid really. And the cheaters?"

"I don't need to remind you detective, how much of a disadvantage you and your baby are at, you shouldn't insult me so easily."

"I'm not fucking pregnant lady!"

The woman laughs, another quick mood swing. "Okay. Whatever you say Mija...just lay off the whiskey."

"Does that mean I get to live?" Marney says with disgust.

"Naw, but that really isn't up to me. I prefer dismembering abusers. Have you abused anyone lately detective?"

"So you think you are doing a valuable thing."

She laughs, "Well, it's something to do."

"For an old lady." Marney insults.

"Hmmm." The Blader doesn't exactly confirm or deny the insult.

"I'm guessing this is something new for you since Olman didn't always have a serial killer."

She drags on her cigarette a moment and then answers, "Serial killers are psychopaths...remember now, I'm a sociopath."

"Oh right, doing society a favor...killing abusers." Marney begins to feel like this torture is never going to end and the monotonous questioning is almost unbearable. Although she is near freezing, nervous sweat runs down her body to her face and drips off onto the floor which sounds very near to her skull.

"You don't have to agree Jade. All you had to do was suck at your job...and look the other way. But, we can see how that went."

Marney feels the weight of her position more and more. Never in her life has she felt so much physical pain. She secretly hopes she will pass out soon. "Yeah, sorry about that. I feel differently about ending life."

"Protect and serve and all that..."

"So, if these so-called abusers didn't directly harm you, how is it you came about knowing them...and killing them?" Marney wishes she was in a courtroom instead of hanging from a dirty basement ceiling...if that in fact is where she is. Basements aren't common in the desert so she isn't entirely sure. She just thinks Eli James knows a thing or two. The pain radiating from her skull confirms she was hit over the head enough to not remember being disarmed and disrobed. Who knows how many hours away from Olman she is. She could be in the next state.

"Let's just say I had a lot of experience with their kind."

"Oh, that's right. And so, this must mean that not only were you a victim yourself...but, you knew the spouses...err, harmed ones of your victims." Marney didn't really phrase it as a question and was leading into the area of the woman's group when the voice interrupted her.

"Detective, your manipulations are elementary. Do you know what it's like to be emotionally abused?"

"Well, I'm hanging from a fucking ceiling with rope and duct tape. You tell me." Marney pulls at her knees but theres no feeling left.

The old woman smiles through her words, "I mean gut-wretching, heart-breaking, soul piercing manipulation sweets."

"Don't you mean Mija?"

"Watch your mouth."

Marney wanted her to keep going so she bit her lip. "Yeah, yeah, yeah...I get the whole narcissist manipulation thing Blader."

"Again, dumb name."

"Narcissist or Blader?"

"You're really trying my patience."

Marney doesn't mean it but says it anyway, "I apologize, it really wasn't my idea...it was your son's...err or is it nephew? The dumb name I mean. Didn't you two discuss it at all?" She is finding it difficult to be respectful.

The chair pushes out and Marney thinks she hears the sound of a cigarette being put out. Scuttled footsteps approach and Marney's heart races. "Do you know what it's like to give your life to someone. To live for only them...breathe for them, only to find out they are a fraud? To suffer the complete devastation that you have been lied to about everything. To be told you are the world to them...then blamed for everything they hate so they can feel better about themselves. To be subjected to comments of how worthless you are, how ugly or fat, to be put down for all your successes because in essence it makes them feel insecure. To be gaslighted at every turn, baited and hooked every day for attention...to watch your child be mentally tortured at the very hand of the person who professes how much they love your kid..."

Marney knows at this point this is Deucen's mother! And she is becoming emotional and weak. She says nothing and hopes she can stay conscious a bit longer. "Why Andres Diaz? What did he ever do to you...or your son?"

"That piece of shit didn't have to do anything to me. None of this is about me. Diaz hurt his wife for years. He had plenty of time to correct his behavior...he decided not to. Its a crime how he functioned in society. Sleeping around, looking at other women, using that sharp tongue to beat up her self esteem, it's appalling...well, was." Her voice trails off and into silence.

Marney takes note that The Blader didn't actually deny that Deucen was her son. She also thinks Andres Diaz' behavior is a crime...but killing him not so much. Marney baits her more, "You cut his dick off right through his pants."

"Yes I did. He stuck it in the wrong women. Hurt his wife...even hurt those women, none of them had any idea about each other. He thought he was slick...well, I showed him how slick he was. He can't hurt any of them anymore." Her voice was smooth and unwavering.

"What about his kids? What about them not having a father anymore?" Marney doesn't really agree with his behavior or hers. She needs to keep her talking.

"They're better off loving a memory than dealing with the dark cloud of a cheating bastard of a father. Can you imagine how they would feel if their father gave those women AIDS or a venereal disease and it got out? Believe me, I was doing those kids and all of Olman a favor."

"Your mind is beautiful..." Marney meant it as an insult.

"Thank you. What else do you want to know detective?"

Marney thinks for a moment. She tries to wiggle her fingers and remembers how bad it hurts. She gets back to the questioning to ignore the excruciating pain and her near death position, "The smudges in your footprints..."

Her voice begins cutting Marney off, "Ah, that's a special secret. Movement I learned early on in life to erase evidence. You wouldn't understand it."

"You mean I'm not a martial artist."

"Something like that."

Marney moves on, "So whats this sheet or outfit you wear along with your latex gloves?"

The Blader exhales, "Sheet? I don't wear a sheet!"

"A witness saw you leaving the scene of Luke Rance's murder. Said you were carrying something in your hand and had your body covered with a black or dark colored sheet." Marney wonders how the incorrect description will affect her.

"Well now, I didn't read that in the papers." The Blader begins to flick the lighter lid again.

"We didn't put everything in the papers after your son was suspended. You can thank him for keeping the public so well informed of your actions. I guess that was his way of supporting your activities. Giving you your due attention so to speak."

The Blader stands and scuffles closer to Marney. It sounds as if she is wounded or limps when she walks. "He's a cop. Why would he disagree with me getting rid of a few degenerates."

*Ah, there it is...the admission.* Marney listens closely to her footing. She sounds far off in the room but, seems to be making her way closer. Marney can tell this is not a small space. There are tiny echo type sounds when they speak so she knows there is not a lot of furniture in the room absorbing the noise. "To protect and serve for one. He is suppose to uphold the law, not support it being broken. You do understand it is against the law to kill another human being yes?"

"Oh come on Detective Jade, aren't all cops a little dirty?"

"The job can be carried out legally. It's a matter of following rules. That's why we have them."

The voice lowers, "So you're telling me you have always followed the rules...never once bent them even the slightest?"

"I'm guessing I'm boring you with my line of questioning. All of a sudden it feels as if I'm being asked the questions." Marney is annoyed, exhausted and losing interest in prolonging the anguish much longer.

The footsteps sound as if they are going the opposite way, The Blader limps in a different direction. "Hmmm yes, it was more interesting when you were trying to get all your little answers. Do go on."

Marney squeezes her eyes, "So, how does one begin killing people? Did this start in childhood?"

The Blader chuckles and hums, "Well, I guess I just got tired of doing nothing."

Marney shakes her head slowly. Her neck feels as if each vertebrae have disconnected.

"I spent forty years in a brutal marriage...surviving painful lies, manipulations, mental abuse, and even a little violence. I had never known anything else. Then...my husband was just gone one day. Killed. Not by me. I was always too scared...but, then came the freedom. The time to live without all that abuse. Time to reflect on it and see how life could be without the constant assaults on my being. The continual uncaring and dismissive treatment was no longer in my every day. False promises and deep disappointments were gone, I was no longer blamed for all the wrongs in his life, the hollow apologies no longer sounded in my head, and best of all my secrets were no longer used as weapons against me. I was finally free...finally." Her pacing started back the other way.

"Sounds like a happier life."

"Much...but, with all the realization and learning came responsibility. Suddenly, I was able to see so clearly how this horrible behavior was happening all around me. How unfair and cruel my husband was...and how others endured the same tortures I did."

Marney asks, "So you lived with a torturous narcissist for forty years and never touched him but, seeing others go through it somehow sparks the serial killer in you?" Marney begins to feel as if she is losing her mind to the pain. Her body is giving up...she has to keep going.

"Detective you are frustrating the shit out of me. I don't know how to get through to you. I'm not a serial killer in the way that you need to frame it. I don't sit around my bonfires and plan out my next killing. Hell, I don't even like the killing part. I much prefer to just see the victims set free...like I was." The Blader lights another cigarette while still limping along the large room. Marney isn't sure she can stand smelling another one. She strains to breathe what little fresh air is left. "You really don't understand the magnitude of your crimes do you? You are murdering people!"

"Am I detective? Or...am I setting a few deserving ones free? Do you know what its like to be tortured mentally day after day after day...by the person who is suppose to love an support you?"

Marney doesn't answer. She's afraid she's starting to commiserate with this crazy woman...and instead feels as if she would prefer death. She wonders if the torture she feels from hanging is so this woman can help her understand what torture she endured for forty years being married to a man who proved at every turn how much he didn't love her. Nausea sets in.

"Going to work every day and hearing the horrendous behaviors of men who had no respect and women just as bad...just..." Her voice fades.

Moments pass, Marney fights to stay conscious. "Blader?"

"Don't call me that. I have a name. I am a-"

"You're a killer lady. No matter how you explain it...you murder people." Marney still antagonizes.

The woman ignores her, "Do you know what healthy is Detective Jade? Marney ignores her. "Emotional intelligence it's called."

"Emotional intelligence..." Marney slurs the words.

"Right."

"You're the fucking...you're the fucking cleaner...from Cordova's office! I know who you are! Marney tries to breathe. "She's got that emotional shit posted up all around her lob...lobby. You're the old lady that cleansssss her place." Marney swallows and tries to stay awake.

"Do you have a healthy relationship detective?"

"Whu-?'

"Do you have a man in your life that tells you the truth detective? Are you able to discuss matters rationally and get through problems? Does he care enough about you to respectfully talk things through without insulting you or attacking your opinions and beliefs...does he take responsibility for his actions? Can he say he is sorry and be genuinely accountable for his own actions without blaming you or making you suffer? Or, detective, does he exact revenge on you in order to feel better about his own sad state? His phoney insides. Does he come from a place of decency or does he prefer to fight dirty...stealing your good energy and faith? Does he love you detective...unconditionally?" She drags long on her cigarette and waits.

Marney feels as if she is going crazy now. How could Deucen be so incredibly stupid with such an intelligent mother? And...how could he be so harmless with a killer so near...then again, he is suppose to return and finish her off... "It...doesn't matter now...does it...Blader..."

"I told you that isn't my name."

"Well, I don't...know what the fuck to call you-"

"Easy now."

"So what, you hang around Cordova's office and listen to all the...the confidential details...then what, kill those...err set the abused free?"

The Blader whispers and startles Marney, "I'm just the cleaner...like you said." She'd silently made her way over to where Marney's naked body hung.

A chill runs through Marney's body and a new anxiety emerges waking her into full consciousness. She squirms and tries to move away from the shadow that nears her. Upside down she can see the short, round woman dressed in what appears to be some sort of martial arts uniform. Marney squints to focus on the blurry vision. She recognizes the uniform! Her brother used to wear the same one...*oh shit! Master Lee's wife? The Blader is Master Lee's wife? What the fuck!* Marney wants to scream. She is standing staring at her, she smells of nicotine! She has a huge sword in her hand! The curvy blade terrifies Marney and she begins to freak out and squirm...going nowhere. Panic takes over and Marney's body convulses uncontrollably.

"It's time detective. He didn't return and I've told you too much. Believe me when I tell you...you are the first unjust one-"

*Wham!* "STEP AWAY NOW! Step away, FBI...STEP AWAY! Step the fuck away from her now or you will be-"

"I'm sorry about your baby detective..." The Blader sinks her sword into Marney. *Bam, bam, bam, bam, bam....*

Marney feels the cold slice into her. She sees movement all around, the shadow fall, and then the blackness closes in. Finally...no more pain. Death is easier...

# 44. Back

Mike stares out the window watching the sun set behind the Mican Mountains. He visits the memory of the time he sat down next to her against the boulder on her Dad's property. He knew then he was already in love with her. He remembers how peaceful her father's home was, how it pained him that she was in love with another...how he felt like a school boy wondering if he was too close to her. He just wanted to hold her then...like he does now. He turns to see her. Her eyes are still shut. He wants her to wake. He wants to tell her of their baby...

He turns again to the window and a tear falls to his cheek. Six days. Six days she has been like this. Six...long, tormenting days. Will she be herself? Will she want the baby? Will she ever want to work in law enforcement again? He clenched his fist, worry hanging heavy on his heart.

The older blonde nurse enters the room, "Hello Agent Taylon. How are you today sir?"

Mike wipes the tear away and tries to smile stepping away from the bed to give her room to take Marney's vitals. Another day has passed and Nurse Elma Basen is starting her night shift. Mike knows that he only has another hour with Marney and visiting hours are over...but, he has decided to stay with her again tonight...he doesn't want to be at the hotel if this is the night she wakes. "I'm just fine Elma." He wants to ask her the same, he can't seem to find the words.

"Will you be needing the recliner again this evening?"

"Yes. I think tonight might be the night. I have to be here to tell her about the baby." He says it for the third day in a row.

Elma nods, her heart breaks for the man. He has been morose since they brought Detective Jade's naked, stabbed body in. She is one tough gal...with an even tougher fetus. So many on the police force have been in and out to visit. The entire town knows about her capture, torture, and bravery. How she left clues to her whereabouts, how local resident

Eli James assisted the ERT to the basement where she was held and how "The Blader" was shot and killed as she sunk the murder weapon into Detective Marney Jade. Jadelock is the top story of the evening news, candlelight vigil are held every evening in her honor, in hopes that she will wake. Marney lays in her hospital bed healing, unconscious, unaware of any of it.

Mike leans against the window sill and watches Elma gently handle Marney. She has done an expert job for the woman he loves more than his own life. He watches as she moves Marney's beautiful long hair away from her ear and takes her temperature, for what feels like the hundred-and-twentieth time. Her arms lay long and still at her sides, the sheets tucked perfectly around her gorgeous body warming her as she cradles and protects their baby. A true little miracle. His heart aches for Marney, for the trauma she and the baby endured while he tried to find her. Fear shoots through him at how she may feel towards him. How being hung and tortured so long could change her forever and there is nothing he can do about it. She may hate him. Blame him for not being there for her...rescuing her too late.

Mike stands and looks out of the window again. The sight of her naked body hanging from the dirty basement ceiling haunts him hour after hour. After he shot The Blader full of holes, he didn't even holster his gun instead, frantically removed his own clothing to cover Marney and stop her bleeding. He remembers how he and Chris lowered her slowly onto the gurney and all he could do was silently pray she would live for all cops know that being stabbed is so much worse than being shot. The bile could have killed her...and the baby...he didn't want to think of it. He chokes back tears at how grateful he is that she survived. He knows he is meant to be with her.

Elma turns down the overhead light and prepares to leave, "Should I send any of her family back Agent Taylon?"

"No Elma. Thank you though. I've told them all to go back home. They know I'll call if she wakes. She would hate for them to stand here and stare." Mike attempts a smile to thank her.

"Okay then. I will have your chair brought in."

"Thanks again."

***

Mike frowns at the piercing sunlight on his face. He inhales knowing he has to open his eyes but, just wants a few more minutes without the hurt. The only time he doesn't hurt, feel regret or guilt is when he finally falls asleep. The warmth on his face is nice yet, not as nice as the warmth on his fingers. They move and he opens his eyes abruptly to see her fingers entwined with his. He looks up at she is staring at him...he opens his eyes wider. Is she really awake?

Marney whispers, "What does that mean?" She points to a small bouquet of flowers across the room. They are from Chris and have a blue balloon attached that says "Congrats. It's a boy!" Chris' idea of a joke. Mike closes his eyes for a moment to gather his answer. He is overwhelmed with elation that she is speaking to him. He wants to scream now that she is awake but tries to figure out how to bring her along slowly, with answers, so as not to traumatize her. "Mike?"

"Marney..." He tries to tell her he loves her...he wants to say the right words. His name from her lips almost brings tears to his eyes.

Marney moves then winces trying to sit up. He stands suddenly to help her and she reaches for him. He comes close, she wraps her arms around him and places her cheek to his chest. Mike feels her and places his hand on her head gently to hold her to him. He wants to take it all away. Erase everything she'll be going through...again. She starts to tremble.

"Is it true? Are we pregnant Mike?"

"That's what the docs say Marns."

"How many months?"

Mike pulls away to look at her, "Months? Sweetheart, only a few weeks...what do you mean months? Only about seven weeks. Most likely from our...time in my room."

Her hands are shaking, she looks at them and tries to put them together to stop the trembling. "Weeks?"

"Yes, wh-" Mike stops and realizes she is in a panic, not at the news of being a mother, but more so at fear of who's baby it is. He has to tell her, "Marney, you were aware that he was sterile right?"

"What?" She is still only able to whisper.

"Sean. He can never have children." Mike thought she knew...afterall, she told him herself there was no way she was pregnant when she threw up in her kitchen.

"How-"

"Sorry, I read his military jacket when I did a background on him...awhile back. I'm sorry, I thought you knew."

"No." She attempts to smile and he realizes he hadn't seen her beautiful smile in so long. He reaches in wanting to kiss her but stops. She pulls him to her and connect their lips, so gently and eager...as if she hasn't been through hell and he is all that matters.

She looks up at him apprehensively, "Do you want a child Mike?"

He pulls away looking at her, shocked at her question, "Marney...I love you."

She stares at him, tears welling up in her eyes. "I'm all fucked up Mike...bad."

Fear runs through him, not at her admission, but, at the thought that she may not want the baby. "I still love you Marns." He shrugs. His heart hanging on his sleeve.

"Okay."

"Okay?"

She whispers again, "Yeah, okay."

He's confused.

"Me too."

"Yeah?" He smiles.

"Yeah. I've loved you from the first moment I met you."

Mike smiles wide and feels relief for the first time since rescuing her. "Well then."

"Its all we need to be a family Mike...its all we need."

*Dear Reader,*

*Thank you so much for reading The Kris. I would love to know what you thought or if you have any questions about Mike and Marney's story. Please feel free to email me at dezigolden@gmail.com.*

*My best, Dezi-*

# ACKNOWLEDGMENTS

Thank you to my instructors, especially Matawguro Louelle Lledo, Jr., for introducing me to the kris swords and fostering my love of weaponry. Thank you for believing in me and seeing my successes *ahead*, instead of my mistakes *during*. You are one of a kind and deeply loved. Never change...Oosh!

Thank you to my editors, my friends, my family and to my fans. Without your encouragement, my stories would still only be ideas swirling around in my mind.

And lastly, thank you to all those who allowed me to use your quirks, your pet-peeves, and your names. Although my characters are completely fictional, without our paths crossing, I would not have been able to build them. I treasure our paths crossing in this lifetime.

# ABOUT THE AUTHOR

Dezi Golden resides in Las Cruces, New Mexico, with her family and many pets. When not writing, Dezi enjoys seeing clients in her private healing practice and traveling. If you're interested in any of Dezi's other books, contact her at dezigolden@gmail.com.

# INSIDE
## Dezi Golden, in her own words

I first began my love of weapons in April 2004 after receiving my first black belt in martial arts. My process was a little different. I had trained for six years! First, I had to master my *mind*, then my *body*...then the weapons came pretty easily. And today? My mind is still my toughest hurdle but I've committed to being a student of life.

If you ever have the chance, explore the arts. Pick the one that feels right, centers you, and stick with it. Any style that grounds you is wonderful. They've been around for thousands of years, like meditation, massage, and natural medicine...and they aren't going anywhere. Why? Because when it works...it works!

Learn for personal growth and enlightenment...not to use against others, *unless you absolutely must*. For me, the best martial artists, and *humans* for that matter, are those who can communicate through respectfully beautiful language...not fists and weapons.

Thank you for reading my story. I have more to tell. I hope I can get them out of this *mind* and down on paper.

-dg

# You've finished The Kris. Before you go....

Contact Dezi Golden on her website or social media pages. Ebook and paperback versions are now available of The Kris. Need an autographed copy? Contact Dezi at dezigolden@gmail.com.

# Don't miss out!

Visit the website below and you can sign up to receive emails whenever Dezi Golden publishes a new book. There's no charge and no obligation.

https://books2read.com/r/B-A-GYDO-EMQNB

**BOOKS 2 READ**

Connecting independent readers to independent writers.

# Also by Dezi Golden

**BreathHealer**
BreathHealer Book I
BreathHealer Book II

**Standalone**
The Kris
Guide to Living with CPTSD
Soul of a Tantric
In a Weekend
My Hero My Love

Watch for more at https://www.dezigolden.com.

# About the Author

Dezi Golden is an American author who resides in Las Cruces, New Mexico. Her unique growth in treating wellness and intimacy coaching clients combined with personal experiences paves the way for her intriguing novels. To learn more or receive your autographed copy contact Dezi at dezigolden@gmail.com.

Read more at https://www.dezigolden.com.

# About the Publisher